JEANIENE FROST

WICKED *All* NIGHT

A Night Rebel Novel

AVONBOOKS

An Imprint of HarperCollinsPublishers

WICKED ALL NIGHT. Copyright © 2021 by Jeaniene Frost. All rights reserved. Printed in the United States of America. No part of this book may be used or reproduced in any manner whatsoever without written permission except in the case of brief quotations embodied in critical articles and reviews. For information, address HarperCollins Publishers, 195 Broadway, New York, NY 10007.

First Avon Books mass market printing: March 2021

Print Edition ISBN: 978-0-06-269566-6
Digital Edition ISBN: 978-0-06-269568-0

Cover design by Amy Halperin
Cover photograph and illustration by Cliff Nielsen
Author photo by Matthew Frost

Avon, Avon & logo, and Avon Books & logo are registered trademarks of HarperCollins Publishers in the United States of America and other countries.

HarperCollins is a registered trademark of HarperCollins Publishers in the United States of America and other countries.

FIRST EDITION

21 22 23 24 25   CPI   10 9 8 7 6 5 4 3 2 1

Wicked All Night

". . . either you respect me enough to have me stand at your side, or you don't, and if you don't, then we are through."

The words tore through me with more destructive power than that silver knife.

"How can you say that?" I whispered. "Everything I've done, I've done because I love you."

"I know that." His tone softened, but his gaze didn't. "I also know you've lived thousands of years alone, so you're not used to having a partner. I've tried to make allowances for both, but there is a limit. This is it. If you want me in your life, no more going it alone when things get dangerous. Not with this netherworld trip now, and not later, either."

Then, he leaned close, until his words fell like the lightest of caresses against my newly wet cheeks.

"Choose us. Together, we can defeat anything in our way."

By Jeaniene Frost

WICKED ALL NIGHT
WICKED BITE
SHADES OF WICKED
INTO THE FIRE
BOUND BY FLAMES
UP FROM THE GRAVE
TWICE TEMPTED
ONCE BURNED
ONE GRAVE AT A TIME
THIS SIDE OF THE GRAVE
ETERNAL KISS OF DARKNESS
FIRST DROP OF CRIMSON
DESTINED FOR AN EARLY GRAVE
AT GRAVE'S END
ONE FOOT IN THE GRAVE
HALFWAY TO THE GRAVE

To Matt, again, because of all the reasons I've listed before, and too many new reasons to count.

Acknowledgments

It's always humbling to write an Acknowledgements page because that means the book is done. Even after all these years, taking an idea and turning it into an entire novel still feels kind of like a miracle. This is why, among many other reasons, I always thank God first. You carried me through another one, Lord! Thank you, thank you.

Endless thanks also go to the other usual suspects who take this journey with me: my agent, Nancy Yost; my editor, Erika Tsang; Pam Jaffee, senior publicity director; Kayleigh Webb, publicist; and to the rest of the fabulous people at Avon Books. Thanks also to Tavia Gilbert, my audio narrator, for bringing my books alive with your talents. Thanks also to Melissa Marr and Ilona Andrews for your invaluable critiques and even more invaluable friendship. Thanks also to my husband, sisters, father, and the rest of my family for your amazing love and support.

Finally, thank you so much to readers, reviewers, bloggers, bookstore staff, librarians, and everyone else who celebrates books. You know they're so much more than just words on a page. Books are escapes, adventures, mini vacations, moments of solace, and times when we catch up with fictional friends. Speaking of that, I hope you enjoy catching up with Ian, Veritas, and the rest of the gang in *Wicked All Night*, so I'll stop rambling and let you get to it. :)

WICKED
All
NIGHT

A week ago, a demon teleporting into my room would've sent me running for the nearest weapon. Now, I barely looked up when the bedroom's shadows suddenly formed into a tall, handsome man with midnight-brown eyes, closely cropped black curls, and skin the rich, dark brown of smoky quartz.

"Did you bring more blood?" I asked him.

Ashael slid a briefcase across the floor to me. I opened it, relieved to see several blood bags inside.

"Thank you." I hoisted the nearest bag onto the IV pole beside me. This was the last ingredient I needed for my spell. Everything else was in place.

Then, I watched as a thin stream of crimson streaked down the IV line toward the unconscious vampire on the bed. *Please*, I thought, fighting to hold back tears. *Please let this spell work!*

Magic flared the instant the blood hit Ian's veins as the spell activated. My nails dug into my palms. *Please, please, please . . .*

A choked sound escaped me when Ian's half-shriveled arm began to change, transforming from a near-skeletal state into his normal, muscled limb. Very slowly, his body began to follow suit, losing the shocking gauntness he'd had for the past ten days to expand back to his healthy, brawny physique.

"Yes!" I shouted, so relieved my knees felt weak.

We'd finally defeated our worst enemy, but Dagon had had one last, evil trick in store for us. At first I thought everything was great. Dagon was dead, Ian had summoned me away from the vampire council, preventing them from executing me, and we were safe at Mencheres's house in the Hamptons. Sure, Ian was badly injured from Dagon's trap, but Ian was a vampire, and vampires healed from everything except decapitation or silver destroying their heart.

Or so I'd thought.

Turned out, there was one more injury that vampires couldn't heal from: whatever dark magic Dagon had infused in his fucking trap. Ian had borne the worst of its effects since he'd been the one to break us out of it. Or my other nature had protected me from the trap's lingering, deadly magic. Either way, I was fine, but Ian fell unconscious the same day that he rescued me.

He hadn't woken up since, and he hadn't healed from his horrific injuries no matter what spell I used to try to counter the lethal magic. Instead, Ian had only grown worse.

Until now.

"It's working." My voice vibrated from the joy rocketing through me. "Thank all the gods, it's working!"

I'd put all my knowledge, every last one of my magic-infused gems, all my power, and more than a few stolen artifacts into this latest spell. Those last ingredients had netted me some new enemies, but I didn't care. Ian's magic-ravaged body was finally, *finally* healing. Oh, I couldn't wait until he opened his eyes again! I also couldn't wait to hear his voice, to see his smile, listen to his laugh . . . wait. What was happening?

Ian's body suddenly began to shrink back into itself.

"No!" I grabbed his arm, as if I could physically prevent him from degenerating again.

I felt as well as saw Ian's formerly healed body reduce itself back to little more than tendon-covered bones. His pearlescent skin now also had a grayish undertone, and his thick auburn hair looked faded and brittle, like discarded straw. If anyone saw him, they'd think they were looking at a corpse.

"No!" I screamed, dropping Ian's arm. If I held it any longer, I would break it from how frail it was.

And Ian wasn't *frail*. He was the strongest, cleverest, bravest, sexiest, most stubborn man I'd ever met. He'd defeated every challenge anyone had thrown at him, every time. He'd even defeated death once, so he *couldn't* end up destroyed by Dagon's spell, after everything he'd overcome. He just couldn't!

Ashael let out a deep sigh. "I am so sorry, my sister."

Only then did I realize I was crying, the kind of deep, hiccupping sobs that no one wanted to cry, let alone with an audience. I couldn't seem to stop, either. I, widely known as the vampire world's coldest, most unfeeling Law Guardian, couldn't even slow my heaving sobs.

I'd put everything I had into this spell, and it hadn't been enough. Even from the grave, Dagon would win. He'd already made me watch Ian die once. Now, Dagon would force me to watch him die again, unless I somehow found another way to stop the magic that was inexorably killing him.

I would, I swore, swiping at my tears. I'd find another way, or I'd *make* another way.

Ashael patted my back in a soothing way. As a demon, he probably wasn't used to offering comfort, but despite his lack of practice, he was pretty good at it.

"I'm okay," I said once I'd shoved my pain down enough to speak instead of sob. Then, I changed the subject because if I focused anymore on how this spell had failed, I'd lose it again. "Have you had any luck finding our father?"

It still felt strange to say "our" father. For thousands of years, I thought I had no siblings. Then, a month ago, I found out that Ashael was my half brother, though Ashael's other half came from the demon race, while I was half vampire.

"No. He hasn't responded to any of my summonings."

"How can he ignore both of us?" I asked. "No, really, *how*? If you draw the right symbols in my blood and called me using my true name, I *have* to come, and I inherited that from dear old Dad. So, how can he ignore both of us repeatedly blood-ritual summoning him?"

Ashael shrugged. "He is the epitome of the river separating life and death. Who knows what he is capable of?"

"Exactly, which is why we need to find him. Our father might be the only person strong enough to heal Ian."

Everything Ashael and I had tried might have failed, but our father was a netherworld god. He'd raised Ian from the dead before, so healing him should be well within his purview.

"I will find him," Ashael said. Then his dark eyes grew more sympathetic. "But I have no idea how long it will take. If Ian does not survive until then—"

"He will," I interrupted, fighting back a new surge of tears.

Crying didn't help Ian. It only took away the energy I'd need to save him. Ian had never let impossible odds stop him from saving me. I wouldn't fail him now.

Ashael didn't argue. He only inclined his head. "As you say. However, Ian's condition puts you at a disadvantage, since many enemies are after you. The vampire council wants you dead now that they know what you are, and you refused my offer to slaughter them—"

"I still do," I said, though I patted his hand.

A human brother might bring me a bouquet of flowers to brighten my day. My demon brother wanted to bring me a bouquet of my enemies' body parts. Gruesome, yes, but his motivation was sweet, even if his method of showing affection was . . . less so.

"Very well, no slaughtering the council," Ashael said, sounding disappointed. "Their death sentence on you aside, you also have Dagon's allies seeking revenge against you, and you have that other concern."

Other concern. That was one way to describe an unwanted celestial fiancé. But that was also the topic I least wanted to talk about.

"I'll deal with that after Ian is well."

Ashael frowned. "Then you cannot attract Phanes's notice by piercing a hole into the underworld again."

Really? There went my after-dinner plans.

I didn't say it out loud. Ashael didn't deserve my sarcasm.

"Thank you," I said. That, Ashael deserved.

A small smile curved his mouth. "Anything for my sister."

It still felt odd hearing it. But also, it felt a little wonderful, and that was the emotion I'd try to dwell on.

"Are you off again?"

Ashael never stayed long. The salt water in the air from the nearby surf burned him. If Ashael wasn't only half demon, he wouldn't be able to stand it at all. That's why we were still at Ian's sire's house in the Hamptons. Its beachside location made it demon-proof, and none of the Law Guardians looking for me would assume I'd choose a ritzy vacation home for my hideout.

Ashael nodded. "I'm meeting an acquaintance that might have information on our father. I should be back before dawn."

I nodded. Ashael hesitated, and then touched my shoulder.

"I'm worried about you, Veritas. You're so busy caring for him, you're neglecting yourself, and Ian wouldn't want you hovering over him until you wasted away. He'd tell you to sleep, to feed, to take a walk, take a drive, or do something other than stare at him every moment as he sleeps. You know I'm right."

He probably was. But when I slept, I woke up screaming from nightmares where Ian degenerated into dust right before my eyes. Plus, every drop of blood I consumed was one less drop that might help Ian regain his strength to fight Dagon's spell. I knew that, even unconscious, Ian was still fighting. I could feel it in his power, simmering beneath the dark magic that was trying to destroy him. Some days, feeling the faint pulse of his power was the only thing that kept me from going insane.

I couldn't say any of that to Ashael without worrying him more, so I said, "I'll walk on the beach for a bit after you leave. I did that the other night, too, so I'm not *only* spending my time hovering over Ian."

He smiled. "Good. I'll see you when I return."

I forced a smile in return. "Be safe, and I'll see you then."

He teleported away. My false smile dissolved the next instant.

STILL, A FEW hours later, I went outside to fulfill my promise to him. The nearby ocean called to my celestial-born nature anyway. Waves grabbed at my ankles like frigid fingers when I reached the surf. I didn't mind. The cold combined with the late hour meant that I was alone on the beach. The Hamptons' other residents were either gone for the winter or safely inside their expensive beachfront homes.

When the next wave rushed over my ankles, I used my power to break it into spirals that twirled around me like mini waterspouts. Then, when the waves departed back into the ocean, I sent the spirals chasing after them. My ability to control water was more second nature than a learned skill. Very second nature, considering that it came from my other half.

When I was in my mid-twenties, Tenoch, my beloved sire, had turned me into a vampire, but I wasn't human before that. I hadn't known, of course. I'd been enslaved by Dagon since I was too young to remember anything except my first death.

Dagon told me he raised me from that death, and from the hundreds—thousands?—of deaths after it. I believed him because Dagon was a powerful demon who could do many incredible things. I only found out decades later that Dagon had nothing to do with my resurrections. My biological father, the Warden of the Gateway to the Netherworld, was the one who'd repeatedly brought me back from the dead. The Warden was also the source of my powers, some of which had scared my sire, Tenoch, so much, I'd suppressed them to the point of forming an entirely separate identity.

For over four thousand years, no one except Tenoch had known what I really was, since being a mixed-species vampire was so illegal that it was punishable by death. No one even knew what I really looked like. I'd concealed my celestial side beneath my rigid, vampire Law Guardian persona, and I'd hidden my true, god-resembling appearance beneath glamour that showed a thin, blonde, young woman to anyone who looked at me. Both disguises had allowed me to lead a safe, solitary life . . . until Ian.

Somehow, Ian had sensed the real me even before we spoke a single word. Later, when circumstances forced me to show Ian what I was, he hadn't been frightened or appalled like everyone else. He'd been intrigued, aroused, and then unstoppable in his pursuit of me. I'd done everything to guard my heart, but I'd failed. By then, I hadn't cared. Falling for Ian might have ripped me in two—literally, considering the emergence of my other side—but it had also been the highlight of my very long life. I'd never known it was possible to be so happy, and now I couldn't bear to lose him. Not again, and . . . what was wrong with the sand?

Seconds ago, it had been grayish. Now, it was every shade of gold. The air filled with golden beams, too, as if the brightest sun were shining instead of the wan streaks from the crescent moon. In the next instant, lights were suspended in the air like multitudes of tiny stars.

It was stunning, but I all I could think was *Oh, shit!*

I'd seen this before, and it had heralded the arrival of the very *last* person I wanted to see.

I flew toward the cottage, only to smack into a muscled chest before I'd made it two meters. Suddenly, I was held aloft by two burly arms framed by huge golden wings.

"My bride!" said my unwanted celestial fiancé.

I looked down at Phanes. Black hair fell over his gold-colored eyes, his skin looked like gold-dusted bronze, and his features were so ridiculously beautiful, most people who saw him would be tempted to stop, drop, and worship.

That's what the ancient Greeks had done, presumably. Phanes didn't just mean "to shine." It was also the name of a primordial Greek god, according to the Orphic cosmogony.

A smug half smile curled Phanes's mouth as I continued to stare at him. *Big ego*, I added to the list of things I knew about him, such as his ability to teleport and how when we'd first met, he had plucked a restraint spell off me as if it were mere lint. But Phanes was wrong if he thought I was admiring him. I was assessing his dangerousness.

Eight out of ten, I decided. Jaw-dropping looks aside, Phanes's wings were a dead giveaway that he wasn't human, yet he did nothing to hide them. Instead, he flaunted them.

If there was one thing my four-thousand-years-plus had taught me, it was that when a creature was this at ease while unarmed and alone in a foreign environment, then that creature was powerful. Worse, my magic bounced right off Phanes, as did my blood-ripping abilities. Whatever ran through his veins—assuming he had veins—wasn't blood or any other liquid I could manipulate.

"Put me down," I finally said.

To his credit, he did. Gently, too.

Potentially not a sadist, I added to my list.

As soon as I touched the sand, it swirled into golden flowers of every variety, until the beach looked like a magical garden. The air was also now so thick with that non-corporeal form of gold dust that I could no longer see the cottage.

Good gods, if any neighbors happened to be up at this hour and looked outside, they'd call the police! Or assume someone had slipped them LSD. Or both.

"Could you please stop making everything look like gold?"

Phanes waved, and the beach, sand, and air returned to normal. "Why did you flee from me before, my bride?"

He crossed his arms over his bare chest as he waited for my reply. He'd been bare chested the first time I'd seen him, too, though thankfully, his aversion to clothes didn't extend to pants. I would have bet they'd be gold, too, but his pants were as black as his hair and made of a material I didn't recognize.

I ignored his question because I had one of my own. "How did you find me?"

Ten days ago, he'd tracked me down because he felt it when I'd used my darkest power to kill Dagon. But I hadn't used that power since I'd killed Dagon, and it's not as if I'd left Phanes a forwarding address.

"Indus told me where you were," he replied.

Indus? Who . . . ? Oh, right, Indus was the ruler of Leviathan—scary, psychic creatures that formed from seawater and could drown anyone they touched. But how did the Leviathan ruler know where I was?

"You've got to be kidding me," I said, putting it together. "Indus tracked me just from my splashing around in the surf these past few nights?"

A sly smile curved Phanes's mouth.

"If you had only splashed? No, Indus could not have felt that. But you used your power on the water. *That*, he felt."

Great. Now, every time I used my power over water, it sent a metaphysical GPS notification to the Leviathan's ruler? That was a complication I didn't need.

"How impressive," I said in a cold voice. "Especially since the last time I saw Indus, he was halfway around the world. Or is he closer now?"

Phanes cocked his head. "I answered two of your questions, yet you haven't answered mine. Why did you flee from me before?"

It took all my willpower not to glance at the cottage behind us. According to my brother, if Phanes found out that his "fiancée" was married, he'd kill Ian. I'd seen Ian defeat powerful enemies before, but never while *unconscious*.

I couldn't let him know about Ian. Fortunately, I had another aspect of the truth to answer with.

"I don't know how things work in your world, but here? People don't get to show up and tell someone they've never met before that they're engaged. That's why I left. I'm not property to be promised to another without my consent."

Interest sparked in his gaze. Not the reaction I wanted, but it could have been worse.

"You wish to be won over by me first, then?"

Not in the slightest. But if pretending that bought me time and got Phanes away from Ian . . .

"Yes. You must prove you are worthy of my consideration. I propose a quest. Find and bring me"— Gods, what? What?—"the thirteen crystal skulls from ancient Mesoamerica, famed for their mystic qualities," I finished, then fought a groan.

That's the best I could come up with? Served me right, for falling asleep to that *Ancient Aliens* episode the other morning!

Phanes's brows rose.

I hid my inner cringe behind a straight face. "You don't find this quest too far beyond your abilities, do you?"

He flashed me a brilliant smile. "If the crystal skulls were genuine, it wouldn't be. But since they're a fable, what you're actually doing is trying to get rid of me."

Dammit! Either Phanes was very clever, or he had access to human television.

"I wonder if the reason has to do with all the energy you're sending toward the house behind me?" he went on.

Ice exploded through my veins. I don't remember summoning my darkest power, but all of a sudden it was there, turning the air around me to shadows of obsidian, while my gaze lit the night with a new silver glow.

"Don't," I said in a voice that now echoed in an eerie way.

A slow smile lifted Phanes's mouth. Then, he spread out his hands while his wings dipped as if they were bowing.

"Daughter of the Eternal River," he said in a newly formal tone, "I mean you no harm."

I wasn't worried about me. I was worried about the vampire who was still near death from what it had cost him to save me. The darkness around me grew with the thought, until I felt its edges touch the very netherworld itself.

"Daughter of—" Phanes began again.

"Veritas."

My voice was sharp, but it was *my* voice again. What I felt for Ian was so strong, it broke through even this.

"Veritas." Phanes held my gaze. "I've lived too long to fail to recognize love when I see it, and I see it every time you send your energy toward that house. Stop," he snapped, flying back when my darkness surged toward him. "I mean its occupant no harm! I do not want our engagement either!"

Oh?

I reined in my power until it no longer sought out Phanes. Instead, it swirled around my feet like inky clouds.

Phanes folded his wings inward the way a bird did when it landed on the ground. Unlike a bird, however, Phanes's wings looked like they disappeared entirely into his back.

"If you didn't want this engagement, why did you come looking for me?"

His approach was wary, but he still didn't look afraid. "When I felt your power, I was honor bound to seek you out."

Bullshit. Just like an annoying text, Phanes could've ignored that.

"So noble," I mocked. "Now, what's the real reason?"

That earned me a reluctant smile. "I wasn't the only one who felt it when you used your power to punch a hole through the veil separating this world from the netherworld. So, if I had failed to respond, others would know, and breaking my pledge to the Eternal River would have consequences."

That, I believed, especially if this match had been my father's idea. You didn't piss off the Warden of the Gateway to the Netherworld without having it come back to bite you.

The darkness around me disappeared as I powered all the way down. "Well, then, good news, Phanes. You can go back home and tell everyone that I released you from our betrothal. If my dad doesn't like that, he can take it up with me."

"I wish it were that simple." Phanes sounded like he was gritting his teeth. "But only your father has the authority to release me from my oath."

Not me, the intended bride? Of all the sexist bullshit—

"And I can't get to him where he is," Phanes went on.

Hope surged in me. "You know where my father is?"

Phanes gave me a surprised look. "You do not?"

If I did, would I be asking? "No, so where is he?"

For a second, all expression cleared from Phanes's face. He may as well have been one of the many statues the Greeks carved in honor of their gods. Then, that blankness disappeared, and the smile he gave me was as beautiful as the rising sun.

"He's an inmate in the bastion of the netherworld."

Guilt blasted through me. As warden, it was my father's job to send souls to their final destination in the netherworld, and he only ferried the souls meant for the netherworld's version of "the bad place." But when my former enemy, Dagon, had hoarded Ian's soul inside himself after Ian died protecting me, I begged my father to free Ian instead of sending him on to the afterlife. My father had, but he'd also inferred that he might lose his position as warden for it.

He hadn't said his punishment would be so much worse.

My father's part of the netherworld contained the darkest souls that this world—and others?—had to offer. I could only imagine those souls' sadistic delight at discovering that their former warden was now a prisoner, like they were.

And I could do nothing about it. I could pierce a hole into the netherworld, but only souls could cross over, and here I was, fresh out of the ability to be resurrected after I died. My head sank into my hands.

I couldn't save my father, and thus far, I'd been unable to save Ian, either. For all my power, I had never felt more helpless.

"I might know a way to get your father out."

My head snapped up.

Phanes rubbed his knuckles under his chin, as if he hadn't just dropped a bombshell. Then, for effect, his wings reappeared and extended to their full breadth, until they wreathed him in twin arcs of gold.

"Enough with the theatrics," I said. "How?"

He smiled. "Come with me, and I'll show you."

Not a chance. "Tell me here and now."

"No."

My eyes narrowed in warning.

Phanes only smiled wider. "You wouldn't believe me without seeing it yourself, so I won't waste my time telling you. And you can only see it if you come with me, so"—a wing extended toward me as if it were a hand—"again I say, come with me."

I might want to save my father from the netherworld's version of jail—and try to get him to heal Ian, plus officially end this betrothal—but I wasn't about to leave Ian behind.

Unless . . . no. No. It was too risky.

Find a way or make a way, I'd sworn earlier.

Well, this was a way. It *was* risky, but everything else we'd tried had failed. Ian might not survive much longer. Doing nothing was just as risky, if not more so.

"I'll go with you," I told Phanes, a desperate sort of recklessness setting in. "*If* you do something for me first."

Phanes gave me a sardonic smile. "Another fake quest?"

"No." My voice turned hoarse as hope and fear roiled within me. "This quest is very real."

He crossed his arms. "What is it?"

"Like you said, it's easier if I show you."

I led Phanes to the cottage, leaving the door open behind me but not inviting him in. Did he, like demons, need an invitation before he could enter a private residence?

No. Phanes crossed the threshold as if he owned the place. Then, he followed me into the bedroom, taking in the IV pole and the prone vampire on the bed without comment. I said nothing, either, but my pet, Silver, looked at Phanes and let out a soft growl.

I didn't know if it was a natural reaction from the Simargl at the sight of a far bigger winged creature, but I decided to add my own warning, too. A silver glow shot from my eyes as I looked at Phanes.

Harm him and you die, my look told him.

His lips curled in acknowledgment.

I pulled back the sheets, showing most of Ian's injuries, though I kept his left hand covered. The ancient horn that adorned it used to belong to Cain, the first of all vampires. More important, it was powerful in a way that defied explanation. It hadn't escaped my notice that the only part of Ian that had healed was his fingers, where the horn was still wrapped around them like a pair of brass knuckles.

Phanes studied Ian with cool appraisal. No sympathy softened his features, but no hostility marred them, either. So much for Ashael's warning that Phanes would kill any romantic rival for me. If anything, Phanes looked bored as he stared at Ian.

Good. I didn't need Phanes to be interested in Ian. I only needed his ability to tear magic off.

I tried not to let any of my desperate hope show. "Can you see the magic that did this to him?"

"Yes." His eyes lifted to mine. "It's very old and very powerful."

Of course it was. Dagon had used his best stuff to take me and Ian down.

"I'm surprised he survived such magic," Phanes went on. "He is, after all, only a vampire."

His dismissive tone rankled, but I ignored it. "When we first met, you plucked a spell off me, so I know you can tear magic from people. My quest for you is simple: tear the spell off him that's wasting him away."

His brows rose. "That magic was hardly the same as this."

"I don't care. If you tear the spell from him, I'll come with you. If you don't, then I won't, and if you do him any harm, I'll kill you."

Sometimes, a warning look wasn't enough. This was one of those times.

Phanes's arrogant half smile returned. "You must

love him very much. How unfortunate. I'm much more powerful, and much handsomer, too."

His ego wouldn't quit, would it? "Ian endured every one of the injuries you see to save me. He even *died* for me once. Can you do better than that?"

"No," he said, and then paused as if surprised by his admission.

Interesting. "You don't care for anyone enough to die for them, do you?"

His arrogant smile remained, but for the briefest moment, something flashed in his gaze. It vanished before I could decipher it, but its presence was telling. That question had made him feel something he hadn't wanted me to see. Under other circumstances, I'd wonder what. Now, I didn't care. I only wanted him to heal Ian, or get out.

Phanes gave Ian's injuries another calculating glance. Then, he moved closer.

I tensed but forced myself not to stop him. Still, it took all my effort to let a dangerous creature?— lesser deity?—something else?—near the man I loved. By the time Phanes ran a hand over Ian's vastly shrunken torso, my cartilage was cracking from how tightly my muscles were clenched.

What if I'd made a terrible mistake? What if Phanes's apathy over our engagement was a ruse, and he was about to murder Ian—?

Phanes suddenly grabbed Ian so hard, I heard countless bones break. I lunged at Phanes, but he swatted me away with both powerful wings. I smacked against the bedroom wall, then immediately lunged at Phanes again. I could barely see him because my otherworldly power had darkened my vision, but I could feel him, and only Ian's nearness kept me from opening a chute to the netherworld right beneath Phanes's feet.

"Get away from him," I snarled.

Phanes let go of Ian to grab me in mid-lunge. It took both his arms and all the strength from his wings to hold me.

"Veritas, stop. Look! The spell is now gone!"

Ian groaned. The sound stopped me in mid-grapple. I hadn't heard any part of Ian's voice for over a week.

I let go of Phanes to stare at Ian.

Muscles and sinews formed on him, filling out his skeletal arms, the awful caverns in his sides, and his formerly shrunken torso before racing to his legs and swelling them with healthy flesh, too. In the time it took me to suck in a choked breath, Ian's body had returned to its normal, well-muscled state, complete with his pearlescent skin and his sunset-hued hair.

I tensed, waiting for it to backfire, and his body to return to that awful, partially skeletized state. Several seconds ticked by. Ian still looked whole and healthy. Silver began zooming around the room while letting out excited yips.

Then, Ian groaned, and sat up.

I fought a sob as I flung myself next to him on the bed.

"Ian? Ian! Can you hear me?"

His eyes cracked open, their vivid turquoise shade even brighter than I remembered. Or maybe it only seemed that way because it felt like an eternity since I'd seen his eyes.

"'Course I can hear you," he murmured. "You're shouting."

I tried to say something else, but it came out as half laugh, half sob. He was healed, gods, fully healed and awake! If I died now, I'd die happy.

His eyes opened all the way, though he still looked a little drowsy, as if his comalike state had left him sluggish. Then his fingers brushed my cheek, and his brows drew together.

"Why are you crying? And who's the wanker with the wings?"

Phanes muttered something in a language I didn't recognize. Then he returned to speaking in an ancient dialect of Greek.

"I've held up my end of our agreement, Veritas."

Yes, he had. Ian was healed, awake, and the air around him was starting to crackle with energy as his power regenerated, too. I was so relieved, I started to tremble.

I allowed myself another moment to stare at Ian while feeling his hand on my cheek. Such a little thing, yet the emotions it generated couldn't be measured.

I couldn't leave him now! Not yet!

But a promise was a promise. Besides, I couldn't risk Phanes taking back this incredible healing if I reneged on my part of our agreement. Nothing was worth that, not even the pain it caused me to pull away.

Ian sat up straighter. "You smell upset. What's wrong?"

"Veritas," Phanes said again.

"Sod off, or I'll rip you in half," Ian snapped.

Any moment, the last bit of mental sluggishness from Ian's coma would lift, and he'd realize who Phanes was. We had to be gone by then.

"I've got to go do something," I said in a voice husky from regret. "But I love you, and I'll be back soon, I promise."

I held out my hand to Phanes right as recognition darkened Ian's features. The look he shot Phanes then was pure murder.

"Wait. I know who you are—"

He never finished the sentence. Phanes took my hand, and at his touch, Ian and the rest of our surroundings disappeared.

$\mathcal{I}$ was too upset to marvel at the whirling darkness around us. Normally, I couldn't see anything while being teleported because the transition from one place to another was almost instantaneous. This wasn't, and it looked like Phanes had swept us up inside a tornado made of black smoke.

I didn't care. All I could think about was Ian's face when he realized I was leaving—and who I was leaving with.

I'd make him understand, once I got back. Hopefully, this chat with Phanes would take no more than an hour or two. Yes, Ian still might be furious with me, but his anger would be a welcome sight compared to watching him hover near death the past ten days.

You did what needed to be done, my newly merged, icily logical half argued. *Phanes healed Ian as promised, and leaving with him was the agreed-upon payment.*

I could have told Ian where I was going and why, I countered.

Only if you wanted to watch the two of them fight to the death, she replied. *Ian wouldn't care that Phanes had healed him. As soon as he realized who Phanes was, he'd try to kill him.*

She—*I*—had me there. Ian was fearless, and he was also the only person that had been more upset than I was to find out that my father had arranged my betrothal to Phanes before I was even born. He absolutely would've tried to kill Phanes, and I hadn't bargained with Phanes to heal Ian only to see him risk his life as his first conscious act.

But, oh, *his face*!

I was so upset, it took a few moments to notice that the whirling chaos had stopped. Clouds now spread out in every direction, lit by rays from a sun I couldn't see because of all the fleecy whiteness. It was nearing 2 A.M. back in the Hamptons. We must be on the other side of the world for it to be daylight here.

Several gleaming marble temples rose up from the clouds at different levels, as if their wispy masses hid the mountain that the temples were built on. I also caught glimpses of forests and rivers. For some reason, this place looked familiar, though I was certain that I had never been here before.

Olympus, I realized as I looked around. It wasn't quite right, but this place greatly resembled how ancient Greeks had described Mount Olympus, the mythical home of the gods.

We must be on some hidden island, possibly in the Mediterranean, considering the knock-off Olympus theme. Phanes or someone else had shrouded this place with glamour so it remained unseen by humans, vampires, demons, and those pesky modern satellites. This wasn't the first magically-shielded island I'd been to. Supernatural creatures of all kinds used magic to keep their private getaways, well, private.

I turned to Phanes, who was staring at me with surprise.

"Your hair, your face, your"—his hand swept out, indicating my body—"*everything* is different."

I glanced down. The glamour I normally wore as my Law Guardian persona was gone. Now, I looked like my real self: mid-twenties, much curvier, taller, with different facial features set off by silvery hair that had blue and gold streaks in it. My bronze skin color was the same, though, hinting at my Middle Eastern heritage on my mother's side.

Phanes stared at me like it would hurt him to pull his gaze away. "You are radiant. Why would you conceal such beauty with that plain appearance?"

My look said I didn't appreciate the disparagement. "Long ago, my vampire sire, Tenoch, disguised me from my enemies by glamouring me with his deceased daughter's appearance. I have been proud to wear her visage ever since."

Phanes was silent. Then, he inclined his head in a formal way. "For my unintended insult, I apologize."

My opinion of him rose. Some people never admitted a fault, which let you know right off that they were untrustworthy.

"Apology accepted, and my compliments on your island's security. It takes a strong magic shield to instantly negate the glamour of anyone entering it."

His expression changed back to his normal, confident one. "My security is the best. Now, come. I'll take you to my home."

We walked on the clouds, which of course couldn't be real clouds or I'd be falling, not walking. But they felt solid and steady even if they looked wispy and formless. Phanes or someone else must've glamoured the ground. No surprise that Phanes wanted people impressed by his island.

As soon as our feet touched the white marble steps leading up to Phanes's ancient-looking temple, the clouds disappeared. Lush gardens replaced them, bordered by a forest that spread out until I could no longer see the other temples. A group of centaurs galloped toward the temple, their humanoid upper bodies in stark contrast to their equine lower halves.

"Lord Phanes has returned!" one of the centaurs shouted.

More people came out from the temple. Some looked like regular humans, some looked part animal and part human, and some . . . damned if I knew what they were.

"Behold," Phanes thundered, hoisting my arm over my head. "The daughter of the Eternal River bridging life and dcath!"

Oh no he *didn't*. I tried to yank my arm free, but his grip tightened. "Don't," Phanes said low. "Our agreement stands, but *they* don't have to know about it."

I'd rather throw up and eat it than act like a trophy being brought home, but if this got me to Ian the fastest . . . fine. I'd never see these people again, anyway.

I smiled and raised my other arm. Our audience cheered.

"Tonight, we feast!" Phanes announced.

Tonight? I kept my smile, but yanked Phanes's head down.

"I never agreed to stay the night," I hissed in his ear.

He beamed as he folded his wings around us. When I could see nothing except those gold feathers, his grin vanished.

"You owe me." A low growl only I could hear. "I accepted your rejection, healed your lover, and soon, I will show you how to release your father from his prison. All I ask in return is that you pretend to be my happy intended bride for one night. Then, leave tomorrow with the information you seek and me as your ally instead of your enemy."

The last thing I needed was a new enemy, but there were limits on what I'd do to avoid that. Still, I could understand Phanes's need to save face with his people.

"I'll give you all the smiles and admiring looks you want, but that's it," I said in an equally low voice.

"And two kisses, plus you share my room tonight. Platonically, if you insist," he added when I drew in a breath to refuse.

Oh, Ian was *not* going to like this!

But would I rather leave my father to rot in the netherworld, plus stay technically engaged to Phanes, *and* have yet another powerful creature out to kill us?

You have no choice, my other half said pitilessly.

Fucking hell. She—*I*—was right.

"One kiss, not two, and we don't sleep in the same bed."

Phanes smiled. Nothing in this strange, hidden place compared to its beauty, but after I got what I came for, I never wanted to see it *or* him again.

"Agreed. Now"—his wings dropped, revealing us to the still-cheering onlookers—"show them that you are happy."

I gave them a bright smile that was the exact opposite of how I felt. Then, I accepted the arm Phanes held out to me, and we ascended the rest of the stairs together.

Chapter 5

*O*nce we were inside, everywhere we walked, reds, purples, blues, and gold swirled beneath our feet, as if our footsteps revealed opals trapped within the marble. A glance up revealed massive ceilings supported by Doric columns topped with ornate capitals. Back at eye level, statues of naked men, women, and nymphs lined the walls while fire braziers cast a golden-orange glow, and the scent of flowers mixed with whatever oil fed the flames.

Phanes must be *really* into the ancient Greek theme, down to using fire instead of electric lighting.

Phanes clapped his hands. At once, a group of women wearing matching blue-green dresses appeared and began to hustle me out of the room.

"My servants will ready you for tonight's feast," Phanes said. Then, he returned his attention to his adulators.

Leaving suited me. It rankled to act as if it were flattering to be treated like a living piece of decoration.

The women led me to a gorgeous, flower-strewn

room with an in-floor marble bath and its own private garden. Once there, I was stripped, bathed, dried, massaged, perfumed, coiffed, and generally treated like a show dog being prepared for the championship round of a competition.

Things almost took a bad turn when one of the hair-styling women leaned in close enough to brush her throat against my mouth. My fangs popped out, and my stomach growled so loudly that all the servants heard it.

They jumped back in alarm, and the apparent head housekeeper, Helena, stared at me with shock.

"Blood Eater," Helena whispered.

"Half Blood Eater," I corrected, since my "daughter of the Eternal River" status was important here. "And I'm not going to bite any of you," I added when the other servants now gave me a wide berth.

Helena snapped out something in a language that sounded like the one Phanes had used earlier. Whatever she said had the servants scurrying back to my couch. Then, one by one, they knelt, pulled their hair aside, and presented their necks.

My stomach growled again, but I shook my head. "No."

They didn't want to do this, and hungry or no, I wouldn't force them. Besides, I could wait one more day to eat.

"Helena, I'd like to be alone, so you and the others may go. Before you do, though, can someone bring me a mobile?"

Helena gave me a blank look.

"Cell phone," I amended. Now everyone had puzzled expressions. "Phone," I stressed, miming holding one up to my ear. "So I can call someone?"

Helena appeared aghast. "We don't have such things."

"What about a tablet? Desktop computer? *Any* telecommunications technology?"

At each question, Helena shook her head. Great. Phanes had brought me to the Greek gods' version of an Amish village.

"Then please just leave," I said with a sigh. "I'm tired, and I want to nap before the feast tonight."

Partly true. I was tired, but I would never fall asleep in a strange place surrounded by people I didn't trust. I did, however, want to be alone.

Helena pursed her lips, but a few sharp words later, and the room was empty of all except me and her.

"I will stay to tidy up," she said.

What part of "alone" did she not understand? "Thank you, but I desire solitude, so please leave."

Color made her dusky cheeks even rosier. "Mistress—"

"Go," I said. Did I have to clap like Phanes next?

Helena pursed her lips. "Very well. I will return after dusk. Be ready to be dressed by then."

With another disapproving look, she left.

I leaned back against the couch with a sigh. I only had to give Phanes his "show off the trophy fiancée" night to rescue my father, end this unwanted engagement, and get back to Ian. One night wasn't so bad. Compared to watching Ian hover near death for the past ten days, it should be easy.

I'll be home soon, I silently promised Ian. *Very soon.*

Chapter 6

*H*ours later, Phanes smiled when he saw me. My gown draped from one shoulder, leaving the other bare before hugging my torso and flaring into soft, individual swaths around my legs. The pale pink material was diaphanous, and shimmered under the glow of the thousand tiny starlike lights that now hung from the ceiling as if suspended from invisible strands. My blue-and-gold-streaked hair was upswept, leaving only a few tendrils free. Jeweled hair combs winked when they caught the light, and more jewels decorated my heeled sandals.

Phanes wore a traditional Greco-Roman-styled tunic, with slits in the back to allow his wings to frame him. Their gold color accented the golden threads that glittered in the garment. He rose as I approached, and I smiled as wide as I'd promised when we made our arrangement earlier.

I sat to his right at the L-shaped table. Cathedral ceilings soared above us, and hundreds of wall sconces lit the shadowed passages as far as I could see. This temple was much bigger than its exterior appearance indicated. No fewer than fifty guests sat at Phanes's table, and there were several more tables as big as this one around the perimeter of the room, leaving the center of it curiously empty.

Phanes clapped his hands. At once the table became laden with delicacies. If I was human and starving, I couldn't consume a fraction of the food in front of me.

Phanes clapped again. Music filled the air, along with an instant fog that covered the empty center of the room. Moments later, a platform crested through that fog, revealing dozens of dancers wearing only jewelry, body paint, and enough oil to make their flesh gleam.

They began to dance. Fog clung to them or dashed away as if it were dancing, too. Some of the dancers were human, some were nymphs, some centaurs, and some were an unknown species, but they all moved with a fluidity that made every leap, sway, and dip mesmerizingly graceful. Soon, the dance took an explicit turn as the dancers began pleasuring themselves and each other with inventive, uninhibited gusto.

Phanes leaned toward me. "Beautiful, are they not?"

"They are," I replied.

He settled back into his chair. "Pick one. Or pick several. Or pick all of them. Whatever you desire."

My brows rose. "Pick them for what?"

"Pleasure." He spoke as if the answer were obvious. "They are the most skilled lovers you will ever find, barring only myself, of course."

It took all my willpower not to roll my eyes. First, Phanes plied me with excessive pampering, then enough food to choke a horse, and now, he was offering me my own harem. Never let it be said that he did anything by half measures.

"Thank you," I said in as appreciative a tone as I could manage. "But you know what I came here for, and it isn't that."

He leaned in, an odd intensity in his gaze. "Very well. Then, tell me what you think about the play. It will begin soon."

The music increased in tempo. The dancers matched the new pace until their movements were almost a blur. Then, with a crescendo that thrummed through me like an artificial heartbeat, the dance came to an abrupt, dazzling end.

Everyone applauded. Then, Phanes clapped his hands, and there was instant silence. The fog around the stage rose, covering the dancers.

Phanes clapped again. The fog cleared, revealing the stage. The dancers were gone, and a temple appeared to loom in the distance, with people and creatures of all types frolicking in a village in front of the temple. No surprise, the frolicking soon turned erotic.

I fought a sigh. I had no interest in watching another orgy, let alone one with a Fifty Shades of

Centaurs subplot, but Phanes apparently didn't offer any other form of entertainment.

Ian wouldn't be bored. He'd be taking notes, my other half thought with more amusement that I had believed her capable of.

She was right, and it only made me miss him more.

It hurt to dwell on that, so I concentrated on the play. Thankfully, the orgy was soon interrupted by a new actor and actress who were clearly playing the part of villains. The actress had fake, frost-coated wings, and she froze several of the revelers in place with a mime of a deadly ice storm. The actor scattered the remaining revelers with a mock earthquake that destroyed the temple. Then, the evil duo set up a new temple, and the remaining revelers now had yokes on them and looked miserable as they mimed serving their new rulers.

A new actor swooped onto the stage wearing large, fake golden wings. He began vanquishing the villains to cheers from the villagers. By the play's conclusion, the villains were in cages in a dark pit, and the actor who was clearly representing Phanes ascended to a duplication of Mount Olympus. When the fog finally rose to cover the stage, the audience broke into wild applause.

I clapped, too, since it was only polite. Once the applause died down, Phanes turned to me.

"What did you think, my lovely one?"

That having an entire play performed to praise you is so arrogant, even Vlad Dracul would tell you to tone it down.

I didn't say that, of course. I just replied, "I'm overwhelmed," which was also the truth.

He leaned in so close that his lips brushed my ear. "Once, before the Great Flood, I saved your world from the cruel deities ruling it. Now, I can give you more riches, pleasure, and protection than you'll ever need. That's why your father honored me by betrothing me to his future seed. He wanted you to be with a worthy mate. I am that mate, Veritas."

It took everything to keep my smile frozen in place, let alone keep my other nature from showing her opinion of being referred to as "future seed." Phanes came from an era where family-arranged marriages were the norm, and where offering to buy my affection with jewels, orgies, and protection was probably a compliment.

"You're a very worthy mate," I told Phanes, which was what he wanted to hear. Then, I kissed him.

He was so startled, he didn't react for a full three seconds. Not used to a woman taking sexual control, was he? He and I would have been the *worst* match.

By the time Phanes recovered and his arms went around me, I was already pulling away and acting as if the brief kiss had flustered me. Our onlookers cheered, and I fidgeted as if I were fourteen instead of several hundred years past four thousand.

One kiss with witnesses, done.

"All the excitement has exhausted me," I said, ducking to tuck my head against his chest. It fit my "exhausted" claims, and also blocked his attempt to extend our kiss.

He hadn't specified in our bargain *how long* the kiss had to last. That was his problem, not mine.

"Let me retire to the bedchamber," I went on, then added in a louder voice so there was no chance he could claim that I hadn't held up my end of the second half of our bargain, "And I hope it won't be too long until you join me, Phanes."

More cheers, this time accompanied by the expected amount of ribald encouragement. Phanes laughed, wrapping a wing around my shoulders as he turned to our guests—

"Sorry, luv, but Phanes is going to be indefinitely detained," said the very *last* voice I expected to hear.

Shock stabbed me. No. It couldn't be.

I felt like I was moving in slow motion as I turned toward that voice. Then my gaze was welded to the tall, auburn-haired man striding through the remaining fog, a red cape billowing behind him as if it were his own pair of wings.

It can't be! my mind continued to rage.

But it was.

At last, my other half thought.

Phanes's wing dropped from my shoulder as if he were shocked, too. Then, his arrogance returned, and he boomed, "Who dares to enter my temple without invitation?"

I'd seen blood dripping from knives that didn't look as threatening as the smile Ian gave Phanes.

"I dare, mate."

For a paralyzing moment, I had no idea what to do. Would rushing over to Ian humiliate Phanes to the point that it guaranteed they fight to the death? Or would staying at Phanes's side incite Ian to do something even *more* rash than barging into a lesser god's temple as if he owned the place? Could I do anything to prevent bloodshed, or were we irrevocably fucked?

"How did you penetrate my security?" Phanes demanded.

"Not without difficulty," Ian replied, sounding faintly amused now. "And I hear you have to defeat the ruling temple's champion for the right to safe passage in your lands, so, whoever the champion is, consider them challenged."

Irrevocably fucked it is! my other half thought.

Phanes met Ian's stare. It hadn't escaped my notice that Ian hadn't deigned to look at me at all yet.

"Who are you, to think you can issue such a challenge?"

Was Phanes pretending he didn't know Ian because he didn't want to admit that this was his fiancée's lover? Or did Phanes not remember what Ian looked like now that he was healed?

Ian certainly didn't resemble the half-shriveled husk Phanes had first glimpsed, especially in his medieval-knight-meets-modern-warrior attire. His auburn hair brushed the shiny armor on his broad shoulders, and more armor covered his wrists, forearms, and calves before a larger piece covered his front like a breastplate. But the rest of him was clad only in black tactical gear, drawing several admiring looks from Phanes's guests at how the form-fitting fabric accentuated his muscled thighs, biceps, and ass.

Ian winked at his most obvious gawkers, proving his peripheral vision was as sharp as ever. Was his power back to normal, too? Or was it still too soon after that terrible, body-ravaging magic? He'd only been healed six or seven hours ago . . .

"I'm a son of noble birth, which is all I need to be to issue such a challenge," Ian replied.

Were those the rules? How sexist *and* classist . . . and how did Ian know this, let alone how was he here in the first place?

Ashael sidled up to Ian, wearing the same Greco Roman–style tunic as Phanes. *That's* how Ian had gotten here!

I glared at Ashael. He flinched, and then spread out his hands as if to say, *this isn't my fault.*

Oh yes it is! I wanted to snap. *All you had to do was* not *teleport Ian to Phanes's home base within hours of my leaving!*

Phanes crossed his arms. "What was your father's title?"

Ian smiled again. "Viscount Maynard, member of the peerage since his birth in the year of our Lord 1731. We're on Wikipedia under 'Viscounts of Great Britain,' if that helps."

Half true. He *was* Viscount Maynard's son, but not a legitimate one. Ian's real name was Killian, and he was the bastard child of Viscount Maynard. The Viscount had forced Killian to serve out his legitimate heir's prison sentence back in the seventeen hundreds since Killian looked enough like his heir, Ian, that no one questioned the switch. Killian had kept the name Ian ever since, and I was the only person alive who knew that it wasn't the name he'd been born with.

"I'm also the vampire offspring of Mencheres, former pharaoh of Egypt," Ian said. "So, I have a noble lineage through my vampire side as well."

I stared at Ian as if I could strike him mute by willpower alone. Why was he spoiling for a fight against creatures he didn't even know how to kill? Sure, Ian was mad, but if he could only holster his rage until dawn, this would all be over!

He did glance at me then. A long, heated stare that made me feel like my clothes flew off and landed at his feet. But beneath the possessive lust, I saw a hardness that sent the wrong kind of shivers over me.

Ian was more than angry. Much more. I just didn't know what else it was, or whether it was all directed toward me.

Then he looked away, giving Phanes his attention again. "Tell me she's the challenger I must face," he said in his most insinuating tone. "Would love some full contact with *her*."

Let the mayhem begin! my other half thought as Phanes stood so fast, his chair upended.

I also shot to my feet. I didn't even intend for my darkness to boil out of me until it transcended shadows and became a flood that drowned the opal lights in the floor, but it did. It also coated my entire chair, making it now resemble a liquid obsidian throne. The netherworld practically throbbed in invitation beneath me, the veil feeling so thin that I wouldn't need much effort to break through it. No, it felt as if I'd able to brush it aside as easily as Ian had brushed away the fog he'd strode through.

Okay, perhaps I'd overreacted, but no one was allowed to hurt Ian for being this reckless except me.

"Stop," I said in a voice that boomed with eerie echoes.

The guests at our table scattered. Even Phanes backed up, avoiding the liquid darkness around me.

Not Ian. His gaze raked me, taking in everything from the inky waters that surrounded me to the new silver beams lighting up my gaze, and his brows only flicked in suggestive invitation.

Ashael stepped forward, clearing his throat. "The daughter of the Eternal River is right. A formal challenge has been issued, and protocol must be observed."

Protocol? I could care less about protocol—

"Long ago, the gods gave us the trials to honor them," Ashael went on. "The challenger has shown his worthiness. Your champion must accept. Let the trials commence!"

Phanes glanced at me and then gave Ian a long look that made me think he did finally realize who he was, either from belated recognition, or my reaction.

Then, with an arrogant smile that made me even more concerned, Phanes clapped his hands.

"If the challenger insists, then bring forth my champion, Naxos, and let the trials commence!"

I TRIED TO find a way to speak to Ian, but everyone started filing out of the room while chanting "to the stadium!" Within moments, I lost Ian in the enthusiastic crowd. Another surge of people later, and Ashael faded from view, too. Then all I saw was wings as Phanes encircled me within them.

"What game are you playing, Veritas?" he hissed.

I was too rattled to object to how he loomed over me. "I have nothing to do with this. If you would stop this challenge and let me speak to Ian—"

"Too late," he cut me off. "As that demon pointed out, even I can't refuse to honor the higher gods by denying a worthy challenger his right to the trials. Your lover insisted on meeting my champion in battle, so meet him he shall."

Phanes was bound by the same traditions that had once led ancient Greeks to consider formal athletic competitions as part of their religion? Interesting, but why was Ian doing this at all? If he'd given me another half day, I'd be home!

"What happens if Ian loses to your champion?"

Phanes gave me a look that required no interpretation.

Ice climbed up my spine and fanned out until even my fingertips felt cold.

"For your sake, I am sorry that he did this," Phanes said, and dropped his wings. "Come. You can watch the trials with me."

My jaw clenched. Yes, I would watch, and if it came to it, I'd also participate, because anyone who tried to kill Ian was dead.

I'll slaughter them without mercy, my other half swore.

For once, she and I were in complete agreement.

"You go. I'll be there in a moment," I said.

Phanes frowned. "You shouldn't be alone now."

I caught a glimpse of Ashael in the crowd. Oh, I wouldn't be alone for long.

"I need a minute to myself." My hard look stopped Phanes when he opened his mouth to argue. "Go. I'll find you."

Phanes sighed. "If you insist, but remember, this was not my doing." He caught my hand, raised it, and brushed his lips over it. "I would never hurt you this way if I had a choice."

Now Ashael ducked out of view. I pulled my hand away.

"I'll see you soon," I said, and headed toward where I'd last seen Ashael.

Chapter 8

$\mathcal{I}$n the back of the temple, a garden path opened up to an impressive stadium that looked like a smaller version of the Colosseum in its prime. The stone benches quickly filled with Phanes's guests as well as people who seemed to pour in from paths between the tall shrubs that surrounded the stadium.

Must be the occupants of the other temples on this cloud-strewn mountain. News about the challenge and subsequent trials had traveled, and it was obviously a not-to-be-missed event.

I felt sick when I heard people placing bets on who would survive: Naxos, or the unknown challenger. So far, everyone was betting on Naxos. I had to get Ian to drop out of this.

I pushed through the crowd, glancing behind me every so often. Yes, Phanes was still staring after me, even as he made his way to a private alcove three rows up in the stadium. Servants scurried behind Phanes, carrying kylixes of wine, silk cushions for him to sit on, and other luxuries.

Phanes didn't want to let me out of his sight. Why?

I grabbed a woman by her arm as she tried to hurry past me into the stadium.

"Where's the challenger?"

"Probably below the arena," she replied, trying to pull away.

My grip didn't loosen. "Take me there."

She couldn't have looked more shocked if I'd stabbed her. "I can't. It's forbidden!"

"Rules are made to be broken," I insisted. "Come on."

She screamed. Now I had the attention of everyone around us, too. I smiled through gritted teeth.

"Just a dispute between friends, people. Carry on."

"Help me, she's insane!" the woman shouted.

"I'm not. I just need to see the challenger—"

"Veritas."

I whirled at my name. Ashael was several meters behind me, half hidden behind a thick stone pillar with a mural of Zeus painted on it.

I released her with a muttered, "Apologies," before I strode over to my half brother.

"Take me to Ian," I said as soon as I reached him. "I need to stop this. Do you know what will happen if he loses?"

"Yes," Ashael said, yanking me behind the pillar. "And if I couldn't talk him out of this, you won't. Besides, if you're caught interfering, it'll be considered as cheating, and his life as well as yours will be forfeit."

Anger and anxiety exploded in me. "Then why did you bring him here, let alone tell him how to issue a non-retractable, lethal challenge? I had the situation with Phanes handled!"

Ashael looked at me the way the screaming woman had: as if I were insane. "Handled? You're *choosing* to be here?"

"For one night, yes! You couldn't give me that before bringing Ian here so he could risk his life for me *again*?"

Ashael's angry, defensive expression melted away. "One night. That's how long you think you've been here?"

"Not even," I began, and then stopped. "What do you mean, that's how long I *think* I've been here?"

Ashael gave me a pitying look. "You don't know where you are, do you?"

My hand sliced the air in an impatient wave. "On a magically hidden island, similar to the one you took Ian and me to when we were looking for Yonah."

Ashael's tight grip loosened. "No," he said very softly. "You're not on an island. You're not in your world at all."

"That's impossible."

His brows arched. "Didn't you notice the celestial wormhole you had to enter to get here?"

Oh, shit.

Yes, I had noticed the strange, extended whirl-wind of darkness when Phanes teleported us here. I'd also never before been to a place where mountains appeared to be held aloft by clouds, the temples were far larger than their exterior appearances accounted for, and creatures from different mythologies were real. I'd discounted the former as glamour and the latter as unusual, but maybe it was more than that.

I took in a breath that did nothing to ease the sudden tightening in my body. "If I'm not in 'my world,' where am I?"

Ashael patted me the way you'd soothe a startled beast.

"Some call these places fae worlds. Others call them the home of the gods. Some consider them purgatory. Technically, they're all correct because no two bubble realms floating on the lip of the netherworld are the same. They become whatever their ruler designates them to be. Phanes modeled this one after the legends mortals told of him, but in all these realms, time passes differently because of their proximity to the netherworld. In some, it speeds up. In others, it slows down. I didn't know which one this was until now."

I'd been shaking my head as he spoke. Logic had nothing on denial. By the time he was done, I was fighting a shriek. Yes, I knew that time passed very differently in the netherworld. I'd been killed often enough to notice that the few minutes I spent in that dark void before my father resurrected me could equate to hours back in the living world. But I didn't know that "bubble realms" like this existed, let alone that I was in one.

"So, how long have I been here, according to you and Ian?" I managed to ask through a new lump in my throat.

Ashael sighed. "A little over three weeks—"

My horrified scream cut him off.

*A*shael clapped a hand over my mouth, giving an alarmed look around before tightening his grip.

"In case Phanes's reaction escaped you, my kind is hardly welcome here. If you scream again, someone will assume I am assaulting you, and it will not go well for me."

I forced myself to stop. To take in a breath instead, and not think about how the whole time I'd been getting bathed, massaged, and then displayed like a trophy for this stupid feast, weeks had passed where Ian was. And he'd had no idea where I was, why I'd left him, or if I intended to come back.

No wonder he'd looked at me with such rage! He must've thought that I'd abandoned him just like I had after my father erased most of Ian's memories of me.

I felt my back hit the wall behind me, and I leaned against it because I suddenly needed the support. Now, I didn't feel like screaming. I felt like weeping.

A new thought shot anger through me, until I straightened as if I'd been yanked up by an invisible hand.

Phanes must have known. This wasn't the first time he'd gone back and forth from my world to his. Oh, yes, he knew, and he'd *insisted* that I come here to "talk." Once we were here, he'd stalled again, telling me that he needed a night of pretending before he'd reveal how to save my dad.

What would his excuse have been tomorrow? That he had to wait until after lunch before telling me how I could free my dad? How long would Phanes have put me off, knowing that every hour I spent in his world equated to being gone for days in mine?

"I'm going to kill him," I ground out.

Ashael gave a wary look around. "Who?"

Phanes! both parts of me replied.

Neither of us said it out loud. Most people who noticed Ashael and me seemed too intent on reaching the stadium before all the good seats were taken, but a few of them had lingered because of my previous scream. I caught their eye and forced a smile as I patted Ashael's arm to show that everything was okay.

No matter my anger, I wouldn't threaten to kill Phanes within earshot of anyone who was loyal to him. Oh, no. I'd continue to pretend to know nothing.

"I have to tell Ian that what he heard was an act, and I had no idea I'd been gone that long," I whispered to Ashael.

He frowned. "I told you, the trials start soon, and

again, if you're caught doing anything that's considered interfering, your life and Ian's life will be forfeit." Then Ashael's tone softened. "But I am his second. If I can manage to tell him without being overheard, I will. Regardless, be ready to leave as soon as the trials are over."

I didn't get a chance to reply before I saw Helena, head of the servants who'd dressed me earlier. From the way Helena's head swiveled to and fro, she was looking for someone. When her gaze stopped as soon as it landed on me, and she practically charged in my direction, I knew I was her target.

Phanes must have sent Helena after me. I glanced around the pillar that concealed us. The onlookers in the stadium were focused on the center of the field, waiting for the action to start. Phanes, however, was staring off in the direction where he'd last seen me.

Oh, yes, Phanes was anxious to get me back. No wonder, too. He must be worried about what I'd discover. Well, too late.

I ducked back behind the pillar. If I couldn't stop the trials, I intended to be there to assist.

I swept away from Ashael without another word. I couldn't risk Helena telling him that she'd seen me arguing with him. Then I clapped my hands at Helena as imperiously as Phanes.

"Take me to Lord Phanes," I said. "I've gotten turned around in these crowds."

She gave me an appalled once-over. "Your hair is askew and your dress is smudged. Come. I will make you presentable first—"

"No, you'll take me to Phanes," I cut her off. Ashael had said the trials were about to start. I couldn't miss a moment.

"At once, mistress, after I make you flawless again."

I couldn't waste time letting her primp me. I hated playing the imperious mistress, but I'd do far worse to save Ian.

"Take me to Lord Phanes, or I'll find him myself, and tell him of your insolence."

With a grimly resigned look, Helena swept out her arm. "If you would follow me."

Chapter 10

*H*elena shouldn't have worried. Smudged dress or no, Phanes looked glad to see me when I ascended the stairs to his private stone alcove. He smiled at me, and I forced a brief smile in return. I couldn't let him see the anger boiling behind my eyes.

As soon as I sat, Helena snapped her fingers, and servants scurried to offer me wine and fruit. I declined, and she gave me another disapproving look before moving to the corner of the alcove behind me.

In the scant time since I'd last seen it, the empty expanse of grass in the infield now boasted a wide strip that ran down the middle like an airplane runway. It ended in a silk line stretched across the ground. A disc made of an indeterminate metal was in front of it, with a finish line about thirty meters away. At that line, a single bow and arrow rested on the ground, its target probably the small, red fruit dangling from the beam that stretched across the top of the stadium, because why else would that be there?

Ancient Greeks had featured foot races, discus throwing, and archery in their early Olympics. This setup vaguely resembled those games. That didn't sound as ominous as Phanes and Ashael had inferred, let alone explained the heavy betting from spectators that Ian wouldn't survive.

A loud cheer from the crowd snapped my attention to the entrance of the stadium. A naked, blond-haired man ran into the arena holding a lit torch. My brows rose. Was this the champion Ian had to face? If so, he didn't seem that imposing.

The naked blond man ran to the end of the U-shaped stadium and touched the flame to what looked like oil-soaked twine surrounding a hatch in the ground. The twine burst into flames, and he ran away to the sound of more cheers that soon became a chant.

"Naxos . . . Naxos . . . Naxos!"

The hatch burst open. Tremors vibrated through the stadium as everyone suddenly jumped to their feet. Something very large, dark, and horned burst from the flame-haloed hatch to a crescendo of cheers from the crowd.

I stared. Naxos was imposing enough when he ran on all fours. But when he stood, topping nine feet tall and about half that length wide, I let out a soft sound that had Phanes glancing over to give me a look that was partly arrogant and partly pitying.

"My champion," he said, as if I needed the clarification.

I took a moment to compose myself before I replied. "You didn't mention that Naxos was a Minotaur."

One of Phanes's shoulders lifted in a half shrug. Right. As if that was of no consequence.

Minotaurs weren't just creatures that—normally—only existed in myth. They were also famed for their strength, ferocity, and most of all, lethality. Looking at Naxos, I could believe all of it. His head was twice the size of a normal bull's, though he had a regular bull's trademark shaggy dark fur, long snout, and sharp-tipped horns. He had a bull's tail, too, a somewhat fragile-looking thing compared to the rest of him.

The rest of his body was humanoid and so slabbed with muscle, it looked like he'd been given injections of supernatural steroids for at least a hundred years. With his immense size, Naxos should have been slow and lumbering. But he switched from galloping on all fours to running on two legs to spinning around with a speed and fluidness that made me want to throw up.

Great. Minotaurs were as fast as vampires. Just as strong, too, judging from how easily Naxos ripped one of the stone statues bordering the arena off its base. He bit its head off, spat it out, and snapped the body in half before hurling the pieces so far, people on the ground level of the stadium had to scatter to avoid them.

The crowd loved his violent showmanship. They

cheered so loudly that my head pulsed in rhythm with the sound.

No wonder people had been betting against Ian. If I didn't know better, I might have, too.

But Ian was far stronger and faster than other Master vampires. He also possessed Cain's horn; an ancient, magic-infused weapon that was lethal to all kinds of creatures. Ten days ago—no, a month for Ian, dammit!—Ian had slain two Anzus with that horn, and Anzus, like Minotaurs, were creatures from mythology who couldn't be killed by normal means.

So, fearsome though he may be, Naxos shouldn't be able to defeat Ian. My nerves settled a bit.

"Bring out the challenger!" Phanes commanded.

At that, a gong sounded so loudly right behind me that I almost jumped out of my skin. I turned and saw Helena, still holding the mallet she'd used to bang on the shield-sized percussion instrument. She gave me a guileless look, but I doubted it was an accident that she'd positioned the gong directly behind my head. If this was her revenge for me clapping my hands at her, I had to admire her pettiness.

I quickly swung back around, because my ringing ears were the least of my concerns. Still, the gong had deafened me to the point where it took a few seconds to hear the boos from the crowd as Ian took the field.

He didn't run out the way Naxos had. In fact, Ian almost strolled, his right hand flitting out in an occasional wave at the booing crowd. His left hand held some kind of wrapped flag on a long, dark pole. When he was halfway across the field, Ian started heading right toward me.

Phanes leaned toward me. "I know this is difficult for you," he said in a low tone. "But if you interfere in the trials, your life and his life will be forfeit. Remember that."

I didn't reply. My gaze was all for Ian as I searched his features to see if I could detect anything that showed whether Ashael had been able to pass on my message to him.

Nothing but a cool mask stared back at me. The carved statues around the arena emitted more emotion than he did.

I ground my teeth. I couldn't give away the game to Phanes by saying what I wanted to say to Ian. Phanes would either call it "interference" in the trials, or refuse to let me watch them.

But, oh, being this close to Ian and not being able to verbalize any of the emotions bursting within me was torturous!

Then, to my surprise, Ian bowed in a courtly way once he reached the top of the stairs.

"Long ago in my world, knights often gave ceremonial tokens to ladies before a battle or competition," he said, not even looking at Phanes. "In honor of my forefathers' custom, I now lay this token at your feet, my lady."

With that, he unfurled the flag and set its pole on the cool, white stone at my feet—

I gasped.

Not a flagpole. Cain's horn, the only weapon that could kill any creature it pierced. Ian was giving it to me before his fight to the death against a Minotaur? Why?

I stared at the horn. The last time I'd seen it, it had reformed itself to wrap around Ian's knuckles. Another of the horn's many dangerous qualities was the ability to form any shape its owner desired. Now, the ancient weapon was as straight as a kudu bull horn could be, which meant that it had a double curve in the middle of its swordlike length.

I recovered from my shock to glare at Ian. Why would he do this? The horn was his only guarantee that he'd survive!

Phanes also gave a quizzical look at the dark, highly polished object.

"Why would you think she'd want such a thing?"

"Because I know how much she enjoys having my horn in her hands," Ian replied in such a bland tone, it took Phanes a second to translate the double entendre.

"By the gods, you have nerve," Phanes said, with a short laugh. "Don't fear, though. With or without that poor excuse for a present, her hands won't be empty for long."

"Will you two stop?" I glared at both of them, and then stepped back from the horn. "You know I can't accept this, Ian, so please. Take it."

Take it, take it, take it! my look screamed at him. If it wouldn't blow the back of my head off, I'd grab the horn and shove it into Ian's hands. But Ian was the only one who could pick it up without activating the horn's defensive mechanism, and I wanted my brains in my skull. Not splattered all over Phanes's stone version of an owner's box.

Ian only turned and descended the steps, giving me a little wave over his shoulder.

"Don't want it? Then keep watch over it for me. This shouldn't take long."

"You're right. It shouldn't," Phanes said with dark expectancy.

If he dies, I will mop the netherworld with your screaming soul! my other half promised.

I agreed with her. Or me. Whatever.

Gods, I'd need so much therapy if Ian and I survived long enough to make it back to our world. That was an issue for another day, though. Until then, I needed the icy resolve that came from embracing my more sociopathic side.

It only took moments to feel more like her than myself, and she wasn't nearly as worried as I was. In fact, she was almost anticipatory as Phanes raised his hand and shouted, "Challenger, face the champion!"

The gong behind me boomed once more. This time I barely noticed the resounding blast to my ears, and I didn't spare Helena a glance for her second petty vengeance. My focus was on Ian, strolling toward the Minotaur that bared his teeth at him while snorting like a bull about to charge.

Simple beast, my other half thought. *You are no match for my sorcerer.*

I latched on to her contemptuous confidence, until I could watch without feeling like my long-dormant heart was about to start beating again from sheer anxiety.

Phanes rose, waiting until every eye was on him before he spoke. "Challenger, if you carry the baton to the end of the first track, then throw the discus past the required point at the end of that track, and then finally, pierce the pomegranate with your arrow, you will have won the trials. However, you cannot utilize any abilities beyond your own strength and speed, or you will have cheated, and your life will be forfeit."

Sonofabitch! What was Ian supposed to use against the Minotaur? Cutting insults?

"The vampire must also be allowed to use his fangs and healing abilities," I said, rising to my feet as well. "Rapid healing is automatic for vampires, and fangs are as much a part of their species as horns are for a Minotaur."

Ian saluted me, while Phanes's mouth tightened. The side-eye Phanes then gave me said that he didn't like being corrected, especially in public.

"Of course those are allowed, too," Phanes finally said.

Ian glanced at Naxos. "What's this bloke supposed to do while I'm busy running, throwing and shooting things?"

Phanes's smile made his next words unnecessary. I knew death when I saw it, no matter what package it came wrapped in.

"The baton, disc, and bow all belong to Naxos, so he will be defending his property. You only get to use them if you are able to take them from him to complete the three trials . . . and no challenger in over three thousand years has been able to do that."

*N*axos pawed the ground again before making a sound like a bull's snort combined with a human's roar. The crowd cheered when they heard it, and Phanes smiled.

"Let the contest begin!"

Naxos charged Ian at full speed. Ian didn't move. My nails dug into my thighs as my darkness pounded against my skin, demanding to be freed.

I held it down with all my strength, silently screaming, *Move, dammit, move!* at Ian.

He didn't.

Naxos's hooves kicked up patches of earth as he ran faster. He bent his head, pointing those deadly, sharp horns at Ian's midsection. My nails dug in harder, and I felt a scream rise. Why wasn't Ian moving? Why? Those horns would shred him—

Ian jumped high right before Naxos's horns tore into him. The Minotaur ran beneath him, howling as he realized he'd been tricked. Naxos tried to swing around, but Ian used his downward momentum to full advantage, and launched a two-legged kick right into Naxos's hindquarters.

The Minotaur sprawled forward face first, horns plowing deep into the earth. The sudden resistance from his horns versus his far heavier body still going forward at full speed had brutal results. The *crack!* as Naxos's neck broke and his body pitched over his head was loud enough to reach me.

"Yes!" I shouted.

Ian heard that and grinned, saluting me again. Then, he ran over to where Naxos had left the baton, picked it up, and ran it back to the end of the track.

By the time Ian picked up the discus, Naxos's neck had healed, and his body was no longer grotesquely folded over the wrong way. He got up, shook his head as if verifying that it was on the right way now, and then glared at Ian while literal steam came from his nostrils.

"He's made Naxos angry." Phanes sounded almost surprised. "I've never seen Naxos angry before. Things are about to become very bloody."

Ian sighted down the field at the line that marked the necessary distance for the throw. Then, he spun in a circle, building up momentum, as if there wasn't an enraged Minotaur now barreling down the arena toward him.

"He won't get away with that jumping trick twice," Phanes said, leaning forward in anticipation.

I'd grabbed the heavy golden wineglass Helena had left for me and raised it before I stopped myself. No, I could *not* bash it over Phanes's head no matter how much I wanted to. Besides, the wineglass wasn't large enough. The kylix would've had a much better chance at splitting Phanes's skull.

Helena filled my glass, making the assumption that I'd raised it in a silent command for wine. I set it down without looking away from Ian as he spun for a second time. Naxos was now so close, Ian should be able to feel the breath from the Minotaur's furious bellows. Why did he only keep spinning?

Jump! Run! Or fight! I silently screeched.

Ian released the discus right as Naxos rammed into him.

Horns ripped through Ian's midsection. Blood and larger hunks flew as Naxos shook his head, resembling a great white shark more than a mythical bull-man hybrid. Ian grabbed at Naxos, trying to get enough leverage to pull free, but the Minotaur rammed Ian into the earth with a vengeful bellow.

A shower of crimson and dirt spurted around Naxos's head. He'd used such force, only Ian's arms and legs were now visible on either side of the Minotaur's head. The rest of Ian's body was in the hole Naxos had made with the horrific impact.

In my peripheral vision, I saw the discus tear through the base of the stands at the opposite end of the field, well past the measuring line. Not that it mattered now.

More gore rose from the hole around Naxos. My power pushed against my skin as if it were a living thing trying to escape.

I would kill Naxos. I would rip him limb from limb, and then command ice shards to riddle his bleeding corpse—

Phanes grabbed my arm. I hadn't been aware of standing, but his hard yank pulled me back down.

"You cannot interfere," he said in an urgent tone. "You will only needlessly forfeit your life. Let him die with honor, not live long enough to see that he's condemned you, too."

Oh, that wasn't going to happen. Screw my more natural powers over water and ice. I'd rip out Phanes's and Naxos's souls like the horrifying creature I really was—

Naxos flew backward, landing on his ass over four meters away. Ian leapt after him, his shoulder armor spattered red from his own guts while the rest of his tunic was torn away.

Phanes's hand dropped from my arm. "How?" he whispered.

I didn't care how. I gripped my bench, exultation shooting through me until I felt drunk with it.

Naxos quickly recovered and charged Ian again. Ian leapt to the side, but swung his fist. It landed dead center between Naxos's eyes, denting the Minotaur's face. Naxos staggered as if he'd been shot.

I jumped to my feet. Naxos staggered forward. Ian pivoted and kicked Naxos's legs out from under him, then landed a brutal elbow to the back of Naxos's head. The Minotaur fell, and Ian pounced, using Naxos's horns to whip his head around until his neck snapped.

Naxos went limp. Gasps sounded all around the arena as Ian grabbed Naxos's ankles and vaulted himself up. Then, muscles in his back bunching, Ian swung Naxos over his head as if the massive Minotaur were nothing more than a sack of grain.

Those gasps turned into stunned silence as Ian slammed the Minotaur into the ground, using Naxos's great size against him once again. Naxos howled as multiple bones broke from the tremendous impact. If they'd been on concrete instead of earth, the Minotaur's skull would've cracked open.

Naxos tried to rear up, only to be slammed down again, harder. Ian's remaining armor flew from his shoulders as he kept heaving the Minotaur over his head, only to slam him down before repeating the brutal punishment. The incredible effort should have slowed Ian, but astonishingly, he seemed to be picking up speed.

I was so mesmerized that it took a second to notice the strange, zigzagging line running up Ian's back. At first, I thought the dark red marking was just more blood. But this marking had sharp angles, unlike the drips and smears from Naxos's goring, and it was also slightly darker.

A scar, I'd think on anyone else. Except vampires couldn't get new scars, and Ian hadn't had this one before.

"How is he doing this?" Phanes whispered. "How?"

I wasn't sure. Yes, Ian was a Master vampire, and Master vampires could throw a car if they wanted to. But they could only do that two or three times, and only if they were old, powerful Master vampires. Naxos had to weigh more than a Chevy Suburban, and here Ian was thwacking him from side to side like the Minotaur was a bag of ice cubes that needed to be broken up.

Then, Ian let go of one of Naxos's legs to snatch his arm. The Minotaur tried to gore him with his horns, but he couldn't reach him. His back and several other bones must have been too badly broken. With a fierce grin, Ian began to spin in a circle with Naxos still in his grip.

What was he going to do? Throw the Minotaur across the field like he'd thrown the discus? That wouldn't stop him for long!

Ian spun faster. Soon, I couldn't make them out as individuals. I only saw a dark blur against a pale one, spinning until it was dizzying to watch. Ian was building up to something more than tossing the Minotaur down the field. I could feel it in the power that now sizzled out of Ian like an erupting volcano, shocking me with its intensity.

He'd never felt like this before. I hadn't even known he could. What was happening?

Ian abruptly stopped spinning, and something dark shot straight up into the air. The crowd jumped to their feet, their roar causing the stadium to shake as they realized what it was. I realized it, too, but unlike them, I didn't move.

Phanes rose, too, shock suffusing his features as he watched Naxos rocket into the sky as if he'd been fired from the world's biggest cannon. Soon,

Naxos was gone, leaving only a hole in the clouds where his body had blasted through them.

Ian's muscles were still bunched from the unbelievable strength he'd utilized to throw the Minotaur so high that Naxos had disappeared from sight. Then, Ian knocked the last of his shoulder armor off, leaving only a few ragged pieces of clothing and that strange, new scar on his upper body. Finally, he turned, flashing a grin my way that shook Phanes from his silent disbelief.

"He couldn't have done that with his strength alone," Phanes said, rounding on me. "No vampire could! If not magic, then how did he do this?"

I didn't know, but I wasn't about to say that. "You saw for yourself," I said in a firm voice that belied my confusion. "He threw him. No magic, no tricks. Just raw power."

Power that shouldn't be possible. Yes, Ian had always been unusually strong and quick, even before his added power from absorbing Dagon's essence when he was trapped inside the demon. But Phanes was right; this was beyond a vampire's ability, even a Master vampire who'd absorbed demon powers. Hell, it was beyond *my* ability, and I could do downright freaky things when I let my other half have free reign.

Another deafening cheer tore my attention back to Ian, who was now retrieving Naxos's bow. He bent the bronze arc, notched the single arrow, and aimed it at the final target, which still swayed from the turbulence left behind from Naxos's exit.

I glanced up. No, Naxos hadn't dropped down yet. How far had Ian thrown him? Five kilometers straight up? Ten?

Phanes squared his shoulders with resignation as Ian sighted the arrow at the round, red pomegranate dangling from the stadium's uppermost beam. Exhilaration and relief washed over me. In another few seconds, this would be over. Ian wouldn't miss. He could make that shot on a bad day, and as he'd proved, he was having the *opposite* of a bad day right now.

Ian drew the arrow back until the string could go no farther . . . and swung right, aiming at me instead of the dangling fruit. I had an instant to be shocked before agony exploded in my back.

The next thing I saw was the underside of the stone bench, followed by a close-up view of Phanes's sandals. Above, I heard Phanes shouting, but I couldn't understand what he was saying. Why did he suddenly sound so far away? Why couldn't I move? And the pain, gods, what was this pain—?

"Don't touch her!"

Ian's voice, cracking like a whip. Then his face, right up next to mine, brows drawn so tightly together, they resembled a dark slash above his glittering green eyes.

"Don't move," he said, gripping me to his chest with one arm. Then another splash of acid tore into my back.

I screamed, twisting in mindless, instinctive need to escape. He held me with brutal strength as that agony dug deeper. Soon, I couldn't hear anything above my screams. My darkness spilled out in liquid form, coating both of us while I writhed in a frenzy of pain. Still, Ian didn't let me go.

Why was he doing this? Couldn't he see that he was killing me? Why wouldn't he stop, stop, stop—

Ice kissed my back and the pain vanished. I sagged, all my strength fleeing along with the pain. Ian pulled back enough for me to see his face. Liquid darkness still clung to him as if he'd fallen into a pit of crude oil, making his smile a white slash against it.

"It's all right. I got it out."

"What . . . out?" I croaked, trying to pull that darkness back inside me. It should have returned instantly, but instead, it moved at a crawl, as if reluctant to leave Ian.

Ian's mouth crushed mine. I only had a second to savor his kiss before that wonderful, bruising pressure was gone. Then his arms were gone, too, as was the rest of him. But when he stood up so abruptly that I had to grip the bench to keep from slumping over, not a drop of my darkness remained on him. I looked down. It was gone from me, too, leaving me in my lovely, diaphanous dress that now dripped with my own blood.

"Who is that bitch?" Ian asked in a deadly tone.

"Helena is my servant."

Hearing Phanes's voice jerked my attention up to him. He was standing on the bench in front of me and Ian, his wings arced on either side like golden curtains, his body and their span keeping everything else from my view.

Or, I realized as my sluggish brain caught up, not keeping me from seeing the rest of the stadium. Keeping all the people in the stadium from seeing me and Ian.

"Helena?" I murmured. "What did she have to do with anything?"

Ian gave me a look I would have called amused, except his jaw was clenched and his eyes were flashing with rage.

"She's the bitch who just tried to murder you by stabbing you in the heart with silver."

What?

Before I could say it out loud, something large and dark flashed in my peripheral vision. Then the ground shook and earth puffed up around a hole in the arena.

Phanes's mouth closed with a click while Ian gave the new crater a single, unconcerned glance.

"Naxos just landed."

I pushed myself onto the stone bench, ignoring the hands that both Ian and Phanes extended to help me.

Maybe I shouldn't have. For a second, my vision swam. Dammit, I felt so weak! The reason why was at my feet, its blood-coated blade looking too small and innocuous to have caused such damage. But small blade or no, the only reason I was still alive was that Helena hadn't gotten the chance to twist the knife. A heart pierced with silver would weaken me for a few hours. A heart destroyed by silver would've killed me.

No need to guess why Helena hadn't made that final, lethal twist. An arrow through her right eye pinned her to the back wall of Phanes's private alcove.

"Nice shot," I murmured, still feeling dazed.

Ian's flash of teeth was too fierce to be a smile. "I know. What I don't know is why she tried to kill you. Any ideas?"

I let out a puff of laughter. "Guess she *really* didn't like me clapping my hands at her."

". . . 's not why," Helena hissed, her single eye opening. Good gods, she was still alive? "Can't let you—"

Phanes's wing shot out sideways. Helena's body dropped from the neck down, arms flailing for a second before her headless body collapsed over the same bench that I sat on. Her head stayed pinned to the wall, mouth opening and closing as if she were still trying to speak.

I saw the flash of metal before Phanes's wing folded back up and his outer feathers concealed it. Razors? I wasn't sure, but he had something very sharp lining his wings, turning the gold-colored feathers into multiple deadly weapons.

Clever, my other half noted coolly.

"Why the bloody hell did you do that?" Ian snapped.

"Because she tried to slaughter my intended," Phanes thundered back. "Had you not saved her, you would be next, for your impertinence in questioning how I punish traitors."

His wrath frightened the people nearest our alcove. They quit staring back and forth between us and the hole that marked Naxos's reentry into the arena and started to leave.

"I believe I earned safe passage in your lands," Ian replied with an edge to his tone.

Phanes's chest swelled as he took a step forward. "Technically, you did not complete the trials—"

Before I knew it, Ian had ripped the arrow out of Helena's eye and hurled it at the dangling pomegranate. The fruit exploded, and the arrow kept going until it drove into the stadium's uppermost stone rim so deeply, only the end feathers remained visible.

Phanes looked like he'd swallowed something foul.

I stared at the arrow before looking back at Ian. He'd hardly glanced at the target before hurling that arrow with sniperlike accuracy. He'd also barely had time to aim before drilling Helena's eye at fifty meters. Had Ian been holding back his true abilities the entire time I'd known him? Or was something else going on?

"There." Ian's tone was light, but his gaze told a different story. A neon sign flashing "Danger!" would've been less threatening. "Trials complete."

Applause swelled across the stadium. It grew until all the onlookers were whooping, clapping, and chanting a new name.

Ian . . . Ian . . . Ian!

Ian's gaze slanted to the crowd before returning to Phanes. His brow arched as if to say, *Hear that?*

Phanes's mouth curled into a sardonic smile. Then, he spread his arms and wings in a gesture that was both magnanimous and commanding as he turned and faced the crowd.

"The challenger has triumphed!"

Ian took the crescendo of applause as his due. He even descended a few steps and stripped the last of his shredded garb from his torso. He tossed it to the spectators at his right, who snatched up the torn remnants as if they were jewels.

I didn't realize I was smiling until I caught Phanes's contemplative look. "I can see why you're taken with him," he murmured. "He is . . . surprising."

He didn't know the half of it. Then again, maybe I didn't, either. Ian had surprised both of us tonight.

"I have to talk to him. Alone," I stressed.

Phanes gave me a hard look. "Unless you're breaking our agreement, allow me to arrange the proper cover for it first."

Stalling me again? I didn't think so. "Fine, as long as you arrange for that cover *now*."

Ian came back up the private staircase. "She sounds testy. Best to acquiesce. Happy wife, happy life, right, mate?"

Dear gods, I needed to speak to Ian *now*!

"Impertinent mortal," Phanes muttered, but louder, he said, "You are welcome in my lands by right of combat, Sir Ian! More importantly, you are welcome in my home for saving my intended. As for the rest of you"—Phanes shouted so everyone could hear—"if there's a drop of wine or morsel of food left in my home at dawn, I shall consider you poor revelers indeed!"

Once again, the stadium shook with cheers. Phanes gave me a challenging look, and then held out his arm to me.

I glanced at Ian, my gaze urging him to understand all the things I couldn't say yet. If I scorned

Phanes now, I abandoned the chance to save my father plus undo this unwanted engagement. Then, everything that had happened to Ian these past three weeks, let alone his death-defying fight with Naxos, would have been for nothing.

One more act. Just one.

I took Phanes's arm, and at once held out my free one to Ian. "My rescuer deserves a formal escort, too," I said loudly.

Phanes looked annoyed, but Ian's gaze gleamed.

"Inviting me to a threesome? How gracious of you."

Ian's tone might fool Phanes, but it sent a shiver through me. He always sounded cheerful right before he engaged in a deadly fight. But where was his ire directed? At me, or Phanes?

We couldn't get alone to talk soon enough.

"You forgot this," Ian said, bending. Then, he held out the ancient, curved horn to me.

I glared at him. We both knew that if I tried to take Cain's horn, the same powerful magic that had "chosen" Ian as its new owner would blow the back of my head off. Guess it was me he was pissed off at after all.

"No thank you," I said curtly. "Besides, that's yours."

A challenging grin curled Ian's mouth. "And now I'm giving it to you, so take it."

What was he doing? If I took that and my head blew apart, Phanes would kill Ian! Or try to. Maybe he couldn't, after what I'd seen. Either way, Ian needed to stop with the games and come with me, so I could explain everything.

"Ian," I tried again.

"Enough," Phanes snapped, and grabbed the horn.

My breath sucked in—and exploded out with disbelief when nothing happened. Phanes tucked the horn under his arm, and the ancient, deadly weapon did absolutely nothing.

What? How? *How?*

Ian grinned at my sagging jaw. Then, he slid his arm into mine as casually as if we were going for a garden stroll.

"You mentioned a party. By all means, lead the way."

Chapter 13

Phanes led us through the temple to a section that appeared to be way off the main, showy path. Once there, stairs seemed to appear in the floor out of nowhere, leading into the darkness.

"How mysterious," Ian said in a mocking tone.

"You'll want to see this," Phanes replied. "It's why she left you to come here with me."

With that blunt statement, Phanes descended the stairs, not waiting to see if we would follow him.

I seized my chance. "Ian, I didn't know I'd been gone so long! I thought it was only one night, not even that—"

"I heard," he said, something hard glittering in his gaze. "We'll discuss it later. Now, I want to see what's in there."

With that, he jumped down into the stairwell, leaving me no choice except to stand there or follow after him.

I followed. The narrow hallway looked different from the rest of the temple. No fancy lights in the floor, no ornate decorations. Nothing but cold, hard stone the color of black glass. It ended in a torch-lit room with more stark black walls. Statues of underworld gods from various belief systems lined the small, rectangular space, and some kind of indoor pool ran down the center of it. It ended in a waterfall that fell from the ceiling as well as the floor, concealing whatever lay beyond it.

As soon as I crossed the room's threshold, I felt a magic barrier pop, and then my senses exploded. The netherworld throbbed around me, so tangible I could have been swimming in it. That feeling pulled me toward the wall of water on the other side of the room. I went, reaching out for the final veil that was the only barrier between me and the world beckoning beyond . . .

Ian snatched my hand back. "Veritas!"

Not now, sorcerer, my other half thought irritably.

The rest of me pulled back at Ian's voice, sharp though it was. It took a moment, but I wrestled free from the drowning pull of power that was only a touch away.

"Oh," I said, surprised to see his face now highlighted by silvery-colored beams. I hadn't summoned that otherworldly power, but it was there, lighting up my gaze with silver.

"Your father is on the other side of that wall," Phanes said, gesturing at the waterfall.

Ian's grip on my hand tightened. "Is he? And where's that?"

"The netherworld." Phanes's tone turned silky as one wing extended toward the watery wall. "This waterfall hides a secret entrance to its prison section. If she goes through here, she can rescue her father with none the wiser. That's why I insisted you come with me," he added with a glance my way. "You must feel how thin the veil is here, so you know that I speak the truth."

I did feel the netherworld so acutely that it reminded me of when I had ripped it open to drop Dagon's soul into it. Ashael had also confirmed that Phanes's realm floated on top of it, so it wasn't inconceivable that Phanes had stumbled across a weak spot in the veil separating the land of the dead from this world.

"Why does your father need to be rescued? He's the bloody warden of the place," Ian said.

Phanes's mouth quirked. "Not anymore, and I confess to being curious as to how he ended up as an inmate. My sources only knew about his new status. Not how he acquired it."

I wasn't about to tell Phanes anything he could use against me. So, I just said, "You know why" to Ian very quietly.

"Ah," he said after a pause.

Did he understand now why I'd had to come? I hoped so.

"So," Ian said, glancing from me to Phanes. "You found her and told her that her da's now locked in his own prison, and offer to help get him out. She required that you heal me first, which you did.

Now, you want her to storm your secret entrance into death's gates. That about it?"

"No," Phanes said before I could reply. "She also seeks an annulment of our betrothal, which only her father can do." His mouth turned down. "She still favors you over me, though why, I have no idea."

"You should be glad of it," Ian said at once. "Saves you worlds of trouble. I've had enemies cause me less stress, and that's on a *good* day of being with her."

"Should I leave you two alone?" I asked in an acerbic tone. "Maybe you'd enjoy discussing me more if I weren't here."

Ian's wrist flicked in an indulgent gesture. "You can stay. Most time I've spent with you in weeks, after all."

So he'd decided on emotional retribution. I wished we could just brawl it out. That would have been quicker.

"I wasn't aware of the time difference until recently," I replied, then shot a hard look at Phanes. "You didn't tell me that when you had me come with you."

"And I should have?" he said with open disbelief. "The difference between our worlds is negligible even to the human race. He's a *vampire*. I'm surprised he even noticed."

Gods, that man! "Even if *you* didn't deem it important, you still should have mentioned it," I said curtly.

Ian snorted. "You're one to talk. You've made it quite the habit to make up my mind for me, haven't you?"

I gave the wall of water a longing look. Flinging myself headlong into the netherworld had never felt more tempting.

"There is one thing I'm unclear on," Ian said, turning his gaze to Phanes now. "Why would you help her storm death's punishment playground? You gain nothing. In fact, you lose a powerful fiancée. What's your real angle here?"

Phanes's wings fluffed, reminding me of an angry swan. "I need not explain myself to you—"

"Did you think I wasn't going to ask the same thing?" I interrupted. "And you *do* need to explain yourself to me, or I'm not going near that watery gateway, let alone through it."

His golden eyes fixed on mine.

"I already told you that I, too, did not want this betrothal, and that was before we met. Now that we have, I know we are not a compatible match." He shrugged. "You are very beautiful, but you argue with my every command, question me in front of my people, constantly make unreasonable demands—"

"Welcome to my world," Ian muttered.

"—and most insulting of all, prefer another to me," Phanes said, with an imperious wing flap at Ian, who winked at him.

"Still, I would have married you if you were will-ing," Phanes went on in a more reluctant tone.

"In your world, you have many chances to elevate your status beyond what you are born with. In mine, there are few. Marriage is one, and you are the daughter of one of the higher gods. In lieu of that . . . alliances are another."

A gleam lit Ian's eyes. "And a higher god would owe you quite the alliance if you were instrumental in his escape."

Phanes tipped his head in acknowledgement. "I would have all the power that a marriage to her promised me, with none of the drawbacks of actually being *married* to her."

I'm going to freeze his innards and stab him with them, my other half thought. *My sorcerer's, too, if his lips keep twitching.*

"Now we all know our motivations," I said through gritted teeth. "But you left out the most important part, Phanes. How am I supposed to raid the prison section of the netherworld to free my father when only the dead can enter?"

Phanes gave me his sunniest smile. "By being dead, of course."

*I*an, shockingly, didn't seem to have the same objection to this notion that I did.

"How dead are we talking?" he asked in a casual tone.

"Only a little." Phanes gave me a slanted look. "You didn't think I meant permanently dead, did you? Even humans know that there's more than one form of death, with how many of them have flatlined and then been brought back."

Yes, but unlike humans, vampires didn't have a heartbeat that could be restored. Our form of death was much more limited, and my father was no longer in a position to resurrect me.

Besides, even if I could pull off only being a *little* dead, I didn't trust Phanes enough to do it.

"And I'm supposed to, what? Wander around the netherworld yelling 'Dad!' until he answers me?" I let out a short laugh. "If that's all you've got, Phanes, it sounds like a terrible rescue plan."

Ian's teeth flashed in a quick smile. "Not to mention, he's yet to show proof that your da is in the netherworld at all."

True. Granted, no one in their right mind wanted to breach the land of death's prison system, plus Ashael had said he'd looked everywhere else for our father. But, if Phanes had any further proof, he needed to show it.

I gave him an expectant look. Phanes saw it, and made an exasperated sound.

"I have done nothing but speak the truth to you and assist you since the moment we met, yet you continue to heap insults and suspicion onto me. You demand more proof? Very well. Look."

The wall of water changed, becoming translucent. It showed a long, deep tunnel surrounded by darkness so thick, I couldn't even see the tunnel's walls. All I had was a dronelike view that zipped down the tunnel with dizzying speed. Several quick turns and zigzags later, the tunnel narrowed to a ledge bordered on one side by a sheer rock face and on the other by a steep drop into darkness. On the other side of the dark expanse, in a tiny alcove that barely fit his tall frame, was my father.

His silver-white hair was so dirty, I could barely see the gold and blue streaks that mirrored my own locks. His eyes were the only brightness around him, those silvery beams highlighting thick chains that bound him so tightly, blood slicked wrists, arms, neck, thighs, and calves where the chains bit into him.

They weren't even necessary. If my father took one step forward, he'd fall into the relentless darkness. The design of his prison trapped him more than those cruel chains that tore bloody grooves into his dark brown skin.

"There," Phanes said, and the image whooshed backward until I only saw the watery wall again. "Your proof."

It was indeed. Few people knew the warden's real appearance. Everyone else only saw whatever god they believed in when they saw my father. But Phanes's spy-drone view showed my father as he was, and that, Phanes wouldn't know unless this was real.

"Interesting ability, to spy into the netherworld," Ian remarked with none of the calm I felt.

I didn't love my father the way most people loved theirs. He'd abandoned me before I was born, ignored me for most of my life, and showed only the barest concern the few instances I had spent with him. But he'd resurrected me every time Dagon had murdered me, and back when I'd been the tool Dagon used for his worship, that had been more times than I could count. My father had also resurrected Ian for me, and he'd warned me that if he did, he would face consequences.

I hadn't cared. I'd argued, berated him, and used massive amounts of emotional blackmail until he gave me what I wanted: Ian alive.

Now, my father was alone, imprisoned, and bleeding in the same place he used to rule, all because of me. If he didn't hate me for it, I hated my-self enough for both of us right now.

Phanes gave Ian one of his arrogant looks. "I have many hidden talents," he replied, answering the question I'd already forgotten about. "Seeing into the netherworld is merely one of them. You're a man of hidden skills, too. Naxos should have defeated you, and he didn't. Moreover, no one's breached my realm in thousands of years, yet here you stand."

That shook me all the way free from my guilt. I didn't need Phanes being intrigued by Ian. I wanted to get the golden demigod out of our lives, not to give him more reasons to stick around.

"You never answered how I'm supposed to get into the land of the dead while only being a little dead, Phanes," I said to redirect his attention away from Ian.

"Spectral projection spell," Phanes said.

Ian nodded as if he'd expected that. "Simple enough under ordinary circumstances, but we're talking about the netherworld here."

"Lucky for us, her father is in the solitary con-finement area," Phanes replied. "Hardly any guards there. If he were in the active punishment section, she could never slip in and out unnoticed. But, with the veil being so thin here, she'll only need the barest extension of her power to crack it. No one should feel that, and no one should be there to see her dash in, grab her father, and dash out."

"So," Ian said in a speculative way. "You're in-tending to spell her into a spectral state, give her your map, and then let her have at this rescue alone."

"Yes," Phanes said.

I fought a sigh. It didn't sound like the greatest plan, but I'd made do with worse.

Ian gave Phanes a sunny smile. "New plan. You're going with her, and so am I."

My gaze swung to him. "Hell no."

He rolled his eyes. "I'd ask which part, but we all know. Yes, I'm going with you. Phanes might be your map, but I'm your security guard, and that's not negotiable."

I took in a breath because I hoped it would keep me from breaking into uncontrollable screams. "Ian, be reasonable—"

"I am," he interrupted, his turquoise gaze now blazing with emerald. "You're always so fixed on trying to save others, it regularly escapes your notice that *you* might be the one who needs protection. Take you running off with this sod, no offense, mate," he added with heavy sarcasm to Phanes, who bristled. "You did it to protect me, and what happened? I had to stop his servant from twisting silver through your heart less than an hour ago!"

"I would have stopped Helena," Phanes muttered.

"Not in time," Ian shot back. "You were watching the duel, same as everyone else in the stadium. Must be why that bitch chose that moment to make her move. I was the only one focused on Veritas. Everyone else was looking the other way."

Shame scalded me. "Yes, once again, I owe you my life, Ian. You keep saving me, and I keep getting you into horrible situations. That's why I need to do this alone. That way, if I fail, I only take out myself."

"Leave me once to protect me, shame on you. Leave me twice, shame on me if I put up with it." His light tone didn't fool me. Diamonds weren't as hard as his gaze. "So, luv, let me be blunt: I will not be sidelined whenever you deem it dangerous, and then retrieved when you once again deem it safe. That's not a partner. That's a pet, and I am no one's bloody pet."

Hurt and anger surged. "I don't consider you a pet! And coming here with him was his idea as the price I had to pay to ensure you got healed after nearly dying to save me, *again*."

He grabbed my shoulders. "I'm not angry that you bargained for my healing. I'd bargain with Lucifer himself for yours, if it came to that. But I wouldn't leave you behind afterward. That is where we differ, and it stops now."

"It was only supposed to be for a few hours—"

He let out a harsh snort. "That didn't work as planned, did it? Even if it had, either you respect me enough to have me stand at your side, or you don't, and if you don't, then we are through."

The words tore through me with more destructive power than that silver knife.

"How can you say that?" I whispered. "Everything I've done, I've done because I love you."

"I know that." His tone softened, but his gaze didn't. "I also know you've lived thousands of years alone, so you're not used to having a partner. I've tried to make allowances for both, but there is a limit. This is it. If you want me in your life, no more going it alone when things get dangerous. Not with this netherworld trip now, and not later, either."

Then, he leaned close, until his words fell like the lightest of caresses against my newly wet cheeks.

"Choose us. Together, we can defeat anything in our way."

I *choose him*, my other half thought at once. *If you're too stupid to, then get out of my way.*

Breath exploded out of me in a shaky laugh. "You've convinced one of us."

His hand slid through my hair, making shivers dance over me. "Little wonder. That part of you isn't carrying unnecessary guilt. Stop thinking you're responsible for everything bad that's happened to me since we met. You're not. I chose, every time, as I'm choosing again. Now, it's your turn."

This was impossible! I couldn't end things between us, but how could let Ian go into the netherworld with me? Any number of things could go wrong! If I didn't make it out, that would be unfortunate. If Ian didn't make it out, it would destroy me.

But what was I supposed to do? Have Phanes show me my father so I could wave good-bye, and then leave him to the literal pit of despair?

"Since you two seem so obsessed with time, I should mention that we're short on it," Phanes said, with a snapping fold of his wings. "The veil is thinnest right before dawn, which is now. That gives us the best chance of slipping through without anyone noticing. Or"—he offered us a cold smile—"we could always postpone this rescue mission until this same time tomorrow. I don't mind waiting."

Spend a full day in Phanes's realm? How many months would that equate to back in our world? Two? More?

"Sod that," Ian said. "We go now."

We. He hadn't used that word by accident. Either we would go together, or I would go alone and stay alone afterward, too. That's the choice he'd left me with.

Don't be a fool! my other half snapped. *You're not leaving our sorcerer. Besides, he successfully navigated the dark void of Dagon's soul when he was trapped inside him, so how much worse could the netherworld be?*

Valid points. Still, they weren't what swayed me. In the end, it came down to the same thing that had led me to my most reckless decisions before.

I loved him. Nothing was greater than that, even my fear.

"Ian," I said in my steadiest tone. "Care to accompany me through the solitary-confinement section of the netherworld?"

His teeth flashed in an instant grin. "Thought you'd never ask."

$\mathcal{I}$ stood in front of the watery wall that separated Phanes's realm from the land of the dead. Or, more specifically, the land of the *punished* dead. The netherworld didn't only contain suffering souls. It also contained peaceful, happily-at-rest ones, too. How I wished we were going to that section instead of the solitary-confinement one.

Ian and Phanes were lying on the ground near my feet, two small, empty bottles next to them. I had a similar bottle in my hand, but it was full. I had to wait to drink until after I cracked the veil.

Then, I'd drain the bottle and kill myself. Temporarily.

I'd be more nervous about that if Ian hadn't made the potion. Phanes had argued that he should do it because he had more experience crafting potions that would release our spectral, astral selves from our corporeal bodies, but Ian insisted. Phanes had been left to sulk, proving there was no age or species limitation to that behavior. Still, to his credit, he'd downed the potion without hesitation once Ian was done with it. Then, his whole body had convulsed before going very still.

Ian hefted his bottle in salute to me before draining it. Seeing him spasm before going completely limp brought back memories that made me lean against the wall for support.

Nothing prepared you to see someone you loved dead. Nothing, not even knowing that it was only temporary. Despite all logic, my knees felt like they'd turned to water, while my throat burned as if someone were holding a blowtorch to it.

Then, Ian's transparent shade sat up, shook his head as if clearing it, and leapt out of his body.

"What's taking him so long to wake up?" he asked, his foot going through Phanes's body when he attempted to kick him.

"No idea."

Ian turned at the new hoarseness in my voice. "We're all right, luv. I'm not dead. I'm only . . . cosplaying, for a bit."

I choked on a laugh. Leave it to Ian to call it that.

"Besides," he said in a tone so confident, I wanted to absorb his certainty. "You're rather like the princess of the netherworld. You want someone in it, you can split through worlds to throw their soul down to the pit. You want someone out, I have every confidence that you could do that, too."

"Except I can't," I said.

Not even death made his smile less dazzling. "You've surprised yourself with your powers before. I've no doubt you're going to do it again."

Phanes's shade groaned, and one filmy wing rose to cover his eyes. "What was in that poison?" he rasped. "My head is pounding. How is that even possible?"

"Eh, different physiology, different effects," Ian said, unconcerned. "Now, quit whinging and get up."

Phanes did, though his real body stayed in its prone position on the floor, of course. Then he shook his wings, smiling in apparent bemusement at how they were now see-through like the rest of him.

"Remember, crack the veil just enough for us to slip through, but not wide enough to attract anyone else's notice."

Right. As if I needed reminding that getting caught would be very, very bad for all of us.

I looked at the wall, and reached out, letting my fingers brush the water that fell in a continuous rush from the ceiling.

Power exploded up my arm. I gasped. I'd been electrocuted with less effect.

Let me do this, my other side thought with no small amount of judgment. *Your emotions are too erratic for the precision required for this task.*

Oh, fuck you, I thought before realizing that I was literally telling myself to get fucked.

Therapy. I needed so much of it.

First things first. I let my other half rise, feeling her cover me like an incoming tide covers sand. At once, my anxiety was replaced by cool objectiveness.

I reached out, touching the watery wall again. This time, the power made me shiver with its delicious ferocity. Such force hidden behind such delicateness. It wouldn't take much to breach this section of the veil. In fact, only the barest effort . . .

A line appeared in the veil, as thin as a thread from a spider. Darkness leaked out, turning the waterfall inky black in an instant. Power rushed out as well, knocking Phanes over while making Ian brace to stay upright. I wanted to bathe in its obsidian flow, but an even more tantalizing power lay beyond it, and all I had to do to partake in that was to drink.

I drained the potion in the small bottle in a single gulp.

Pain ripped through me. I barely noticed. Power washed it away, making the spasms convulsing my suddenly heavy body more an inconvenience than anything else. When those convulsions stopped, I exited my body as easily as if I were discarding a garment. Then, I stared down at it.

Despite all the times I'd been murdered, I'd never seen my body before. Normally, it burst into flames when I died, mimicking my very first death, when Dagon's lackeys had murdered me by throwing me into a blazing fire.

I'd been so very young back then. A toddler, the modern term for it. That death should have been the end of my story. Instead, it was the beginning. After I came back to life, Dagon's lackeys took me to him, knowing he'd have a use for me. And oh, Dagon did. I spent the next two decades being ritually murdered to bolster Dagon's claim that he was a god because he took credit for my continually rising from the dead.

Then, my father sent Tenoch to rescue me, and I realized Dagon hadn't been the one resurrecting me. My father had. Now, he was the one who needed saving. I supposed even if my father hadn't brought Ian back from the dead, I'd still owe him one.

Time to repay him.

"Come," I said, sliding through the faint rent in the veil.

Once on the other side, my vision crystallized in a way it never had before. Darkness was everywhere, but it was also so clear. Like staring through crystalline, obsidian waters. Oddly, the other side, where Ian was, now looked grayish and fuzzy.

I pushed my hand through the slight rent in the veil, making sure that I could go back as easily as I'd come through. At once, Ian took my hand. Neither of us had fleshly bodies anymore, but somehow, I could still feel him. He laced his fingers with mine, his grip just as strong and real as ever.

"I've got you," Ian said, voice sounding farther away even though we were mere centimeters apart. "If you want me to pull you back in, just say so."

Phanes let out an exasperated noise. I ignored him. So did Ian. He continued to hold my hand, the veil shimmering and rippling between us.

I didn't want him to pull me back in. Incredibly, after all my arguing about him staying behind, I wanted to pull him in here with me instead. This entire place vibrated with so much power. I wanted Ian to feel it the way I did.

"No," I said. "I'm doing this."

Ian's mouth curled. "That's my demigod."

Then, he released my hand and turned around to face Phanes.

"After you, mate."

Phanes gave Ian a sour look. "Don't you trust me to go through after you?"

"No, I don't," Ian replied with a brilliant smile. "Besides that, I also wouldn't leave you alone with our helpless, mostly-dead bodies even for a second. So, again I say, after you."

Phanes muttered something I didn't catch, but then moved in front of the faint seam in the veil. I moved back, allowing him room. He hesitated for a second, and then went through the seam.

He seemed to have more difficulty than I did, but I also didn't have a large pair of wings to contend with. Once on the other side, he shuddered before visibly steeling himself.

"Well?" he said in a challenging way to Ian. "Your turn. Unless you've changed your mind?"

Ian snorted. "No. Just need to do one last thing."

He turned his back. I saw the muscles in his

shoulders working, but due to the angle of his body, I couldn't see anything else. After a full minute, Ian turned around and slid through the crack in the veil as if he'd been sneaking into the netherworld his entire life.

"Christian fundamentalists will be so disappointed about the lack of fire," were his first words.

A smile hovered over my lips. "I won't tell if you won't."

"They were right about the darkness, though," Ian continued. "Can hardly see a meter in front of me."

"I can see," I said simply.

Ian grunted. "No surprise that your abilities are still active. Ah, well, let's see if I can give my vision a jolt."

His fingers worked, forming a complex spell. Tactile magic had always been Ian's strong suit. But when he was finished, nothing happened. He frowned and tried again.

Phanes laughed. "Magic doesn't work in the netherworld."

Interesting . . . and how would Phanes know that? By spying? If so, what a macabre hobby, staring into this section of the netherworld through his little personal peephole.

Or was it something else?

Maybe. I still knew so little about Phanes. At least here, I had the upper hand. If Phanes tried anything, I could leave him behind and seal up the veil after Ian and I.

But for now, I'd give Phanes the benefit of the doubt.

"Which way?" I asked him.

Phanes moved ahead of me. From the sureness of his steps, his vision was better than Ian's.

"Follow me."

Chapter 16

The ground sloped, taking us down as well as deeper into the solitary-confinement part of the netherworld. Soon, the walls around the tunnel changed to jagged rocks. They looked like a mix of metamorphic and igneous stone, but streaks glowed through them when I touched them, as if something bioluminescent in the rock responded to me.

Ian glanced at the streaks before looking back at me. Then, he gave a barely perceptible nod.

I nodded back, and kept running my hands over the rocks every several meters, leaving gleaming patches behind us. Having a metaphysical trail of bread crumbs meant we wouldn't be wholly dependent on Phanes for our location. Even if he didn't have nefarious intentions, men *were* known to get lost even if they insisted that they knew where they were going.

Phanes glanced at them with a sardonic curl to his mouth. "Don't you trust me to see us back safely?"

"What if you're incapacitated?" I countered. "Anything could happen down here."

"That it could," Phanes said in an easygoing tone.

Ian gave him a sharp look, but Phanes didn't elaborate.

Nothing dangerous had occurred so far, beyond the ground becoming scattered with rubble, making our steps uneven. How odd that the worst part of "the bad place" so far was the risk of tripping over loose rocks.

"Stinks in here," Ian commented.

From the wrinkle on Phanes's nose, he agreed. I didn't notice any bad smell. In fact, I didn't smell much of anything, which was odd since the regular world was continually awash with various scents.

"I don't smell any stink."

Ian's brow rose. He looked like he was about to say something, but with our next few steps, the jagged walls fell away, revealing a narrow path with a steep drop on either side. Inky darkness ran along the bottom of that drop, reminding me of rivers within ravines.

"Single file from here," Phanes said. "Careful of the drop, and don't let the wails distract you."

"What wails?" I asked.

Now Ian stared at me in disbelief. "You can't hear them? It sounds like every condemned soul in this place is caterwauling at the top of their lungs."

I didn't hear anything beyond the echo of our steps on the stony floor, which was already interesting since we didn't have real bodies, so how were our steps making enough of an impact to cause echoes?

"I don't hear any wails," I said, growing frustrated.

"Lucky you," Phanes muttered. "Even luckier if you still can't smell the stench. Naxos's farts weren't this noxious, and he was half bull."

Charming, but more important, why couldn't I smell or hear what they could? It didn't make sense, but so far, not a lot did in this place. I'd have to rely on Ian for scents and sounds, and he'd have to rely on me for what he couldn't see.

On the bright side, I hoped the people making those horrible sounds deserved whatever they were enduring, but perhaps not. My father's only crime was freeing the souls that Dagon trapped inside himself, and I didn't think that was a deed worthy of this place, but here he was.

"This way," Phanes said, gesturing to the left side of a new fork in the tunnel.

"Why can I hear that, but not the other things?" I wondered out loud.

"Not to worry, luv," Ian said. "I'll be your nose and ears for whatever you miss."

It was so close to what I'd thought moments ago, I smiled.

Ian smiled back, giving my hand a light squeeze. "Least this part of the netherworld only smells like decay; an improvement from the stink tunnel."

I didn't catch a scent of decay. I did detect a faint scent of sodium and rock, reminiscent of an abandoned salt mine. It was so odd that I could smell that and not what Ian mentioned, and I could hear them, but not the wails.

Phanes went to the far side of the tunnel, where a chain was bolted along the wall leading down a dark passageway.

"We follow this to the end," he said.

I was glad of the makeshift handrail as we descended. Within a few meters, the rest of the floor dropped away until we walked on only a narrow ledge. A vast expanse spread out beyond the ledge, so dark that even I couldn't see far into it.

I paused to pick up a small rock, and then tossed it into the darkness. The rock clattered as it bounced off the wall below the ledge we stood on. I strained my ears to hear more impact sounds, but after several seconds, still nothing. After a full minute, Ian tugged my arm.

"Come on, luv. No point dwelling on how long the drop is when we're not going to fall."

We continued along the narrow ledge. Soon, the ground became slick, making me keep a hand on the chain as I walked. I couldn't see where the new slickness was coming from, and I couldn't hear the sounds of a stream or other water source. Was that my hearing failing me again? Or something else?

Either way, I might not be able to hear the source of the water that slicked our narrow ledge, but I could hear a strange, scrabbling sound coming from the darkness below our ledge.

"Stop," I said, going very still. We were no longer alone in this place. Hearing aside, I could also feel it.

"Something's coming," I whispered.

A surge of air rushed up, feeling like fingertips brushing across my ankles. I looked down, and gasped.

A creature clung to the sheer wall below me. It had two arms and two legs, but the humanoid similarities ended there. It was eyeless, and its slick, pale skin resembled the bioluminescence some fish in deep waters had. It opened its mouth, revealing rows of sharp teeth, and then skittered up the wall at an incredible speed.

Instinctively, I tried to summon magic as a defense, but it felt like ashes within me. Right, magic didn't work here. Dammit! My other vampire abilities might not, either, and for once, my Death's Daughter powers were useless, too. I couldn't send this creature to the netherworld: we were already here.

"Everyone, pull the chain tight!" I ordered.

Ian snapped the chain back, yanking up the slack. A moment later, Phanes did, too. I grabbed the chain with both hands and braced my feet against the wall. In the next instant, the creature swiped at me with razorlike claws—

I shoved off the wall and kicked it in the head with both feet. My momentum briefly sent me into the darkness with it, but my grip on the chain and its new tautness swung me back. I landed painfully against the ledge before Ian pulled me up.

"Bloody hell," he muttered as the light from the creature's bioluminescent flesh illuminated its fall.

"What was that? I didn't even see it until it was right upon us!"

"I have no idea," I replied.

More than two hundred meters below, I saw the creature land in what at first looked like water. Then its flesh sizzled, and its body broke apart before disintegrating entirely.

"Shit," I said resignedly.

"What?" Impatience coated Ian's tone.

"You can't see that?"

"If I could, would I ask you about it?"

With my other side flowing through me until I couldn't tell where she ended and I began, I was able to meet his eyes without my usual amount of panic over his safety.

"There's a lake of supernatural acid below this ledge, so whatever you do, don't fall in."

Instead of being concerned, Ian laughed.

"Lake of acid? That's more like it. Was starting to be very disappointed by the lack of horror in this section of the netherworld."

"It *is* only the solitary-confinement area," Phanes said with a quick, grim smile. "The active-punishment section is sufficiently horrifying, I assure you."

Good gods! Did he spend all his time spying in here? As the modern saying goes, Phanes obviously needed to get laid.

"Good to know," Ian said in a mild tone. "Now, let's get her da out of here before any other critters notice us."

Phanes continued to lead along the narrow ledge, which curved into a corner up ahead. Either he could see as well as I could, or he knew this route well from his incessant spying.

"Her father is this way," Phanes said.

I kept one hand on the chain as I walked, not wanting to risk being caught off balance by another charging creature. As I walked, I strained my senses for any indication that another attack was coming from below.

So far, nothing. Just our footfalls and the soft scrape of Phanes's wings against the wall from how narrow the ledge was. After we came to the other side of the sharp bend, Phanes stopped. I followed his gaze to the other side of the cavern.

I recognized the alcove from Phanes's previous spy-cam vision. It was still cut into the rock wall as if some giant had swung an ax and cleaved off the small space before growing bored and abandoning the project. But the figure chained inside the short ledge that made up the entirety of his prison wasn't my father. He also wasn't alone. Someone with wings was behind him.

"Who is—?"

Phanes suddenly leapt up before slamming down on the narrow ledge with stunning force. The ledge crumbled beneath the impact, sending the three of us catapulting into the darkness.

*M*y arm wrenched painfully as my fall was abruptly stopped. I looked up. Ian was dangling by the chain we'd been using as a handrail, his grip on my arm keeping me aloft. Rocks that used to be firm ground now pelted me as they fell around us.

I didn't see Phanes, damn him. I hoped he'd tumbled right into the acid lake, but with those huge wings, he'd probably flown away. I tried to fly, too, and cursed in several languages when I couldn't. Why were my powers so restricted in this place? I was supposed to be in my element in the netherworld, not as helpless as a human!

"I can't seem to fly, can you?" Ian ground out as the chain creaked in an ominous way. Despite not having real bodies, it didn't seem capable of holding our combined weight.

"No, but—"

A large form bashed into us from behind with tremendous force. Ian's grip tore free as feathers surrounded me. I twisted, trying to pummel Phanes, when he hurled me downward.

I grabbed at the nearby rock wall to try to stop my fall. It was slick from the same substance that had made the ledge so slippery, and I couldn't get a good grip. I kept trying, but either my non-fleshly fingers weren't strong enough, or I was falling too fast. I could no longer see Ian, and a quick glance down revealed that the acid lake was getting closer.

"Ian!" I screamed.

"Part the lake!" I heard him roar. "Do it now!"

If this were regular water and we were back in our world, that would be easy. But none of my abilities had worked here. Still, I sent my senses downward, seeking out the liquid that made up the acid lake. When I felt it, I wrapped everything I had around it and thought a single word.

Back!

Liquid shot out in every direction, splashing the rock walls that bordered the acid lake. More creatures I hadn't seen before that moment screamed as it hit them. Then, they dropped into the acid and dissolved on contact.

I'd made the lethal lake move, but not enough to part it. The rock wall rushed by me, faster and faster. Another twenty meters, and I'd be enveloped by the roiling liquid that coated the walls in repeated splashes.

Obey me! my other half bellowed at the lake. *Now!*

The liquid scattered right before I hit it. I fell onto dry stone with enough force to shatter all my bones, if I'd had any. In this form, I didn't. It still hurt, though, not that I was complaining. Pain meant that I wasn't dead.

A light spray coming off the acid waves swirling in every direction around me burned even though none of the actual acid touched me. I ignored the feel of daggers in my eyes as I stared upward, desperately trying to get a glimpse of Ian.

"If you can, land right on top of me!" I shouted. "Only this small area is dry!"

". . . not falling," I faintly heard back.

Relief crashed through me. Ian was still alive. Still alive, and somehow, he'd managed to stop his fall.

Other sounds drifted down to me. A series of clanging, and then voices, too fragmented for me to discern words. Moments later, I heard laughter distinctly enough. I shaded my eyes from the burning, half-blinding spray to see golden wings circling in the air well over a hundred meters above me.

"You truly are surprising," I heard Phanes say, but he wasn't talking to me. "I expected she might survive the fall, but I was certain that you would die."

"I don't die very easily," Ian replied, his voice garbled.

Another laugh. "I'm starting to realize that."

I wished I could see Ian, but the burning spray limited my vision. It would be hard to see Phanes, too, except his huge golden wings provided a splash of color against the darkness.

"I'd finish you off, but as you can see, my hands are now full," Phanes continued in an amiable tone. "Besides, you won't last long. Before you die, do give Veritas my regards."

"I can hear you, you duplicitous bastard!" I shouted.

A graceful dive later, and Phanes was close enough for me to see that he held two people in his arms. It was too dark to make out much about them, except that one of them had wings, and they both slumped as though unconscious.

"Remember when you said I didn't love anyone enough to die for them?" Phanes asked. "You were right. Long ago, I abandoned my friends when I should have fought to the death with them. I even claimed *I'd* been the one to defeat them in order to raise my status among my kind. I received all the acclaim I'd craved, yet guilt made it meaningless. I thought I could never undo that mistake . . . until the first time you used your powers, when the veil separating my realm from the netherworld cracked."

What? I thought my powers only ripped a single, *temporary* hole into the netherworld that closed as soon as I was finished! It had cracked other veils between worlds instead?

"You were gone by the time I traced your power to your location," Phanes went on. "Thousands of years passed without a reoccurrence. I thought you must have perished. My powers allowed me to see into the netherworld, so I watched my friends suffer, and could do nothing to save them. Then, ten days ago, the veil bordering my world cracked again." Phanes paused to smile. "I knew it had to be you, and this time, I vowed to let nothing stop me from finding you and convincing you to open the veil. It was easier than I thought. I only had to tell you that your father was trapped here for you to insist on entering the netherworld. I even pretended to want to stay behind to further lull you into trusting me. Now, finally, I have freed my friends. You gave me that gift, so for that, I thank you."

Thank you? What did the fucker think I was going to say to that? You're welcome?

"You come off like the misunderstood hero, but you're full of shit," I said coldly. "You're not here to save your friends so they can live quiet, peaceful lives. If that were the case, you could have *asked* for my help. But no. You've got bigger plans, don't you? Let me guess: these two are the gods that your circle-jerk play showed you defeating?"

I didn't need to see his expression to know I was right. His silence confirmed it since Phanes was so rarely silent.

I let out a contemptuous laugh. "What, you think now that you've busted them out of their eternal jail, they'll let you back into their conquer-Earth club? Is that why Helena tried to kill me? Because she knew what you were up to? Now her last words make sense. She said, 'Can't let you,' but you killed her before she could finish the sentence, didn't you?"

"Soon, you'll be dead, too," Phanes said in silky tone. "Pity. You'll never see the good that can come from real rulers assuming control. Humans have wrecked your world almost beyond saving, but now the gods are back, and mortal rule is over."

I dropped my hand. No matter the additional burning from the acid wall that spun around me like a hollow geyser, I wanted Phanes to see every bit of my expression when I spoke.

"It'll never happen, Phanes. I will get out of here, and when I do, I will come for you."

He only snorted. "That sort of disagreeable attitude is why I'm leaving you behind. If you would have been more biddable, I would have honored our betrothal and taken you for my wife."

Biddable? "I would rather bathe in this acid lake than become your wife."

"You *will* bathe in it once your power falters."

Rage made the walls swirling around me shoot high enough to almost reach Phanes. He flew away at once.

"Until then, thank you as well for the bodies you and Ian left in my world," he tossed down to me. "If it's any comfort, they will live on even though you won't. My friends will make good use of them since they need new vessels for their souls."

"You won't get away with this!" I shouted, which wasn't the most original response, but I was too furious to be creative.

He continued flying away, soon becoming only a dark speck against an even darker background.

"Yes I will," I heard him reply. "I'm closing the veil behind me, and in case you haven't realized, your father was never imprisoned down here. That was only an illusion. No one knows where he is."

Sonofa*bitch*! No one since Dagon had fucked me over this thoroughly. My power blasted out, but then had nowhere to go, so it flooded back into me hard enough to knock me over.

My most fearsome abilities were useless. I couldn't pull someone into the netherworld when we were already here.

"I'll find a way out, and I *will* come for you!" I shouted again, although I doubted he could hear me anymore.

Then again, maybe he could. Laughter faintly drifted back down to me. After that, I heard nothing at all.

I allowed myself a moment to feel all the rage, frustration, and need for revenge boiling in me. Then, I forced it all down. I couldn't get revenge until we got out of here, and we couldn't do that until we figured out a plan. Good plans required thought, not raging emotions.

"Ian?" I called out when I felt calmer. "Where are you?"

"Here," I heard him say in a strained tone above me.

I followed the sound. After a moment, I caught sight of him. Height-wise, he was about halfway between the acid lake and the ledge that Phanes had destroyed, but much farther left from where I'd landed. Phanes must have flown me away for a bit before he hurled me down. Ian's body was angled oddly against the wall, too, with his arms hanging almost loosely and his head tilted all the way back.

How could he hold on to whatever he'd used to stop his fall like that? Unless he'd found a double foothold . . . no. His feet were dangling free. What the hell was holding him up, then?

I tilted my head to get a better look . . . and gasped. "You rammed your *fangs* into the wall to stop your fall?"

It looked like his cheek creased into a smile. "Felt like giving a mountain a blow job, but it did the trick."

His sense of humor still being intact was almost as remarkable as him hanging there by only his fangs. I couldn't imagine the painful effort it had taken him to smash his face into the rock wall hard enough for his fangs to anchor him, let alone the twisted imagination it had taken to think to do that.

But he had. *Hard to kill, indeed.*

Still, Phanes was right. Ian couldn't hang there forever, nor could I keep this swirling wall of liquid acid at bay for an indefinite length of time.

"We need to get out of here," I said, looking around for anything I could use as climbing tools.

Nothing but flat, hard rock in the small space. My teeth ground. I had to find something more useful.

I began to walk, pushing my power at the liquid acid swirling around me. At first, it didn't move, and irritation merged with my growing sense of desperation.

A little help, please? I thought at my other half.

Quit fighting me, and the power would be there, was her pointed response.

I wasn't trying to fight her. My heightened emotions had pushed her away—a side effect of a merging process I still didn't fully understand. I'd thought smashing the inner cage I'd long housed her in would make everything, well, blended between us, but it hadn't. In some ways, my relationship with my other nature was more complicated than ever.

We need to work together or we'll die together, and so will our sorcerer, I said, using the moniker she'd chosen for Ian.

That won't happen, she thought, sending a wave out to knock down one of the eyeless creatures crawling up the wall toward Ian. It fell back into the remaining lake and disintegrated.

Shame, I thought. *We could have used its claws.*

I felt her shrug. *We still can.*

"We can, can't we?" I said out loud. I'd seen several of these creatures down here, clinging to the wall like bats to the sides of a cave. All I needed to do was get over to where they were, and one of the crawlers would come to me.

"Who are you talking to?" Ian asked.

"Myself," I replied, adding, "Both of us," with a stab of dark humor.

The wall muffled his laugh, but it was there. He'd never been frightened by my other half, even when I'd been terrified of what she could do.

What we *can do,* she corrected me.

Yes, we. Or both sides of me. Or . . . I gave up.

"Hang on," I said to Ian. "I'm going to get climbing gear."

I could practically feel her cracking her knuckles in anticipation.

Step back. This won't take a moment.

IT TOOK HALF an hour. Or, at least, that's what it felt like, although time stretched differently in the netherworld, so who knew how long it actually took? First, I had to move the dry space my power had made over to the wall that Ian was on. Then, I enticed two of the crawlers to get close enough to attack me. Once they did, I sliced them in half with an acid wave, grabbed their bodies, and held everything except their hands into the swirling wall of acid around me.

Now I had my climbing gear, in the form of four hands with razor-sharp claws. I tied two into a pocket I made from my dress, and then used the other two like climbing axes to scale the steep wall to reach Ian. The creatures' preternaturally sharp claws slid into the rock as if it were butter. No wonder the things were so fast when they attacked.

Ian gave me a hard kiss when he was finally able to free his fangs from the wall. Then, he used his pair of severed hands to scale the wall alongside me.

"Phanes didn't knock down the whole ledge," I said, squinting in relief when I spotted the intact portion farther ahead. "I can see where it picks up again."

"Good. Can't wait to see his face when we catch up with him. Then, I'm going to rip it off and feed it to him."

"If we have bodies left to do all that in," I muttered.

"We will."

Ian's confidence made me stop climbing to look over at him.

"What do you think your brother's been doing this whole time?" Ian said, with a short laugh.

"I've been a little too busy to wonder," I said, stress making me snippy.

"Yes, well, Phanes will be sorely disappointed to discover that his friends won't get to wear our bodies like he intended. Must be why Phanes didn't object to me coming down here with you. But the last thing I did before passing through the veil was send a message to Ashael so he could come collect our bodies. Didn't trust leaving them there when anyone could come upon them and do whatever they pleased."

I remembered Ian turning his back before joining me in the netherworld, his muscles flexing as he did something neither Phanes nor I could see. His "message" to Ashael must have been sent via tactile spell. Good thing Ian had sent it off before we crossed into the netherworld, or it wouldn't have worked.

And him doing it spoke volumes. "You suspected that Phanes was going to double-cross us, didn't you?"

I hadn't trusted Phanes, but I'd been so desperate to save my father—and so confident that Phanes couldn't best me with my soul-ripping ability—that I hadn't been as cautious as I normally was. What was the saying? Always pride before a fall? I had proved that, ending up at the bottom of a nether-world pit because of my overconfidence.

"Yes." Ian's tone turned to ice. "Though I did think we had the advantage down here with your lineage, so Phanes surprised me by using the nether-world's traits against you when I thought they'd work in our favor. But, yes, I knew you were in danger as soon as you ran off with him. Felt it more strongly than I'd felt any of my prior premonitions. That's why I did what I had to do to get here. Knew you'd die otherwise."

What had he done to get here? Before I could ask, Ian's expression brightened.

"Ah, now I see the ledge. Let's not tarry any longer. Our clawed, toothy friends are back, and we're too far up for you to swipe them away with an acid wave again."

He was right. I could hear them skittering up the cave wall, though slower now. Maybe they knew we'd killed several of their brethren and were warier as a result.

Ian and I quickly scaled our way over the remains of the ledge. Once there, I kept one hand on the chain lining the wall while the other held my clawed weapon. Ian did the same, and we had to use those weapons four times before we made it to the tunnel. Once we were there, the strange creatures gave up pursuit.

It was easy to determine which fork in the tunnel to take. Phanes hadn't bothered to get rid of the bioluminescent streaks in the rock that marked our way back. His arrogance was a blessing in this case. When I saw him again, I'd thank him for that . . . before ripping his wings off.

Ian had already called dibs on ripping Phanes's face off, so I'd leave that to him. Who said I couldn't be agreeable when the situation called for it?

We ran down the tunnel, the faintly glowing blue-green streaks leading the way. When they ended and we came upon the narrow strip between the "wailing waters," as Ian called them, we slowed down, but only slightly. Then, once we were past them, our steps quickened again.

One more tunnel, and we'd be back at the entrance to Phanes's world—

I stopped and yanked Ian back so hard, his feet skidded out from under him. He recovered without falling, managing to fling me behind him in an admirable, if annoying, display of grace.

"What is it?"

I pushed him away until I was at his side, not his back. "You don't see them?"

His head swiveled around as he snapped the two severed creatures' hands up until their claws extended outward like unsheathed knives.

"See what?" he asked tightly.

This couldn't be a case of diminished vision. The scorpions were *right in front of us*, big as well-fed lions and twice as vicious, from the way their stingers kept stabbing at the ground as if saying, *Come closer, I dare you.*

A normal scorpion was no danger to a vampire. But a group of huge netherworld scorpions? I didn't want to find out what getting stung by one of those would do to us.

"See what?" Ian repeated.

"Half a dozen scorpions bigger than I am," I said.

A laugh escaped him. "This place is finally getting interesting."

Phanes had probably flown right over them, if he'd encountered them. Damn him and his useful wings. I tried to fly, hoping it might work now that we were closer to the exit, but no, nothing happened.

Next, I tried to feel for anything that I could rip out of the scorpions since my control over liquids still worked in this place. But whatever was under those glossy amber shells wasn't liquid, so I came up empty there, too.

"I've got nothing," I said in frustration.

"Don't fret." Ian sounded so calm, I envied him. "We'll treat them like any scorpion, and cut their stingers off."

"You can't even *see* them," I pointed out.

"You'll be my eyes."

Total confidence filled his tone, and the new tightness running through his body was his muscles bunching with anticipation. He was relishing the upcoming fight.

"Are you incapable of being afraid?" I asked with admiring exasperation.

"No." Now his tone was clipped. "When you vanished with Phanes, and every prophetic feeling I had screamed that you'd die if I didn't find you, I was terrified."

One of the scorpions lunged, cutting off any reply I might have made. Time to be his eyes.

"Back two meters, left one!" I shouted.

Ian followed my instructions with lightning swiftness. The scorpion's stinger missed both of us. Then, Ian watched me as I stared at the creature, waiting for the scorpion's next move.

"Three meters ahead, one to the right?" Ian whispered, following my gaze.

I nodded without looking away.

"Stinger up or down?"

"Down now, but—"

Ian sprang forward. I tried to snatch him back, but he was too fast. He leapt at the scorpion. It raised its stinger, but it was too slow. Ian landed on its back and spun around to grab the base of the stinger, forcing it forward.

"Strike!"

I swung my cave-crawler weapon. Those sharp claws cleaved all the way through, and the severed stinger fell to the ground. The scorpion's instant screech felt like it knifed through my brain. The others took it as a battle cry.

Ian twisted off the screeching scorpion. Then, he grabbed it and flipped it on its side, using the creature's body as a makeshift shield against the others.

Clever, creative, and . . . "Are you crazy?"

He tossed a grin over his shoulder at me. "Since the day we met. Now, less talking and more stinger slicing!"

I did, shouting out instructions for him to raise or lower the scorpion he held according to the onslaught of new stinger attacks. If not for the narrowness of the tunnel, we'd have no chance, but the scorpions couldn't get behind us to attack from both sides, and they couldn't get past the screeching bulk of their companion to overrun us from the front.

I'd sliced off three more stingers before I felt a rush of air at my back. Something was coming. Fast. That's what I got for being smug over the scorpions not being able to attack us from behind! Now, something else was coming.

I swung around . . . and froze.

"What?" Ian demanded, hefting the scorpion's body as if about to hurl it at the final one with the stinger.

He needn't have bothered. There was no danger. Probably.

I heard several thwapping sounds, and glanced back. All the scorpions had crumpled. Even the one in Ian's grasp went limp. For a second, I thought they'd all spontaneously died, and then their heads lifted despite their many-legged bodies staying supine on the ground.

Not dead. No, they were bowing at the tall figure that glided toward us on a stygian river that hadn't been there moments before.

Ian whistled. "Look who's down here after all."

I swallowed, trying to control the myriad of emotions that sprang up inside me.

"Hello, Father."

$\mathcal{T}$he incarnation of the Eternal River between life and death looked different to everyone since beliefs dictated what you saw. Mencheres had seen Aken, the ancient Egyptian ferryman. Ian had seen the Grim Reaper the first time he met my father; Bones had called him the Angel of Death, and I used to see Dagon because he was both my first god and my greatest fear. Now, however, I simply saw my father.

His skin was deep bronze versus my more golden shade, but his hair was the same silver with gold and blue streaks. His eyes also looked like mine when my other nature took control: piercing silver, and so bright they made it difficult to hold his stare. Not that anyone would want to stare at him for long. His gaze held truths that even the bravest shuddered to know.

"You're not in chains," I said, then instantly fought a groan. What a stupid remark. One, Phanes had already told me he'd lied to me, and two, the lack of chains was obvious.

The Warden of the Gateway to the Netherworld didn't arch his brow. That would be too expressive of him, but he did twitch his brows by the most imperceptible of margins.

"Why would you expect to find me chained in my own domain?"

"Your would-be son-in-law Phanes showed her a vision of you imprisoned down here, so she came to rescue you," Ian summed up.

That silvery gaze flicked to Ian before landing on me with almost tangible force. I fought the urge to take a step backward. If he wasn't happy about that news, wait until he found out about the *other* prison break I'd participated in.

"It was a very convincing vision," I said. "Phanes knew your real appearance, how I have no idea. Also, you said there would be consequences for you helping Ian, plus you've ignored every summons that Ashael and I conjured up. Also, Ashael was unable to find you anywhere else. Put all that together, and I believed Phanes when he said you were being held here against your will, especially when he showed me a vision supposedly proving it."

His head tilted; his version of bursting into laughter, probably. "And you came to rescue me?"

"That was the plan," I said, grinding my teeth against my sudden urge to apologize. I wasn't wrong for wanting to save my father from torturous imprisonment. If he had anything close to normal emotions, he'd realize that.

He gave me another look that somehow reduced me to a child on the inside despite my vast age. Then, features that were sharply defined and frighteningly handsome eased a bit.

"It is unfortunate that you were susceptible to Phanes's illusion, but I suppose it is . . . touching that you sought to save me."

I must still have some acid spray clinging to my face. That was the only reason I'd accept for the new sting in my eyes because I would *not* cry over such faint praise, even if these were the first quasi-affectionate words I'd ever heard from him.

"Still, two prisoners are now gone, so you have stolen from the dead," my father said, his voice becoming harder than the jagged walls around us. "And the dead require repayment."

Damn. Guess he knew about the other prison break after all.

Ian dropped the scorpion's body and strode over to my father. "She didn't steal from the dead. Phanes did, so you should be directing your ire at him."

I almost flew in my haste to get between them. "What Ian means is, there are extenuating circumstances—"

My father pushed me to the side. "Your rash act might protect you from most deaths, should you succeed in absorbing it, but it will not protect you from me," he told Ian.

What? And, oh, *shit,* Ian needed to stop pissing him off!

"Spying on me, were you?" Ian said with a gleam in his eye.

"Only because I was seeking her," my father retorted. "Her repeated summons made me wonder if she was in need. I might not be able to use my abilities to find her, but when I find you, I tend to see her as well."

Ian let out a harsh laugh. "Then if you saw what I was doing, you should've known she was in danger. A better father would have interceded to help her. If you had, I wouldn't have needed to eat that fruit to come here."

I yanked on his shoulder, saying, "Stop talking!" even while wondering, what fruit?

"I won't stop," Ian flared. "You only went with Phanes to save your da, and Phanes couldn't have tricked you if your father had answered even *one* of your summonings. Did you know *you* were trapped as soon as you entered Phanes's realm? Of course not, but your father did, yet he promised you to that wanker anyway. Were you that desperate to get rid of her?" he asked, switching back to my father now. "Most uncaring fathers simply ignore their children, but you ensured she'd be trapped by her worthless fiancé instead—"

"Stop!" I demanded, reeling from Ian's recklessness. No one talked to my father that way. It was akin to slapping Death in the face, and Death always slapped back.

Ian spared me the briefest glance. "No, because I'm not talking to the god of the netherworld now.

I'm talking to *your father*, and if he can't handle hearing criticism about what he's done while in that role, then he shouldn't have done it."

Where was that lake of acid when I needed it? Dissolving into nothingness sounded like a vacation right now.

"If anyone gets to bitch at him for being a bad father, it's me, not you," I said through gritted teeth. "Though what do you mean about me being trapped in Phanes's realm?"

Ian gave me a brief, pitying look. "Phanes's realm is normally impenetrable to everyone except him and whoever he brings in with him. Part of his security system. I couldn't use your blood to summon you from it, and on my own power, I couldn't teleport into it to get you. Neither could Ashael, and he's a demigod, like you are. So, when your dear ol' da promised you to Phanes, he knew you'd be trapped in his world the moment he brought you there."

I pushed Ian aside. This time, he let me. Then, I got in my father's face, so hurt and angry that I didn't care about the consequences. When he freed Ian's soul from Dagon months ago, I'd thought my father had cared for me, in his own cold, strange way. Clearly, I'd been wrong.

"You not only set me up to be married to Phanes without my consent, but you also set me up to be trapped by him? Why?"

He said nothing. A sharp laugh escaped me.

"I'd ask what I did to deserve this, but I hadn't even been born yet when this was arranged. Did you even have a reason, beyond bestowing a 'gift' on Phanes for defeating those other gods—which, by the way, he lied about! So, if you only meant me to be his Good Behavior trophy, the joke's on you, because Phanes just used me to free those same gods from your prison."

"Making you just as liable for that theft from the dead that you said needed repaying," Ian drawled.

My father gave him the same look he'd given people right before he ripped their souls out. "I would kill you for your hubris, but then she would only beseech me to raise you again, so I will spare myself the effort."

"Don't you dare hurt him," I muttered.

"Dare?"

I'd never heard my father laugh before. After the sound, I never wanted to hear it again. Even Ian winced. Thousands of condemned souls shrieking at once would have been more soothing.

"'Dare' is the least of what happens when a god loves," my father said in a frightening tone. "You are only starting to realize that. Your control is gone when it comes to him, is it not? As is your reason and sense of proportionality, because everything shatters under the weight of your love."

I'd never heard him speak this way. I hadn't thought he was capable of understanding raw emotion, let alone feeling it in the way his words implied. I nodded, too stunned to speak.

His voice darkened. "Love is the worst of curses for our kind. That is why I sought to protect you from it. I knew you could never love someone such as Phanes, so I promised you to him to spare you the pain our kind feels when we lose someone we love. Phanes also cannot be killed, so with him, you would never be alone, and once inside his realm, none of the gods who seek to use your power for themselves could reach you. Phanes was not meant to be your trap, daughter. He was meant to be your shelter."

Emotions knotted me up inside. My father's arrogance in arranging my life before I was even born enraged me, yet at the same time, I was touched that he'd cared enough to bother. Was this what it was like to be on the receiving end of a clusterfuck that started out with good intentions? If so, no wonder Ian was so often furious at me.

"Yes, well, despite your intentions, terrible things often happen when we make up other people's minds for them while trying to protect them," Ian said as if reading my thoughts.

I winced. *Yes, I finally get it! Trying to control the ones you love will only backfire!*

My father made a sound that, from anyone else, I would have called a snort.

"I once laid waste to an entire world for my beloved. That is how deeply our kind feels when we love, yet you are indignant when she merely tries to protect you? If I had that much discipline, I would not have needed to put myself into exile as Warden of the Gateway to the Netherworld. Now, only the dead require my attention, yet even here, I am not safe from my heart. I tried not to love you," he said, turning that burning silver gaze back to me. "I abandoned your mother when she became pregnant, and I bound my power so that I could not see you the way I can see every other mortal. Even then, I should have sent you away when you came to me after your first death. I knew what would happen if I brought you back to life, but I looked at you . . . and it was already too late for me not to love you."

A sob choked out of me that I tried to force back. My reaction to hearing the Warden say that he loved me made no sense. Tenoch had been my father in every way that mattered. I'd also lived for almost five thousand years without the Warden's love, so it was hardly as if I needed it. But oh, someplace deep inside me must have *wanted* it, to feel what I did now!

"Despite that, I will not let myself become what I was before I consigned myself to this place," he went on, his gaze turning into that fathomless one where staring into it felt like endlessly falling. "No world deserves that. I will hold to the balance I have maintained these many millennia. You must right the balance as well. Return the two escaped gods to me before they wreak havoc in your world, else I will not be able to hide your complicity in their escape."

"Done," Ian said, as if catching two runaway gods being helped by an unkillable asshole was easy.

My father lasered a look at him before his gaze rested on me. "He has agreed, but you have not."

"You know I will," I said. "Those gods escaped because I cut the hole in the netherworld. The least I can do is clean up my mess before countless innocents pay for it."

"And before you are punished by the gods above me for your involvement in their escape," he pointed out.

That was the least of my motivation. If I let my world get destroyed, I'd deserve whatever punishment came my way.

I met my father's eyes and said, "I understand."

He gave the barest nod. "You should make haste, but first . . ."

He moved so fast, I only saw a blur of inky water. Then, the scorpions that had spent this entire time bowed before him were back on their feet, their severed stingers now healed and regrown. They let out happy, chittering sounds and practically danced around my father on their many legs.

"Lucifer's bouncing balls, *now* I see them," Ian said.

"Yes," my father said, stroking one of the scorpion's glossy amber heads. "I have given you the ability to discern what is real from what is illusion. You will need that to face Phanes again. Illusion is one of his greatest strengths."

Late, but better late than never telling us this, I thought. Still, he was letting us go, and he was giving Ian an anti-illusion upgrade. It could have been much worse.

"What about me?" I asked.

"You already have that power," he replied. "That is why you were not fooled by the false sounds and scents that distracted Ian and Phanes here. Being inside the netherworld enhanced your true nature. Phanes was only able to deceive you with an illusion of me earlier because of your vampire side. I cannot erase that, but I did ensure that when you leave here, your true nature will remain enhanced enough to overcome his illusions."

I goggled at him. "You heard us as soon as we entered this place, but you let everything go down the way it did anyway?"

"I was hindered by restraints I implemented onto myself after I freed *him*." His voice darkened. "I told you, there would be consequences for that. The balance must be maintained. Thus, I shackled my own powers so that I can no longer leave this place, or move about it as freely as I once did. In another millennium or so, I will restore my powers to their full capacity, if my judgment is clear again."

He'd punished himself because he'd bent the rules for me by bringing Ian back? I was both flattered and appalled.

Ian snorted. "That's why you didn't respond to her or Ashael's summons? Because you'd put yourself under the supernatural version of house arrest down here?"

My father's gaze became so bright, Ian had to look away. "If I did not restrict myself, her world might not survive what I would do to its occupants to ensure her safety."

I once laid waste to an entire world for my beloved, he'd said before. I couldn't imagine doing such a thing, but then again, I had ripped a hole between two worlds, and look where that had gotten me. Maybe a little restriction was a good thing.

"How do I get those gods back to you, since using my netherworld powers apparently cracks veils in a number of places and could possibly cause more breakouts if I do it again?"

My father fisted his hands. When he opened them, he now had two pairs of crystalline shackles that he held out to me.

"Put these on them. They will pull them down to me without disturbing any of the veils between worlds."

Suddenly, we were right in front of the veil that bordered the netherworld and Phanes's realm. True to Ian's word, our bodies were no longer lying on the floor on the other side. Or, if they were, I couldn't see them. I couldn't see anything past the piles of collapsed stone and marble.

"The fucker collapsed the room behind him after he left!" I said with a new surge of fury.

"Can't fault him for his thoroughness," Ian replied.

My father gave us a look that was almost—not quite—amused. "Only here, in the land of the dead, do spirits still have mass and weight. Once outside it, spirits are merely air, so stone cannot stop you until after you reenter your bodies."

Right. Of course. I hoped I wouldn't get used to not having a real body. That would ruin my plans for stopping the two runaway gods, let alone my revenge on Phanes.

"However, Phanes did seal the veil behind him," my father noted. "That would have taken an impressive amount of power. Perhaps that is what brought down the ceiling."

That got Ian's full attention. "How could Phanes do that? He has none of your powers, or does he? Is there more to Phanes that you're not telling us, besides him being unkillable?"

"Yes," my father said bluntly. "But he has none of my powers. Still, many gods can strengthen a door to the dead, though only those with a key can unlock one."

One question answered, one ignored. For the warden, that was a gracious ratio.

My father stared at the veil. A seam in it parted as if he'd cleaved it in two with a sword. Then, he turned to me.

"Good-bye, daughter. I hope I do not see you again for a very long time."

From anyone else, that would be insulting. Coming from the Warden of the Gateway to the Netherworld, it was almost a benediction. I shouldn't push him for more, but I did.

"Before we go, we need to know about the two gods Phanes let out. Who are they? How can we defeat them?"

He was silent for a full minute. I was about to take that as a "no" when he said, "Morana's powers lie in ice and death. Ruaumoko can shake the earth and has power over volcanoes."

Just like Phanes's play had depicted. I'd hoped that Phanes had been exaggerating. Apparently not.

"Morana and Ruaumoko will strike at the humans' protectors first," my father went on. "Vampires and ghouls banded together to fight Morana and Ruaumoko back when the gods reigned before the Great Flood. You must rally the protectors to fight together again alongside you. Then, you will have a chance."

My faint hopes sank. Get vampires and ghouls to put aside their differences and unite? That was impossible—

My father thrust Ian and me through the seam in the veil before I could tell him that. I didn't even get a chance to say good-bye. When I turned around, the Warden was already gone.

Chapter 20

Finally, I could fly again. Sure, I was a disembodied spirit, but hey—progress, not perfection, right?

Ian gripped my hand and led me through the piles of stone that immediately turned my vision into various shades of gray.

"Do you even know where you're going?" I asked him.

"'Course. If you concentrate, you can feel where your body is. Learned that after Dagon ate my soul, and I had to tunnel out of him and find my way back to it. It helps to think about how your body feels. You know: the weight of your limbs, the feel of your skin, your hair sliding through your fingers . . ."

I did, and felt an inner ping, as if a locator beacon I didn't know I possessed had gone off. I concentrated on it. Soon, I was flying past the rubble and up the hidden staircase to the main level of Phanes's temple . . . which looked very different from the last time I'd seen it.

The ornate décor and all that gorgeous, opalesque marble was gone, replaced by empty rooms and plain white stone. It was also much smaller, with only a few people scattered about, wearing worn clothing that bore no resemblance to the opulent attire I'd seen everyone wearing before.

Everything I'd seen since I arrived here had been an illusion. Or, at least, most of it. Yes, there were people, yes there was a temple, but that's where the similarities ended. All the grandness of the rest had been a mirage of what Phanes thought he deserved, not what he actually had.

Fool, my other half thought. *If he'd worked harder on bettering his conditions instead of masking them, he could have had a lifestyle that closely resembled his illusion.*

She was right. That meant Phanes had a lazy side. It wasn't quite the weakness I'd hoped for, but I'd remember it.

It didn't take long to pass through the entirety of Phanes's temple. Once outside, I saw a high-school-sized stadium instead of the Colosseum lookalike from before, bordered by overgrown bushes instead of stately, manicured hedges. But that's not what I was focused on. That inner ping intensified, leading me below the stadium to the single door at the end of a hallway.

Ian and I passed through it, entering what looked to be Naxos's lair, of all things. The Minotaur was lying next to a broken bed that might have been beautiful once but was now a pile of smashed wood and torn silk, while every other piece of furniture was either broken or overturned.

Most important, our bodies were on the other side of the room, with Ashael standing between them and the Minotaur.

". . . told you, if he doesn't bring my sister back soon, I'll let you eat him," Ashael was saying while Naxos snorted and pawed at the floor.

Ian rolled his eyes before diving into his body, which was now clothed in the same sort of plain garb that Ashael wore.

My body was also clothed in new, serviceable trousers and a tuniclike top. I chose a more graceful reentry into it, settling over my body like I was preparing to stretch out on a comfy bed. Then, I dropped down into it. For a few disconcerting moments I couldn't move, and all I saw was darkness. Then, I felt suddenly heavy, and light exploded across my vision.

". . . is she?" I heard Ashael demand, and turned to see him gripping Ian by the shoulders.

"Right there," Ian replied. "And thanks ever so much for telling Naxos that he could eat me."

Ashael grabbed me, picking me up in a hug that turned into a twirl. At first, I was more startled that he *could* do it than I was at him choosing to. Every other time I'd come back to life, I'd been a pile of ashes first. This was the only time I'd returned to a fully intact body, no reassembly required.

"I was so worried!" Ashael said. "It's been more than four days since Phanes and the other two returned."

"Are they still here?" Ian asked at once.

"No, they all left immediately, only pausing for Phanes to tell his people to kill me on sight," Ashael replied.

Ian's brow rose. "And you chose *here* to hide?"

"It's the safest place," Ashael said in an arch tone. "No one wants to be around Naxos right now. He's never been defeated in battle before, and he's taking it rough, even though I told him that you had an unfair advantage and it wasn't his fault, no it wasn't, no it wasn't," Ashael finished in a singsong way at the Minotaur, who sidled closer and whined as if wanting more consolation.

I shook my head. Another few days, and Ashael could've probably made a loyal pet out of Naxos. Between that and the way those fearsome scorpions had obviously adored my father, my family had a way with deadly creatures. I only wish I'd inherited it, but that ability seemed to have skipped me . . .

"Oh, shit, where are the handcuffs?" I said, smacking at my new clothes to see if they'd somehow gotten tangled in them.

Ian came over, plucking at my sleeve. "Stop. Look."

New markings on my forearm caught my eye. I pulled my sleeve all the way up, revealing silver-colored links twining around my arm before connecting to two larger sets of cuffs.

Ashael frowned. "You didn't have a tattoo when I dressed you earlier . . ." Then his voice trailed off, and when he came closer, a hiss escaped him. "That is our father's magic."

"Yes." My voice was hoarse. "It is."

I didn't have to worry about losing the handcuffs now. My father had embedded them inside my very skin. I wasn't clear on how to get them out, but something told me that I'd know when the time came.

"We need to get back at once," Ian said. "If you've been hiding our bodies for over four days, that will translate into months back in our world."

I winced. Phanes, Morana, and Ruaumoko had such a head start on us. I only hoped it had taken time for them to regain their strength since they hadn't been resurrected the normal way. I certainly felt like shit, and usually I felt great when I came back to life. But I hadn't regrown a whole new body this time. I was back in my old one, and it felt starved and sluggish.

"I'm ready to leave, if you're up to it," Ashael said.

"Only one way to find out," Ian replied, taking my hand.

Ashael took Ian's free hand. Naxos let out a loud, snorting whine and rose to his feet.

"Sorry, you can't come with me," Ashael said. "I'll come back for you if I can. Until then, farewell, my friend!"

Naxos ran toward Ashael, but the whirling darkness took us all away.

SEVERAL DIZZYING MOMENTS later, it felt like the three of us were vomited out of the vortex. We landed in a forest. Luckily for Ashael, it was night, so he didn't have to immediately run for cover. I rolled onto my side, my hand slipping from Ian's, who had also landed in a sprawl.

"Worst. Headache. Ever," he said with a groan.

Headache? Vampires didn't get those . . . "What *is* that?" I gasped, catching my first good look at Ian.

Ashael jumped to his feet, drawing a curved dagger. "What?"

"Ian's head," I said, shock making me sway. "What is that?"

A new, ragged scar zigzagged from Ian's ear all the way down to the back of his neck. For a second, it glowed with the brightness of a lightning flash. Then, it turned into the same dark red color as the other strange new scar on his back.

"What the fuck is going on with you?"

Worry sharpened my voice. New scars were impossible for vampires. At least, they should be. Sure, some vampires had old, faded scars from back when they were human, but once you changed over, any new injuries healed without a trace.

"Don't fret about it," Ian said, sitting up.

"Oh, she has cause to fret, all right," Ashael muttered.

"About what?" I nearly shouted.

Ian gave Ashael a look that had my brother turning around as if suddenly fascinated by the tree behind him. Oh, shit. Whatever this was, it was bad.

"Nothing we're going to discuss now, until I'm sure of where we are," Ian said, holding a hand up when I immediately began to argue. "We might not be safe, so a bunch of noise giving away our location isn't a good idea, don't you agree?"

My mouth closed with a click.

Ian flashed me a grin that made me angry as well as worried. Bastard knew I couldn't bear to needlessly put him in danger, even if everything in me was screaming for answers.

"Does your mobile still work?" Ian asked Ashael.

My brother took out his cell phone, pressed some buttons, smacked it against his hand, and then finally tossed it aside.

"Dead," he said. "Told you it couldn't survive inter-dimensional travel. I'm surprised it wasn't smoking from all the electromagnetic interference it must have absorbed."

"The old-fashioned way, then," Ian said with a sigh, getting up and starting to walk northward.

"I could teleport ahead and tell you what I see to verify if we're where we're supposed to be," Ashael offered.

Ian let out a sardonic grunt. "Then you might get your eyes stabbed out with demon bone, giving Veritas something else to be cross with me about. No, mate. Stay close."

"Where do you think we are?" I asked, keeping my voice low.

"Hopefully, just inside of Durham," Ian replied.

"Durham, North Carolina?"

He chuckled. "No. Durham, England."

We continued to walk. After twenty minutes, I saw lights beyond the trees. I floated up until I was past the forest canopy to get a better look, surprised by how much effort it took. I must have exhausted most of my energy splitting and holding that acid lake in the netherworld.

Oh, well. No deadly lake to deal with here. Just a stately manor with flowering vines creeping up past the second floor, giving the manor a red hue even though it was constructed from beige and gray stone. Some of the architecture dated to the fifteenth century, while other additions were clearly newer.

"English manor ahead," I said when I was back on my feet.

"Good. Then I didn't miss my mark."

I shot furtive looks at Ian as we continued to walk. He must be in worse shape than I was, not to have flown up and checked for himself. Was it exhaustion from the effort it took to teleport us?

He'd said Phanes's realm had extraordinary shields blocking all from entering except Phanes and whoever Phanes brought with him. Ian had clearly found a way around that, but how? And how did his strange new scars factor into that?

As soon as we were safe, I intended to find out.

Lights blazed from several directions as soon as we left the shelter of the forest and stepped onto the manicured grounds of the estate. I gave a slight wince at their brightness, but Ashael cursed and leapt back into the tree line like his ass had suddenly been set on fire.

"High voltage UV!" he snarled. "What the fuck, Ian?"

"Eh, those must be new," Ian replied in an unperturbed tone. "Still, this is why I told you not to go ahead of me. There are multiple salt bombs stationed around the manor, too."

Even from the tree line, I saw Ashael's glare. "Where have you brought me? A demon-killing headquarters?"

I raised a brow at Ian, too. Motion-sensor UV lights were not your average backyard décor.

He waved an unconcerned hand. "Nothing so dramatic. They've just had unpleasant experiences with demons before and don't want any repeats. Still, stay here until I have them turn off their UV lights."

With that, Ian continued toward the manor house. After an apologetic look at Ashael, I followed. Ian walked straight down the middle of the wide stretch of grass between the tree line and the manor; another security feature, though more subtle. Still, the lack of hedges, gardens, gazebos, and other lawn décor commonly found on such properties meant that anyone approaching the manor from the yard had nothing to hide behind.

We had just reached the portico that bridged the driveway and the steps leading to the front door when I caught rapid movement in my peripheral vision.

Ian caught it, too. He stopped and raised his hands in the universal gesture for surrender.

"Don't get antsy, lads. If I were an enemy, I wouldn't walk straight up to the house. Tell Charles that Ian is here."

Must be Charles DeMortimer. My former dossier on Ian had included his closest associates, so from it, I knew that Charles had been a member of British aristocracy back when he was human. Guess he'd kept his ancestral estate these past three centuries.

One of the guards repeated Ian's directive into his communications device. Moments later, the manor's front door swung open, revealing a tall man with spiky black hair and ivory-colored skin.

"Ian!" Charles said, sweeping down the stone steps.

"Double-check!" a feminine voice shouted from inside.

Charles stopped before he reached us. Ian saluted in the direction of the open doorway behind Charles.

"Good on you, Denise, for making sure I'm not an imposter, especially now that we have more than shape-shifting demons to fret about. An illusion master is on the loose, so don't settle for only seeing if I can cross the threshold without invitation. Demand more proof."

With that, Ian hopped up the stairs, walked inside, and walked back out; something no demon could do.

"Now," Ian said. "Ask me something only I would know."

"Where's your piercing?" Charles asked.

Ian laughed. "Mate, thousands of people know *that* answer. Try again with a less obvious question."

"Now I know it's you," Charles muttered. "Since you insist, what's the name of the ship that took us to New South Wales?"

Ian's face tightened in recollection. "The *Alexander*."

Charles closed the space between them and embraced Ian. "Good to have you back. After so long, we feared the worst."

Then, Charles let Ian go and turned to me. "Your turn. Tell me something only the real Veritas would know."

"Ian said he'd make you eat your own ass for insulting me the last time we met," I said.

A burst of laughter came from the doorway, where a brunette woman now stood. "Tell me that's true. I'll crack up all night imagining the look on Spade's face."

This must be Denise, Charles's wife. Her accent was American, and she'd called Charles by his vampire name, Spade. Must be his preference. I'd have to remember that.

"It's true, and I'm Veritas. Pleased to meet you," I said.

Denise came closer, staring at me with avid curiosity. "You, too. I've heard so much about you, but none of them said how beautiful you were. And your hair! It's stunning."

It felt odd saying thank you because I had nothing to do with either. My looks and my hair color came from my father.

"How kind of you," I settled on. She was beautiful herself, with long mahogany hair, hazel eyes, and roses-and-cream skin.

"Now that we're done with tests and introductions, I need you to turn the UV lights off and invite my other companion inside," Ian stated.

Instantly, Denise stiffened and Spade's gaze frosted over.

"You're barking mad if you think I'd let a demon into my home," he told Ian.

Ian sighed. "He can be trusted—"

"No demon can be trusted," Spade cut him off.

Their heads swiveled at my snort. I must be getting punch-drunk tired because I should have squelched it.

"It's just funny," I said in explanation. "For thousands of years, I believed the same thing. Then, I found out that I had a demon for a brother. Karma's a bitch, right?"

Denise's eyes widened. "You're half *demon*?"

I was too focused on the wonderful new smell in the air to be insulted by her tone. "No, but I have a demon half brother. His mother was a demon; mine was human, hence the difference."

"More importantly, I trust him," Ian said, staring at Spade. "You know how rare those words are from me."

Spade unleashed a tirade of profanity that would've sounded more offensive if not for his upper-crust accent and British colloquialisms. I mean, telling Ian to get rodgered by a daisy chain of knives was almost poetic compared to how an American would simply say, "Fuck you in every hole!"

"At least meet him," I interrupted, and then raised my voice. "Ashael! Come out!"

My brother materialized next to me, holding his coat up like a makeshift barrier against the lights. Ian and I moved behind him, blocking the UV glare from that side, but the marble portico we were under did the rest of the shielding.

After a second, Ashael lowered his coat and gave Spade a pointed look. "Now you know your home's weak spots when it comes to demons. You're welcome."

Denise shivered. Her scent soured, too, making me realize the luscious aroma I'd caught before had come from her. Now, however, she smelled mostly of fear.

"Tell them you won't hurt anyone," I said to my brother.

Ashael bowed to Denise. "There's no need to be concerned. I come in peace. I'm simply here to support my sister."

He must've heard me reveal our family tie earlier. From the quick look he gave me, he was pleased by it. Right then, I decided to reveal our tie to everyone it was safe to tell. Ashael needed to know that I wasn't ashamed to call him my brother. If anything, I was ashamed of myself for my prior bigotries.

"See? That's settled," Ian said. "Now, can we come inside? I have something important to discuss."

"I imagine you do, what with suddenly reappearing after months of no word," Spade said, still eyeing my brother warily. "Veritas called you Ashael. I'm Spade."

Ashael laughed. "Impressive nerve, using that name to a black man's face."

"It wasn't a racial slur in the seventeen hundreds, when the prison-colony overseer only ever called me 'spade' because it was my assigned tool," he replied in a flat tone. "Later, I kept the name because I never wanted to forget what I could overcome if I refused to let circumstances defeat me."

A slow smile spread across Ashael's features. "More than a pretty face and a fancy house, are you?"

"Much more," Spade said bluntly. "But are you more than a race best known for damning people's souls?"

Ashael laughed again, this time lower. "I am, and to prove it, I'll tell you my race's most closely guarded secret: we actually can't damn anyone's soul."

"The fuck you say?" Ian sputtered.

My mouth dropped open in disbelief, too.

Ashael gave us a negligent wave. "Yes, I know— it's a dirty trick, but a good one, right? Holds up well, too, because ninety-nine percent of the time, *nice* people don't make deals with demons. Only terrible people do, barring the rare exception. So, when those people die and their souls go straight down? Boom!" Ashael clapped, and Denise jumped. "Reinforces our claim that we had the power to damn them. But we don't. People damn themselves by their own choices. We have nothing to do with it, but far be it for us not to take the credit."

"Then how did Dagon eat Ian's soul after he died?" I asked, reeling.

Ashael grimaced. "It's forbidden, but some demons have the ability to hold souls inside themselves to absorb their residual energy. Like temporary housing, with benefits. But they can't do it permanently. Eventually, Dagon would've had to release Ian's soul as well as the others inside him to their final destination, which he would have had nothing to do with."

"You're swaying," Denise said in alarm.

I hadn't been aware of it, but with how I was suddenly leaning against Ian's new, tight grip around my shoulders, I must have been.

"You're the one who should be shell-shocked," I murmured to Ian. "You thought you were damned, and all along, it was a trick."

"Yes, and that's information that would have been very helpful *before*," Ian said, with a hard look at Ashael.

"Don't glare daggers at me," Ashael said in a mild tone. "Dagon's claim on you had already been dealt with by the time we became family through Veritas."

Ian still wasn't finished. "What's the point in making deals with people, if in truth the demon gains nothing?"

"I didn't say demons gained nothing," Ashael corrected him. "I said that demons can't damn souls. But the brands demons put on people after a bargain is akin to sticking a hose into a car's gas pipe to siphon petrol. We obtain a tremendous amount of energy through the brand, all while leaving the vehicle—or person, to abandon the car metaphor—intact."

"Nathanial," Denise whispered. "For centuries, he thought a demon owned his soul. When he finds this out—"

"Don't tell him." Now Ashael's voice was sharp. "Don't tell anyone. You needed something to prove I could be trusted. I gave it to you, but if you start bandying this knowledge about, other demons will come after you like the proverbial wrath of hell. There's a reason this secret has been kept for eons. People who talk about it soon find themselves permanently silenced."

"Veritas needs to sit," Ian said, which I thought was an odd change of subject, until I realized my legs were buckling.

"I'm just tired," I said, surprised that my fangs popping out made me lisp the words. My fangs hadn't caused me to lisp since I was a brand-new vampire, and . . . Mmmm. Denise smelled *good*.

"Mmmm," I said out loud, leaning to take a deeper whiff.

Spade shoved himself between me and Denise, giving me an appalled look. "What do you think you're doing?"

"Smelling your delicious wife," I replied without thinking.

Denise blanched. Ian tilted my face toward him, which I fought because the pulse in Denise's throat was mesmerizing.

"When's the last time you fed?" Ian asked me.

Gods, had Denise bathed in blood and baked goods before coming out here? She must have, because she smelled like a Cinnabon-flavored artery.

"Don't know." Dammit, I lisped *again*! That's what I got for being so tired, even my tongue felt heavy.

"Judas's bleached bones!" Ashael snapped. "Didn't you feed from some of the blood bags I brought you?"

Spade flew Denise away before I replied. Statues on pedestals around the doorway smashed to the ground from his swiftness.

I swallowed. "I'm sure that wasn't necessary—"

"It is if you haven't fed in over two weeks," Ian said, exasperated. "Why didn't you feed from the blood bags Ashael brought?"

"I took sips here and there, but I didn't take more because you needed them. I also didn't count on being in stasis for almost a week."

Ian rolled his eyes. "Endangering yourself to protect me yet again! I wouldn't have died if you'd have fed from one or two of those bags, but you might've died if you'd ripped out Denise's throat, because not even our centuries of friendship would have stopped Charles from trying to kill you for it."

"Ian is right," Spade said, returning after slamming the door behind him. "Now, if you can manage to control yourself for a few minutes, I'll have some other blood brought to you."

"I wouldn't have ripped her throat out," I muttered. *Probably not.* "Even if I had, I couldn't have killed Denise, with what she is," I added defensively.

Charles glanced at Ashael before giving me a warning look. My brother caught the exchange and snorted in amusement.

"There's no secret to be kept. Even if I couldn't smell what Denise is—and I can—I can see it. Must be why you have all this anti-demon security. Raum branded her, eh? If so, relax. No one's seen Raum for years, so that means he's probably dead."

"He's very dead," Spade said with cold satisfaction.

"Killed him, eh?" Ashael shrugged. "Good for you."

"What makes you think it was only I who killed him?" Spade asked in a silky tone.

Good for Denise, then, too, I thought. And surprising. She hadn't struck me as the demon-killer type, but that's what I got for making a snap judgment.

"Don't expect me to weep," Ashael said. "Raum was an asshole. If demons were allowed to kill their own kind, one of us would've ended him centuries ago. But enough talk about the past. We have present issues to discuss."

"Indeed," Ian said. "Charles, if you would?"

Spade gave Ian a baleful look. Then, with an obvious edge, he said, "Ashael, won't you come inside?"

My brother flashed a grin Spade's way. "Don't mind if I do."

Chapter 22

The interior of Spade's house resembled the exterior, with its mix of old and new. In the drawing room, shields that dated from the Elizabethan era hung under the antique crown molding, but a widescreen TV filled one of the recesses in the paneled walls opposite the modern couches. When Spade flicked a switch, the embroidered silk-and-taffeta draperies closed by automation.

We'd barely sat down when a male, blond-haired vampire brought me a tray containing a china teapot and a cup. The server poured warm, delectable blood into the cup, and I almost twitched from need as I watched. Spade didn't trust me near any of his live-in blood donors, to feed me this way. His caution was probably a good idea. I might accidentally take too much if I tried to feed from someone's vein right now.

I'd drained my little teacup before the vampire server finished putting the teapot back onto the tray.

Ian took the teapot from the blond vampire and handed it to me. In other circumstances, I would've argued against being so uncouth, but since I'd nearly leapt on Denise, I downed the teapot's contents, not caring that I probably resembled a college frat boy chugging a beer.

Ian shot Spade a look. "Really, Charles? Expecting a starving vampire to sip from a teacup is presumption soaked in privilege and then deep-fried in stupidity."

Spade had the grace to look abashed. "You're right. I should've specified a more suitable method to serve her."

The teapot was now empty, and I was still so hungry that I could chew on the fancy china just to get the extra droplets. Then again, that might be the last straw for Spade.

"Bring more blood, in large glasses this time," Spade directed his vampire server.

I didn't cheer, but it was close. Spade must have several human donors living nearby to have access to so much fresh blood.

"So, what's the date today?" Ian asked in a casual tone.

Spade's brows rose, but he said, "September nineteenth," as if that wasn't an unusual question.

My hands clenched, and the teapot shattered. I apologized as I picked up the larger pieces, waving away a new vampire servant who immediately rushed over to help.

September nineteenth! I'd only left yesterday, but here, it had been over six months since I'd gone with Phanes.

"Where's Silver?" I blurted out.

A silly thing to focus on with three gods running amok, but I loved that little winged fluff ball, and he probably thought I'd abandoned him. How could he not, after this long?

"With Cat and Crispin," Ian replied. "Having a grand time annoying her kitty, last I saw. Don't fret. He's fine."

I let out a sigh of relief that had Spade's mouth curling.

"Not such an ice queen after all, are you?"

I ignored the backhanded compliment. "Speaking of ice, have there been any strange cold-weather incidents lately? Or any significant earthquakes or volcanic eruptions?"

Spade frowned. "Another odd question, but yes. Last month, temperatures at the arctic circle suddenly dipped below normal after years of record highs, and Iceland had a volcanic eruption that disrupted air travel all the way from there to Asia."

"Fuck," Ian said.

My sentiments exactly. I'd hoped it would take Morana and Ruaumoko longer to become strong enough to flex their powers in noticeable ways, but it appeared not. It would only get worse as they got stronger, too. Ian and I had just gotten back, and already, we didn't have much time to stop them before they grew too powerful to contain.

"There's also been a deadly pandemic," Spade said.

My father hadn't mentioned the power to spread diseases when talking about Morana and Ruau-moko. A deadly pandemic was horrible, but it probably had nothing to do with them.

The blond vampire returned with two pilsner-style glasses filled with blood. I took one, and handed the other to Ian.

"You haven't fed in days, either, with both our bodies lying in stasis. So, drink."

Spade's brows shot up at that, but all he said to his server was, "We'll need another round immediately, Jefferson."

"I'll wait for that," Ian said, handing the glass back to me. "Now, drink both."

I did, feeling like I absorbed strength with every swallow. I was still tired, but after the second glass, I no longer felt like my body was committing mutiny against me, and I'd never mourn the loss of my short-lived lisp.

I set both of the empty pilsner glasses on the tray and said, "Denise can come back in now, and I need a computer."

A nod from Spade to his other servant, a russet-haired vampire, had that man leaving to comply.

"Checking your email?" Ian asked with amusement.

"Checking my knowledge of Russian mythology," I replied. "I recognized the name Morana from old Slavic tales of a goddess who personified ice and death. In some cultures, they still drown effigies of Morana to herald the coming of spring."

"You now care about old wives' tales why?" Spade asked.

I heard a person with a heartbeat descending from the third floor. When I caught Denise's scent—thankfully no longer intoxicating to me—I waited until she was back in the drawing room before replying.

"That particular old wives' tale is true. Morana and a god named Ruaumoko escaped from the netherworld with help from a lesser deity named Phanes. If the three of them get up to their old tricks again, humans won't be the only ones who suffer."

Spade was silent. Denise dropped onto the couch next to him and said, "Things were quiet too long to last, I suppose."

"Morana and Ruaumoko," Ashael said, whistling. "That's who Phanes broke out? How ambitious."

That's right, we hadn't told Ashael who we were up against before now. He only knew about Phanes, and he hadn't asked about the rest before offering his full support. I needed to be a better sister, because he was already an incredible brother.

"I saw our father down there," I told Ashael softly. "He hadn't responded to our summons because he basically put himself on house arrest and couldn't leave."

"He was there, and he let Morana and Ruaumoko escape?" Ashael asked in astonishment.

I sighed. "He said he couldn't stop them in time because he'd 'restricted' himself too much."

As soon as the words were out, guilt attacked. If my father hadn't done that, Morana and Ruaumoko never would have escaped. If I hadn't brought Phanes into the netherworld, none of this would have happened, either. And, if I hadn't used my darkest powers, Phanes wouldn't have gotten the idea to begin with.

If, if, if . . . all laid at my feet.

Stop whipping yourself, my other half said.

She'd been silent since our meeting with the Warden, but now she was back, her cold irritation sliding through my guilt.

Did our father tell us that using our power would crack the veil in places? No. Did our father need to restrict himself to the point of being an ineffective warden? No. Did Phanes have to trick us? No. Do Morana and Ruaumoko have to try and rule mortals? No! I could almost feel her huff before she went on. *Everyone has their own culpability, yet only we are tasked to fix this before it gets out of hand. That is more than enough punishment, especially since what we did was accidental, and the rest of these vainglorious fools acted on purpose.*

She was . . . right. Moreover, I should have realized that myself. I used to stand on logic instead of the shifting sands of feelings. When had that changed?

Ian drummed his fingers against the side of the couch, and I closed my eyes.

Of course. Falling in love had changed me, to the point where grief at losing him—however briefly— had literally split me in two. My father had said that our kind felt too much when we loved. I'd say that he was being melodramatic, except I was currently having a pseudo-schizophrenic debate with a part of myself that had only manifested *after* I fell in love, so . . . yeah. My father might be onto something.

Jefferson returned with two more tall glasses of blood while the red-haired vampire came in holding a laptop. Ian took one of the glasses of blood, and I took the laptop.

"I'd love a scotch, if you have any," Ashael remarked.

Spade looked startled at the reminder that he'd neglected to offer him any refreshment despite bringing us multiple libations. Then, he almost stammered as he said, "Of course."

Ashael grinned. "Not used to being in the position of playing host to a demon, are you?"

"No, I'm not," Spade said, recovering. "Not when a demon branded my wife against her will after slaughtering most of her family. Or when another demon simultaneously possessed me and several of my best mates. Or when another demon tried to kill my oldest friend, or when yet *another* demon tricked Ian into thinking he'd damned his soul after Ian tried to bring our sire back from his presumed murder."

Ashael's reply was a shrug that seemed to say *shit happens*.

"Ashael didn't do any of that," Ian said, setting his glass down and leaning forward. "Instead, Ashael brought me blood when a spell knocked me unconscious, helped me find Veritas when no one else could, and he's now helping us fight against gods who have no quarrel with him. Save your anger for those who deserve it, Charles. He doesn't."

"I will never trust a demon," Spade said flatly.

"Oof, now I won't sleep a wink," Ashael mocked.

Spade started to rise. I beat him to it, my finger poking into his chest before he was fully on his feet.

"You don't have to like him, but you *do* have to show him some basic respect, because you owe me."

Spade eyed my finger before saying, "How do you reckon that?"

"I saved Denise's life, and the life of your friend's child," I replied with all of the cold logic that had evaded me recently. "You weren't at the supposed execution of Cat's child, but I was. I could have revealed that the child the council *thought* they were executing was really Denise using her shape-shifting abilities to look like Katie. Instead, I made sure the council never knew that by giving Cat the sword coated with Denise's blood, and by demanding the council give Denise's body to Cat before Denise regenerated and the council realized they'd been duped. What is that worth to you? More or less than your ability to insult my brother at will?"

Spade's eyes blazed green and his fangs came out. I held out a hand to Ian and Ashael when I felt their power coil like snakes readying to strike. If I couldn't handle one pissed-off Master vampire, I had no business going up against two gods and an unkillable lesser deity.

"Well?" I said to Spade.

Spade's eyes darkened back to their deep bronze shade, and he took a deliberate step backward.

"You're quite right," he said. Then, he looked over my shoulder at Ian. "Wouldn't have thought it possible for someone to be more ruthless than you during an argument, but here she is, and you married her."

"Best decision I ever made," Ian said lightly.

"Perhaps."

Spade's gaze returned to me. Then, he looked away, and held out his hand to Ashael.

"Based on the priceless debt I owe your sister, allow me to welcome you into my extended family. Expect frequent rows and at least one potential apocalypse per decade, but also, you can now expect me to fight for you as I would for one of my own people."

Ashael gave me a look that made me glad I'd fought for my brother. Then, he grinned as he rose and accepted Spade's hand.

"I love a good fight, and life would be boring without the occasional apocalypse."

Denise pushed past Spade and surprised me by enveloping me in a hug. Spade stiffened, but I was well past my bloodlust, so Denise was in no danger despite her neck brushing my mouth.

"Spade told me you knew what I was, but he left out the part where you'd helped save me and Katie," she breathed into my ear. "Thank you, Veritas. You, Ashael, and any other member of your family are *always* welcome here."

If she knew our father was the very embodiment of death, she'd leave that last part out, my other half thought.

I stifled a laugh. Was my other half developing a sense of humor? Or were we merging more into each other than I'd realized? Whichever it was, I was glad of it.

"Thank you, Denise," Ian said. "Now, let's get the rest of our extended family here so we can fight against two power-hungry gods and an arsehole with wings."

"Here's a bonus to having a demon as an honorary member of your family," Ashael said, releasing Spade's hand. "Tell me where they are, and I'll have them here in five minutes."

*I*t might have taken Ashael only his promised five minutes, but Ian had had to argue with Bones and Cat over the phone for nearly half an hour before they agreed to let a demon bring them here. At least Mencheres had required far less persuading. Ian had only to tell his vampire sire that he was back before Mencheres demanded to see him, brushing off demon teleportation as inconsequential. When Ashael returned from his first round of guest-fetching, he didn't have only Cat and Bones with him.

"Silver!" I said in delight, vaulting toward the Simargl.

Silver saw me and burst from my brother's grip. Then, I was blinded by light gray feathers as Silver flew around my head with so much excitement that I couldn't catch him. When I finally did, I hugged and kissed him while Silver let out a series of loud, happy yips.

"Guess we know where we rank," I heard Cat drawl. "Hugs and kisses for Silver, but not even a hello for us."

I supposed that was a bit rude of me, especially since she and Bones had taken care of Silver these past months.

"Sorry. I'm happy that both of you are here, too, of course," I said, finally letting go of Silver.

He immediately resumed flying around my head, turning everything I saw into streaks of gray. Then, Silver must have finally realized that Ian was here, too, because he left me to fly in happy dips and whirls around him.

I smiled at that before returning my attention to Cat and Bones, since I could now finally see them.

"Your hair looks *much* better," I said to Cat before I could stop myself. Then, I fought a groan. *Thank you, heightened emotional state, for ruining my verbal filter once again.*

Cat snorted. "I know, right? That other shade should've been called 'weaponized drab.'"

It really should have. Now, her naturally crimson hair was dyed a pretty cinnamon shade that set off her alabaster skin. Bones had changed his hair as well. The former ash blond was gone, replaced by a shade of mocha so dark, it matched his eyes. Next to that, his cream-colored skin almost glowed.

"Good to see you two as well," Bones said, looking more at Ian than me. "We were very concerned."

Ian gave Silver a final pat before going over to Bones. "I know you have questions, mate, but let's wait until Mencheres gets here. Then, I won't have to repeat myself."

"I'll be back shortly," Ashael said, and vanished.

Cat hugged Ian, wrinkling her nose when she let him go. "Why do you smell like you were wrestling with a wet buffalo?"

"Minotaur fight," Ian replied. "Haven't had a chance to bathe since then."

It felt like forever since he'd battled Naxos, but yes, he had gone right from that duel to lying in stasis to here, so Naxos's scent would still be all over his body. I must have gone nose blind to it.

Cat touched the back of Ian's head. "A Minotaur? Is that what caused the weird-looking dried blood trail on the back of your head?"

Ian casually batted Cat's hand away. "Don't fuss over me, Reaper. We have much bigger concerns than my appearance."

Cat could be forgiven for mistaking the new scar on his head and neck as a dried blood trail. If Ashael hadn't redressed Ian in a new tunic while he was in stasis, she'd have seen his other scar, too. I hadn't forgotten about Ian's inexplicable new scars, and I intended to drag the truth out of him about them as soon as we were alone.

But that wasn't now, especially since Ashael returned with a whoosh of shadows. Mencheres was on his arm, and the former pharaoh's power punched the room with a shockwave of energy; the only outward indication that Mencheres hadn't enjoyed his experience of being teleported.

"Hello, everyone," Mencheres said.

I was glad that he was here despite our complicated history. Among other things, I'd once been tasked to arrest Mencheres in my official capacity as Law Guardian, and Mencheres had once nearly ripped my head off when he thought I was a danger to Ian. Still, Mencheres was almost as old as I was, so we shared many of the same memories of the ancient Middle East. We also shared the same vampire sire, the same bronzed-sand skin color, and we both had powers that made others fear us.

His obsidian gaze flicked to me, and he nodded. Then, he looked at Ian, who smiled despite tensing ever so slightly.

"Hallo yourself, Mencheres," Ian said. "See? I'm safe and sound, just as I promised."

"Yes, but if all was well, we wouldn't be here," Mencheres said while nodding to Bones, Spade, Cat, and Denise. Spade had cleared out the rest of his house, giving his servants the night off. The last one had just left minutes before Ashael returned.

"Let's get to why we're here," Ian said, and filled them in about Phanes, Morana, and Ruaumoko. He left out how Phanes had tricked me into thinking I was rescuing my father when I was aiding in their prison escape, and also left out how me using my power had weakened an untold number of veils between this world and the netherworld.

The omission felt like a hole that the truth was

being buried in, and I couldn't bury it and ask for their help at the same time.

"I opened the veil that Phanes used as an exit to break Morana and Ruaumoko out," I said, to Ian's instant groan of, "Can't bloody help yourself, can you?"

"They need to know," I insisted to Ian. "I had no idea what Phanes was up to," I said to the rest of them. "I thought he came into the netherworld with me to curry favor with my father, and to break our engagement."

"Engagement?" Cat repeated in disbelief.

"Yes, my father set it up before I was born, and only he can break it, but back to the point. Phanes nearly killed us, and while we were saving ourselves, he broke out the two gods."

"What an asshole," Denise said in a flat tone.

"Couldn't agree more," Ian said, giving me a look that said, *Done spilling your guts? Or do you have more?*

I held up my middle finger at him.

He grinned. "Promises, promises. Now, these gods might have powers we haven't faced before, but they are not unbeatable," Ian summarized to our audience. "Long ago, vampires and ghouls banded together and defeated Phanes, Morana, and Ruaumoko when they ruled parts of this world. If they did it, we can, too."

Silence followed. I didn't know whether everyone was still processing the information, or if they were just thinking of all the different ways that we were probably fucked.

"So . . . different gods really exist," Cat finally said. "All that time I spent praying to one feels like a waste now."

Ashael smiled. "Of course it wasn't. There are many other worlds outside of this plane of existence. Every so often, beings from those worlds break through into ours. 'Gods' is what we call them since compared to us, they are. Still, they didn't create this world or any of the others. Something far beyond them did. So, keep praying; beings like Phanes, Morana, and Ruaumoko are no threat to your faith or anyone else's. They're only a threat to your life."

Cat laughed. "Oddly enough, I find that comforting. Who knew a demon could make me feel better about my faith?"

Ashael grinned with enough charm to make Bones bristle. "I am a man of many, many talents."

Bones gave Ashael a look that said, *Don't even think about it.* Then, he said, "Yes, well, we might all need to pray, because getting vampires and ghouls to suddenly forgo their enmity and join forces is near impossible."

He wasn't wrong. Our races had been in conflict since their creation, when our side claimed that Cain was the first vampire, after God cursed him to drink blood in retaliation for killing Abel, and ghouls claimed that Cain was the first ghoul, because he'd eaten his brother after he killed him.

I didn't know who was right. That was well before my time. I only knew that vampires and ghouls had vacillated between a wary peace and the occasional mass slaughter ever since.

"We have a plan B if ghouls refuse to ally with us, but we'll need the vampire council's help," I said.

"You mean the same council that branded you a fugitive?" Denise asked, before muttering, "Good luck," under her breath.

Denise was right. At best, I had an "arrest on sight" edict against me. More likely, it was "kill on sight." But if I had any chance at convincing the council to overturn thousands of years of settled law, I couldn't do it by text or Zoom meeting.

"My father said that Morana and Ruaumoko's reign ended 'before the Great Flood.' Magic was flourishing among vampires then, so our ancestors had to have used it when they fought them."

Mencheres rubbed his chin. "You think enough magically powerful vampires can make up for the loss of ghoul allies, if they refuse to join us?"

"I think it's worth a shot," I said in a steady voice. "I still want to reach out to the ghoul queen, though. Perhaps Marie will agree that three power-hungry gods with conqueror complexes running loose here is a problem that needs to be dealt with. But it's only been a few years since the last ghoul uprising against vampires, so . . ."

"Tensions are still high," Cat said, her lip curling. "Yeah, I know. Sorry."

"That's not your fault, Kitten," Bones said at once.

"It isn't," I agreed. "I was there during the prior ghoul uprising in the fifteenth century, remember? Warmongers look for any excuse to flare tensions."

I should remember that when guilt struck me over Phanes, Morana, and Ruaumoko. I wasn't making them do anything they didn't want to do. But oh, I still felt responsible.

"I'll call Marie and set up a meeting," Cat said.

"I could speak to Marie," Ashael offered.

Cat waved him off. "A demon presenting this might make Marie less receptive toward helping. No offense," she added when Ashael opened his mouth to speak. "Marie's very prickly. But, she and I left on semi-good terms, so I have that in my favor."

It sounded like Ashael stifled a laugh, but then he simply said, "As you prefer."

"Get Fabian involved, too, Kitten," Bones said. "Might be that some of his people could be persuaded to join us, too."

"Yes, we should rally the ghosts, too," Cat said, sounding much more hopeful. "Some of them have incredible power."

Some did, indeed. "I'll summon my friend Leah," I said. "She can assist with any plans for recruiting ghostly help."

Ashael rose. "Then I'll see if there's any chatter among demons about these gods. Maybe one of my kind has seen them."

The word "seen" gave me an idea. "Can't you find out where they are with one of your blood-spying spells?"

That garnered several interested looks, but Ashael was already shaking his head.

"That doesn't work on gods, demigods, lesser deities, celestial creations, or anything else that didn't once begin as a human. If it did, I would've found our father right away, and we wouldn't have wasted all that time trying to summon him."

Of course. I wasn't thinking clearly. Maybe I was more tired than I realized.

"I also would have found you, as soon as I heard rumors of a Halfling with silver eyes who ripped people's blood out," Ashael said in a softer tone. "But that ability doesn't work on you either, sister, because you were never human. Not fully."

I was about to reply to that when a mechanical ping drew my attention back to the laptop. BREAKING NEWS, a new banner read. DEVASTATING EARTHQUAKE ROCKS NEW ZEALAND'S SOUTH ISLAND.

"Oh, shit," I whispered, grabbing the laptop.

"What?" several voices asked at once.

"New earthquake," I said, clicking the link.

Cat, Denise, and Bones pulled out their mobiles. Spade turned on the TV. Ian moved closer, reading over my shoulder.

Early estimates ranked the earthquake at a catastrophic 8.4 on the Richter scale. It also appeared to involve all four major fault lines in the Marlborough Fault system. Many buildings had collapsed, and rescue groups were rushing to the scene . . .

"You think this is them?" Denise asked in a hushed voice.

New Zealand hadn't been hit with an earthquake like this in over a century. Ruaumoko's origins were in New Zealand. If this wasn't him, it was a hell of a coincidence.

"Those poor people," I whispered. Trapped under buildings because Phanes had duped me into helping his lethal friends escape. How much blood was on my hands?

I stood. "Ashael, take me to the epicenter. I can help with rescue efforts."

"No," Ian said, holding out a hand to ward off Ashael. "Others can do that."

"A vampire can do what human rescuers can't," I snapped with all of the guilt eating at me.

"Yes, they can," Ian said in a patient tone. "But it doesn't have to be you. I have vampires under my line in New Zealand. Charles will contact them and send them to help."

With a nod of assent, Spade left. Bones exchanged a look with Mencheres, who pulled out his mobile.

"Between my line and Bones's, we have many people there, too. They will also assist."

I hadn't thought of sending other vampires. Then again, I had no line of my own like they did. How could I? Any vampire I created could feel my feelings through the sire connection, which would've posed too great of a risk to me, with my secrets.

"You see?" Ian said in a soft voice. "As I've reminded you, you're not alone anymore, Veritas."

Yet once again, I'd acted as if I were. Would I ever unlearn nearly five thousand years of my solitary mentality? Or was it more than that? Was it that wonderful things, like having people to genuinely trust and rely on, would *always* be harder for me to adjust to because I knew how rare they were?

"Thank you," I said, my voice huskier from emotion.

"Don't worry," Cat said, giving me a sympathetic look. "You'll be at bat for other stuff, but this part, we've got."

I had to change the subject before I did something disgraceful, like burst into tears at all the unfamiliar love and support.

"All right, if Ruaumoko and Morana are behind this, maybe we're lucky and they're not smart," I said in a brisker tone. "Showing off in such big, seismic ways before they're up to full strength must be burning through their limited power reserves. Unless," my voice trailed off as an awful thought hit me.

"Unless what?" Cat pressed.

"Unless doing these things doesn't drain them."

A chill raced up my spine when I thought of what happened after I ripped Dagon's soul out and threw it into the netherworld. I hadn't felt drained after using my most formidable ability. Instead, I'd never felt more powerful.

"Morana and Ruaumoko might be doing these things to power *up*," I said, my chill increasing. "If

I'm right, and this is what they're capable of when they're at the weaker end of their abilities, we don't want to know what they can do when they're at full strength."

"No, we don't," Cat said, rising too. "I'll call Marie to set up the meeting, and then I'll call home to have Tate send Fabian here so we can get the ghosts in on this."

"I will reach out to my allies," Mencheres said. "Many of them have exceptional abilities even without magic."

"I'll call mine as well," Spade said, coming back into the room. Then, he turned to Ian. "Going to let your people know you're back and resuming Mastership of your line?"

My mouth dropped. "What do you mean, resuming? You gave up control of all the vampires and humans in your line?"

No one else looked shocked, even though such a thing wasn't done unless a vampire believed they were about to die, and didn't want to leave their line unprotected.

"Helm it a little longer, Charles," Ian said, his voice casual despite the seriousness of the topic.

I rose. Everything else could wait another hour. I had to find out what Ian had done to himself *now*.

"Would all of you excuse Ian and me?" I said in my sweetest tone. "We're overdue to have a private conversation."

"Oh, we are indeed," Ian said, with a glint in his eye that reminded me of lightning strikes during a storm. "Groom's quarters still next to the stable, Charles?"

"It is—"

That's all I heard. Ian took my arm, and everything slid into chaos.

*T*he world righted moments later. Ian and I were now in a small room with a slanted roof. The wooden floors, walls, and ceiling beams were aged but so well cared for that their rugged appearance added charm to the otherwise Spartan space. One combo desk and bookcase with a chair comprised the makeshift office next to a small, empty fireplace. A tiny table for two next to a set of cupboards was probably the former eat-in kitchen, and the single bed in the corner needed no explanation.

Groom's quarters, Ian had called this place. Soft neighs coming from nearby would've told me we were next to the stable even if the faint smell of horses didn't permeate from the very walls. But no groom had lived here for a long time. I knew that more from the feel of the place than the dated furnishings. A fastidious cleaning service might've kept the room dust free, but abandoned places all had a certain stillness to them, as if their space grieved the loss of those who'd once lived there.

Ian pulled out the chair from the tiny office, turned it backward, and straddled it while facing me.

"We're down the hill from the manor, so we should have relative privacy here."

Good, because I might scream from everything I'd been holding back. Judging by the still-dangerous look in his eyes, so might he.

I went first. "How do you have new scars when that should be impossible for vampires?"

"Used a relic with side effects," he replied dismissively.

"*That's* an understatement."

Both our heads swiveled to the chimney, where Ashael popped out of the fireplace as if he were a demon version of Santa Claus.

"Get out," Ian said at once.

"Only after you tell my sister what you really did," Ashael countered. "No? Then I will. This numbskull—"

Ian's fist swung. Ashael teleported away before it connected with his jaw. Ian teleported after him, still swinging. Ashael avoided him again. Soon, they were both teleporting in and out so fast that I could hardly track them. All the while, Ashael never stopped speaking.

"—talked me into letting him see my relic vault. I *told* him not to touch anything because all my relics are powerful enough to be deadly. I intended to trade some for information on how to turn one of Phanes's people against him—"

"Which would've taken too long," Ian snarled.

"—but this numbskull refused to listen, and what did he do with the most ancient, deadly relic this world has ever seen—"

"Shut your bloody face hole!" Ian shouted.

"You should have shut *yours*!" my brother roared back. "But like a naughty toddler sticking everything into its mouth, you took the most dangerous relic ever and *ate it*!"

My hands clapped over my face in horror. "What?"

"Ate it!" my brother repeated.

Ian swung again. Ashael teleported away at the last moment, leaving Ian's fist to smash into the antique desk instead. Books and wood littered the floor.

"Too slow," Ashael taunted as he avoided another swing. "What's the matter? Have an upset stomach? You should considering that no man since Adam has been reckless enough to eat that fruit, and here you swallowed it without even chewing!"

No man since Adam . . . No. Ashael couldn't mean *that* fruit?

"Didn't need to chew such a little piece, though it's clearly larger than both your balls combined," Ian snapped.

Ashael shoved him. "I am not a coward because I sought a less suicidal way to save my sister!"

"Stop!"

Shadows erupted behind me and darkness spilled out of me in liquid rivers as my other half registered her anger and disbelief over what Ian had done, too. Ashael teleported onto the bed before any of the growing inky substance touched his shoes. Ian spun around, saw me, and let out an exasperated sigh as he slogged through the now ankle-high puddles toward me.

"Put the netherworld theatrics away. You're not ripping out anyone's soul, and we both know it."

"How are you moving through that?" Ashael asked, stunned.

"How are you cringing on the bed?" Ian retorted. "Half of that same power runs through your veins."

Ashael stared at Ian, now calf-deep in the pools of darkness that had swelled within the confines of the small room.

"Yes, we share the same bloodline, and yes, I can manifest darkness, but I cannot summon the river." Ashael's voice was almost reverent. "Only she and my father can, and anyone caught in it should be filled with all the panic of impending death."

At that, the inky substance snapped back into me so fast, it splashed my face before disappearing beneath my skin.

"Are you all right?" I asked Ian at once.

He snorted. "As if any part of you, even the scariest ones, would ever frighten me. But check on the horses, Ashael. Charles will lose his mind if they break out and run off because some of that leaked through the walls and touched them."

Ashael either loved horses, or he'd had enough of this, because he vanished without another word.

Ian and I were now alone in a room filled with broken or toppled furniture. Not the first time that had happened, but this time, I hadn't enjoyed any of its destruction. At least none of the netherworld "river" had stained the floors or walls. When I pulled that liquid darkness back into me, all traces of it somehow vanished.

Good thing, since it was apparently dangerous . . . except to Ian. I must be able to control the terror aspect of it on a subconscious level. I should have realized that before. Ian had been covered in this same liquid after Helena had stabbed me, and he hadn't suffered any ill effects from it.

But Phanes had backed away from it. Both times, now that I thought about it. He must know what it could do.

The irony of it all pierced me. Even my darkest parts had found a way to avoid hurting Ian, but the rest of me had still been responsible for him doing something lethal to himself.

"Ashael had a piece of fruit from the Tree of Knowledge of Good and Evil, and you ate it because you thought it would give you the power to break into Phanes's realm," I said, stricken.

"'In the day ye eat thereof . . . ye shall be as gods,'" Ian quoted with the barest of smiles. "Ol' Scratch wasn't wrong. It did give me godlike power. Even drained all the magic from Cain's horn and funneled it back into me, so it was the gift that kept on giving."

I barely registered the news about Cain's horn, even though it explained how Phanes was able to touch it without the horn's defensive magic blowing the back of his head off.

"It also gives death," I whispered. "That's why you're scarring. You're a vampire, but somehow . . . you're dying."

Ian flicked his wrist as if that were inconsequential. "We found a way around death before. We will again. Besides, I'm only in danger when I utilize that power, such as when I used it to enter and exit Phanes's realm, or when I fought Naxos."

How could he be so cavalier? I grabbed his shoulders and shook him. "It might be all the same to you, but *I* can't go through your death again! How could you eat that cursed fruit, knowing what would happen? How?"

I screamed the last words as memories strafed me of Ian lying at Dagon's feet, his skin so shrunken and dry that it pulled away to reveal his bones. I'd see that again, and this time, my father would refuse to raise him. This time, Ian would stay lifeless and cracking like a broken branch on the ground . . .

He covered my hands with his, his gaze now bright green.

"How? Because I knew if I ate that, everything *might* be okay, which it damn sure wouldn't be if I didn't eat it. I told you my premonitions are never wrong. As soon as you left with Phanes I knew, without a doubt, that you'd die if I didn't get you away from him. So, I did what I had to do."

"And now *you'll* die!"

Harsh laughter struck my cheeks as he leaned closer. "Maybe. But don't act as if you don't understand doing anything to protect the one you love.

Yes, saving you might mean my death. If so, been there, done that, wasn't so bad. But letting some arsehole trap and kill you? I refuse to do that, and while we're on the topic, stop abandoning me under the mistaken belief that you're protecting me. You're not, because if nothing else, this shows that I'll do whatever it takes to get back to you, *especially* if I know you're in danger, too."

I could hardly see through the sheen of tears. "I was *not* abandoning you! You won't let some arsehole trap and kill me? Back at you, Ian! I only thought I'd be gone an hour, maybe two, when I first left with Phanes. That seemed a small price to pay for your healing after Dagon trapped and nearly killed you, or have you forgotten about that?"

"No," he said with a frustrated sign. "Perhaps I'm stricken with the same lack of control, reason, and proportionality your da accused you of. I love you too much to care what happens to me as long as you're safe, yet I'm angry at you for endangering yourself because you feel the same way. It's insensible and unreasonable, and I can't bloody help myself."

I had never understood anything more.

"I can't help myself, either," I said, and threw my arms around him, needing to feel his skin, his body, and his vitality that sparked against me with static-like currents.

"Then let's not help ourselves." His voice deepened. "Let fairness and reason go to wreck and ruin. We can have the world's most dysfunctional marriage for all I bother. As long as I have you, I have everything I need."

So did I, which was why I could not, *would* not let him die. *Somehow,* I swore, *I'll find a way to undo this.*

No, we will, my other half thought at once.

We will, I agreed.

Out loud, I said, "There has to be some kind of a loophole negating the deadly effect of eating that fruit. We just have to find it before you get worse."

Ian's hands slid along my back, caressing their way under my tunic to stroke my skin.

"We will. But come now"—his voice turned teasing—"if a bloke isn't willing to eat the fruit of the world's most cursed tree in order to save his love, is he even worth her time?"

"You're insane," I breathed, turning my face toward his.

He kissed me, deep, slow, and so passionate, everything spun as if I'd become drunk. I gave myself up to every stroke of his tongue, the sharp brush of his fangs, and then the luscious, hard length of his body as he pulled his clothes off.

I pulled mine off as well, needing the silken feel of his skin. I needed his muscles bunching beneath my hands, too, and I got it as he reacted to my touch. Then his groan filled my mouth as my fangs scored his tongue, drawing blood we both swallowed.

He took us down to the floor, me underneath him. His hands roved over me, making my skin tingle at his touch. Then his mouth left mine to tease my breasts. Soon, my nipples were so oversensitized from each skillful lick, suction, and graze of fangs that I ached in places he hadn't even touched yet.

My thighs slid along his hips, urging him between them. His laugh teased my skin as he sucked harder on my nipple. I felt pleasure erupt everywhere, and that inner ache grew.

I twisted to the side and reached down to grab what I needed inside me. His shaft overflowed in my hands, hard as the silver stud that pierced its tip. I pushed him away, bent down, and tried to encase him in my mouth. His husky laugh taunted me as he teleported away, leaving me grasping only air.

He materialized by my knees. Then, he opened them and pulled me on top of him. I had the barest moment to feel his hair against my thighs before his tongue twisted deeply inside me. I gasped, arching at the fiery sensations. Inner bands clenched as he repeated the deep, greedy stroke. I moved against him, needing more even as I was frustrated by him stymieing me from pleasuring him this way, too.

"I want you in my mouth," I moaned, stretching back and reaching behind me. I couldn't see my goal from this angle, but I could feel for it.

Ah, there it was. Even harder, if that were possible, with the tip now slicked by pearls of moisture.

He responded with more deep, twisting licks. I let go of his cock and my arms slammed to the floor because the pleasure almost knocked me over.

He wasn't teasing me with seeking flicks or playful delves. No, he was fucking me with his tongue, and gasps stole my voice at the merciless pleasure.

My hands fisted as I rocked against his mouth, forgetting about changing positions to make this a mutual pleasuring. I also couldn't stop my gasps, or the way my hips moved even faster, until he'd be concussed by the hard wood floor if he were human. He wasn't, though, and he gripped me tighter, urging me to move faster as his tongue swirled deeper, harder, fiercer . . .

"Oh, gods, yes!" I shouted as those bands snapped and rapture broke through. Its effects bent my back until I sagged forward from the overload, my upper arms now resting against the edge of the bed that we were somehow now in front of.

Suddenly, Ian disappeared beneath me. Before my lower half hit the floor from suddenly having nothing beneath me, he was behind me, holding me up on my knees. I leaned against him, and he craned his neck until his mouth closed over mine in a kiss erotically flavored with honey and salt.

I reached for his cock again. He gave a throaty laugh and pushed me forward until my torso draped across the bed, while the rest of me was still kneeling. To entice him, I rubbed my breasts against the bed as if the quilt was the finest of silks, and then spread my legs and lifted my hips.

The sound he made would've been foreplay enough, if I wasn't already so wet from his exquisite mouth.

He grasped my hips, his cock sliding along my crease. I pushed against him, whimpering when he denied me. His other hand wound in my hair, tilting my head to the side.

"Show me your face, little Guardian."

"You'll need a new nickname," I said in a breathy voice as I turned toward him. "Pretty sure the council fired me."

His gaze had never been brighter, bathing me in rays of emerald. "No," he said as he pushed into me. "I won't."

I arched at the intensity of the pleasure. How could this hit me with the same emotional impact as our first time? It shouldn't, but it did, and I felt lost in the sensations.

"What you are to the council has nothing to do with what you are to me," he continued with another deep, sinuous thrust.

What was he talking about? I'd forgotten. Nothing existed except his body against mine, the delicious burn from his silver piercing, his girth stretching me, and then his fingers teasing my clit as he reached between us. Between that and each new, rapturous thrust, I was soon right at the edge again.

"I want you to feel this, too," I said with a moan.

His laugh vibrated through me, punctuated by deeper thrusts that curled my toes.

"How can I not feel this?" he said thickly.

"I mean, I want you to come with me," I managed between gasps. I was almost there, but he wasn't.

He hadn't even snapped the bed we were leaning on, and it was made of fragile wood.

"I'm close, and I want you to feel what I do when I come," I said while grinding harder against him.

He pulled me up until my back pressed against his chest. His arm slid up between my breasts, holding me to him. Then his mouth was at my neck, finding my sensitive spots and devastating them with pleasure. All the while, his fingers never stopped teasing my clit, and those mind-shattering thrusts never slowed. When his fangs finally sank deep, ecstasy exploded, and I came with a shout that made the nearby horses restless.

"I'll come later," I thought I heard him say, but I wasn't sure. I was still drowning in bliss.

He turned me around and flung me onto the bed. The light impact from that was nothing compared to the slam of pleasure when his body covered mine, and he filled me in one stroke.

"But right now," he said with a wicked grin. "I'm going to shag you until you're too sated to scream that loudly again."

Two hard knocks on the door woke me. I hadn't intended to fall asleep after Ian made good on his promise to fuck me into a state of temporary muteness, but I had. Then again, I'd done a lot of things I hadn't intended to do over the past two days. What was that saying about making the gods laugh? All you had to do was tell them your plans?

"Sod off, whoever you are," Ian said without opening his eyes.

The door burst open in a shower of wood, revealing Cat.

Ian cursed as he leapt up from the bed. "Really, Reaper? Kicking the door in? This isn't even your house."

"I know, but this news is important and I drew the short straw, so I'm here and Spade isn't," Cat replied, looking anywhere except at Ian. "Figured it was the best time to interrupt since the horses finally quit stomping up their stalls from all the racket. Unless that banging around was you two and not the horses? Wait, don't answer that. I don't want to know."

I got out of bed, too. Now Cat was almost staring at the ceiling to avoid looking at our nakedness. How silly.

"We don't have anything you haven't seen before," I said before adding dryly, "even if I *am* Death's direct descendant."

"It's not you," Cat said, her strained tone proving that, if she were human, she'd be blushing. "It's just his . . . you know."

"You barged in for a reason, so spare us your puritan modesty and get to it," Ian said impatiently. "Besides, you must have seen a cock piercing before, and if you haven't, Crispin owes you an apology for being such an unimaginative lover."

"Fine, let's get this over with," Cat muttered, and dropped her gaze below Ian's waist.

"Wow," she said after a stunned moment. "Really jammed that thing in there, didn't you?" Then, her head tilted to the side. "Is that one bar straight through the tip? Or are there two different piercings on either side—?"

"Focus, Reaper," Ian interrupted.

"Right," she said, shaking her head as if to clear it. "I came in here because we're in deep shit. The ghoul queen is refusing to meet with me. Marie didn't give a reason, either. She just had her lackey reply, 'This is Jacques. Regrettably, Majestic's schedule prohibits new appointments at this time.'"

Ian gave a humorless smile. "And Marie tends to murder people that barge in without appointment."

"Oh, yeah," Cat said, with a shudder. "I did that once, and believe me, I barely survived."

"I'll go."

Both heads swung toward me. Then Ian looked at his wrist as if checking a watch that wasn't there.

"'Course you will. It's been, what? Five hours since you threw yourself into certain death? Well past time, then."

I ignored his sarcasm. "I've known Marie longer than either of you. She's big on protocol, but she values the well-being of her people above all. She'll want to know that rogue gods are on the loose. Since I saw them and you didn't, it should be me telling her versus you, Cat. If I hadn't been distracted by other things, I would have said that earlier."

"You keep saying 'me,'" Ian said in a warning tone.

I gave a wry snort. "Don't you know by now that when I say 'me,' that's still plural?"

"I don't mean that," Ian purred in the same don't-test-me tone.

"I know what you mean," I said, brief humor fading. "Of course I assumed you'd be going with me. Aside from meaning my former promise not to abandon you, I also admit that leaving you behind even briefly doesn't seem to protect you. Either you do something reckless, or someone dangerous finds you, or both."

"Not to mention all the times you've done reckless things when you're alone, or someone dangerous finds you," he pointed out.

"We're a mess, aren't we?" I asked, smiling in memory at his earlier vow.

He smiled back, and pulled me to him. "The worst," he agreed, and kissed me.

Cat banged on the door frame hard enough to dislodge more wood. "Get freaky later. We have gods to stop now, remember?"

Reluctantly, I pushed Ian back. "She's annoying, but correct. We only have time to shower and feed since we have more than Marie to contend with today. We also have the council."

"I'll get you two some robes," Cat muttered. "Don't want you streaking through the house because neither of you cares about covering up what you've got."

"I agree we need to warn them, but we shouldn't go to the council directly," Ian said, ignoring Cat, who left after another disapproving glance at us. "They won't listen if you call, and if you go to them, they'll try to kill you on sight. Your safety aside, they're more likely to believe what's happened with Phanes, Morana, and Ruaumoko if they hear it from someone they trust."

I let out a soft snort. "Anyone the council trusts will probably try to kill me on sight, too."

"One won't," Ian said in a confident tone. "Your former girlfriend, Xun Guan."

———

THE LAST TIME I'd been to Athens, Greece, I ended up fleeing it after Ian had proved our marriage to the vampire council. Now, I was returning with Ian to convince my former lover, Xun Guan, that my unwanted fiancé, Phanes, and his previously deceased celestial besties were about to unleash supernatural mayhem.

I wouldn't blame Xun Guan if she didn't believe me. I'd have trouble believing this, too, if I wasn't living it.

"Why is Xun Guan in Athens?" I wondered out loud as Ian and I drove away from the Larissa train station. We hadn't taken a train to get from England to Greece; we'd teleported, but I didn't want Ian burning through needless energy when there were perfectly good rental car places near the train station.

"The vampire council isn't in session now, and Xun Guan hates Greece," I continued.

"She must have found some reason to be here, because this is where Mencheres's hacker traced her mobile to," Ian replied.

My confusion deepened several minutes later as we reached the address where Xun Guan's mobile signal had pinged from: a derelict building on a street with mostly closed businesses.

The Xun Guan I knew would never stay here. In addition to being a Law Guardian, she was a savvy investor who'd accumulated quite the portfolio. Even if her investments had suddenly tanked, she could become rich again simply by selling a few personal effects from her time as a human during the Western Jin dynasty. She still had the sword she'd wielded at thirteen against Du Zeng's armies, and that item alone was priceless.

"Something's wrong," I said as we drove past the building to avoid attracting notice. "That building has to be a front."

"Hope so," Ian replied, parking out of sight of it down the street. "Otherwise, your getting married and revealing yourself to be a demigod must have sent Xun Guan into such a downward spiral that she's now useless to us."

My look told him what I thought of the callous comment. "She's too tough for that, so she must have a good reason for staying here the past two days. Be on guard, but stay out of her sight. I don't need to remind you that she hates you."

He smiled coldly. "The feeling's mutual."

I shook my head as I got out of the car. "It's almost admirable that you can be jealous at a time like this."

"She had you for centuries." His tone was light, but his turquoise eyes glinted with emerald as he exited the car, too. "If you think I don't envy her to the point of hatred for that, you vastly underestimate your worth to me."

I paused. This wasn't the normal territoriality that all vampires felt over what was theirs. It was something else.

"She had my flesh," I said very softly, coming around to his side of the car. "She never had *me*. Only you have."

He stroked my face while the barest of smiles creased his.

"I used to believe there was no difference between the two. Now, I know there is." His voice deepened. "That's why, despite my very extensive past, I can honestly say that you and you alone have touched me, Veritas, and those are words I never expected would cross these sin-stained, sordid lips."

I kissed him, feeling more from the simple brush of his mouth than I'd felt from every relationship before him. Oh, I never thought I'd have this! In all the years of my life, I hadn't even dared to wish for it. No wonder I lost my mind on a regular basis when it came to Ian. Everything else could be replaced. He couldn't.

"Unless you want to continue this in the backseat, we need to stop," Ian said, breaking the kiss. Then, he opened the backseat car door with a grin. "You already know my preference."

"Later," I said with a laugh.

His eyes flashed a brighter shade of green. "I'll hold you to that."

I was still smiling as I walked down the street toward the building. Silver and other metal objects in my coat pockets slapped against my legs with my brisk movements. Denise and Spade had loaned us clothes and, more important, weapons.

I didn't want to use any of them against Xun Guan, but I didn't underestimate her, either. She'd been a warrior for the past two thousand years. She wouldn't stop being one despite her feelings for me . . . if she even still had feelings beyond anger.

Right before I reached the building, I used a quick glamour spell to change my appearance back to my blond Law Guardian disguise. This was the appearance Xun Guan knew. She'd only ever seen my real one twice, and I didn't want to remind her of the last time, when I'd ripped Dagon's soul out right in front of her.

Then again, she probably didn't need my real appearance to remind her of that. It was doubtless seared on her memory.

Several windows in the three-story building were broken. It looked abandoned, and I didn't hear any heartbeats, but her cell was here, so it couldn't be empty. I sent my senses out, searching for the aura of energy all vampires emanated.

There. On the third floor.

I felt only one vampire, but I had my energy tamped down to where it was undetectable, too, and I was far from the only vampire who knew that trick. After a quick glance confirmed that no one on the street was watching me, I jumped up to the second floor, entering through one of the smashed-out windows.

I felt the snap of magic as soon as I did. I tried to leap back out the same window, but it was suddenly a wall. So were all the other windows that, moments before, had been empty square spaces that let in the cool night air.

Nice, I thought even as I jumped up because the floor now felt like quicksand. I couldn't go far, though. Magic-infused webs hung from the ceiling, nearly reaching the floor.

At once I stretched out until I floated horizontally above the floor. This sparse, half-meter-high space was the only section of the room free of both webs and the quicksand-like floor . . . and both should have been invisible to me. Since Law Guardians were allowed to practice defensive magic, I'd taught Xun Guan the web spell myself, so I well knew its strengths. Invisibility was one of them. But somehow, I caught glints of the magic that infused each strand of the complex nets.

Such beauty, my other half thought. *Like raindrops on a spider's web when the moonlight shines through them.*

That's why I could see the spell now! Thanks to my father's enhancement, my other half must now be able to see magic as well as see through Phanes's illusions.

We *can see through magic,* she corrected. I could almost feel her huff as she added, *Will you never learn?*

Don't you mean will we *never learn?* I countered.

Her laugh bubbled in my throat, until I found myself chuckling out loud.

"How can you be laughing?" a feminine voice asked in an ancient dialect of Mandarin. "And how did you avoid my traps?"

I turned my head. Xun Guan was in the doorway, wearing a tactical-style gray unitard with a scabbard belted at her waist, and throwing knives holstered around her thighs and upper arms. She'd swept her long black hair into a bun—her usual style when fighting so it didn't restrict her vision and no one could use its length to grab her. Her sword was drawn—not a good sign—but for the moment, it was also pointed downward.

"Xun Guan," I said in the same language. "We need to talk."

*H*er midnight brown eyes were hard, as if I was nothing to her and never had been. I hadn't expected a warm welcome, but it was a bit disconcerting to see her look at me that way. We'd been more than on-again, off-again lovers over the centuries. Long before that, we'd also been friends.

"You insult me, wearing this false image," she said.

I dropped my glamour, then immediately had to tie my hair into a knot after its much longer strands touched the floor and that quicksand magic tried to grab them and pull me down.

"Should've worn it in a bun like you do," I commented.

She just stared at me, her features as tight as her coiled muscles, while she continued to hold herself in a fighter's stance. She was so still, she resembled a beautiful statue, but my wariness increased. She only held herself this immobile right before she executed someone.

"I mean you no harm," I said, in case that was the issue.

She didn't even blink. "I cannot say the same."

"Xun Guan—"

Silver knives ripped through the air from an unseen third trap. I shot away to avoid them, but I could only move in a horizontal line, while they came from all directions.

Very good! my other half noted as several blades sank home. *We'll kill her quickly in appreciation of her cleverness.*

We're not killing her, I snapped.

Why? Because with you in charge, we'd already be dead?

I ignored that and concentrated. This building might be abandoned, but it still had plumbing. I didn't have to kill Xun Guan to stop her.

Trust me, I told my other nature, then grabbed the water in the pipes with our combined abilities and pulled.

The pipes exploded as it burst free. Xun Guan turned at the loud sound, her sword rising. Another blast of concentration turned the water into ice shards that tore through the ceilings, walls, and floor, aiming for Xun Guan. Her sword spun in a blur, but not even her incredible skill and speed could stop them all.

She fell to the floor as the shards ripped through her, too numerous for her to heal from their damage. The knife trap that had been razing me ceased. Her will must have powered the spell, and now she was unconscious, her body strafed from so many ice shards that her ripped unitard revealed more than it covered.

At the same instant, a car crashed through the wall opposite Xun Guan, hitting her and sending both of them hurtling through the other wall and into the next room. I turned in disbelief. Ian was floating in front of the huge new hole in the wall, a torn-off fender still in his hands.

"What the hell?" I managed to say.

His brows shot up. "Did you think I'd watch her cut you to shreds with that knife trap? Knew I couldn't teleport in without getting caught by her spells, so I stopped her another way."

I love him, my other half said with smug satisfaction.

So did I, but all of us would have a *real* hard time getting Xun Guan to help now.

"Go back down and mesmerize the bystanders that will *definitely* show up after this racket," I said, wincing as I began pulling the silver knives out of me.

He rolled his eyes. "You're welcome."

"Okay, thank you, but I did have it handled! She was on the ground, wasn't she?"

He snorted. "You're saying I overreacted in order to protect you? If gods struck hypocrites with lightning bolts, your arse would be on fire right now."

I shot a quick grin at him as I finished removing the knives and zoomed over to check on Xun Guan. "True, but you still have to deal with any bystanders.

Everyone has camera phones now, and we can't afford to make someone YouTube famous by proving the existence of vampires."

"You get five minutes," I heard him mutter before he vanished from the hole in the wall.

I flew into the second room, keeping a careful eye out for any new spells. So far, nothing. Just Xun Guan trapped under a smashed sedan that I didn't recognize. Figures Ian wouldn't use our rental car. That had been insured. Now, I owed some poor stranger a check because this car was a total loss.

"Two gods escaped from the netherworld with the help of a lesser deity named Phanes," I said as I pulled the car off Xun Guan's upper body. I left it on her lower half because I wasn't about to make it easy for her to try killing me again. "All three are here, and they *don't* come in peace."

"Murderer," she rasped in reply.

"Yes, I killed Dagon, but you don't know how much he had it coming. To summarize, he used me to murder thousands of innocent people back when I was human, and that's not even mentioning what he did to me."

"Not . . . the demon."

Her voice gained strength as the bones in her upper body healed. They must have splintered after Ian basically swatted her flat with this car.

"You murdered Claudia and Pyotor," she finished in a much clearer tone.

"Claudia and Pyotor *from the council* are dead?"

My raised voice made her wince. Her head must not have finished healing yet.

"Do not feign surprise with me!"

She swiped at her fallen sword as she spoke. I kicked it away, and then stood on both her wrists to hold them down. Between me and the car, she wasn't moving anytime soon.

She gave me her opinion of that in a rage-filled glare.

"I saw the security footage. It was you, in your real form, murdering Claudia and Pyotor two days ago. That is why I messaged you, telling you to meet me here for battle instead of slaying others in their sleep the way a coward would!"

"I didn't get your message, and I *didn't* kill them, because I wasn't even in this world two days ago," I snapped.

But Phanes was, and he knew my real form.

A simple glamour spell could have duplicated it. He wouldn't have even needed his powers of illusion. Oh, the clever bastard! He'd used my appearance to create chaos in the vampire world by having it appear that a former Law Guardian had assassinated two council members, all while Ruaumoko was regaining power by setting off volcanoes in Iceland and earthquakes in New Zealand, and Morana was leveling herself up by refreezing the arctic circle!

I had to hand it to the trio: they'd been busy, and smart. If Ian and I hadn't returned, no one would know they were behind all of this, and we shouldn't have returned. Minus a few lucky breaks, we'd still be stuck in the netherworld or dead.

"It might have looked like me on that footage, but it wasn't me," I said to Xun Guan. "I told you, I wasn't even in this world. I was in the netherworld until last night."

"Liar," she hissed. "Only the dead can enter the underworld, and the dead do not return from it. And *if* you were with the dead, how did you know where I was, if you were not in this world to receive the message I sent you?"

She'd challenged me to a duel. No wonder she'd had this place rigged with traps from top to bottom. It also explained why she'd been staying in an empty building in this nearly abandoned, derelict section of Athens. She hadn't wanted any innocent people to get hurt when we fought.

"I never got your message," I told her in a steady voice. "I had a hacker trace your mobile to this location because I needed to speak to you, and I was able to travel in and out of the netherworld because my father is its warden."

The truth I never thought I'd tell her hung in the air between us. She stared at me, unblinking.

"King Yan is your father?"

I sighed. "That's one of his names, yes."

Granted, King Yan, or Yanluo, was the ruler and judge of the underworld in Chinese mythology and my father claimed not to judge anyone. But he did rule the punishment section of the netherworld, and I didn't think Xun Guan wanted a discussion on religious minutia right now.

"I should have known." Her voice lowered to a whisper. "When I saw you tear that demon's soul out and hurl it into the underworld . . . I should have known what you were."

I almost missed her staring at me with murderous intent. The new, almost reverent horror was worse. With one admission, I'd ceased being a person to her. Now, I was a thing. A feared, honored thing with her beliefs, but a thing nonetheless.

I steeled myself against how much that hurt. She'd been one of my oldest friends, but my feelings were irrelevant right now.

Then, she looked away. "What you are still does not prove your innocence. You lied to me for over a thousand years. How am I to believe you're not lying to me again now?"

I sighed. "Because you know me. I might not have told you *what* I was because I knew you'd feel honor-bound to report me, but you know who I am, Xun Guan. That hasn't changed."

Sadness clouded her gaze. "I thought I knew you. Once."

Frustration sharpened my tone. "You refuse to trust in my character? Fine, then trust in my methodology. We fought many battles together. Have I ever killed an enemy in their sleep?"

Her silence confirmed my point.

"And if I *were* going to murder a council member, it wouldn't have been Claudia or Pyotor," I added with brutal honesty. "It would've been Haldam, and you'd better believe he'd be awake, because I'd want to look that sexist, malignant narcissist in the eye when I twisted silver through his heart."

A wheeze escaped her that she stifled too late. I wasn't the only one who disliked Haldam for those same reasons.

"I might not be *what* you believed me to be, but I'm still the person you know and loved," I said. "I still care for you, too, Xun Guan. I also trust you. That's why I came to tell you that these gods are real, they're here, and they need to be stopped before they do much worse than kill two council members. You have to warn the remaining council about them because they will no longer listen to me."

"No, they won't," she breathed out. "They are meeting now to appoint two new members, and to determine the bounty they are placing on your head for assassinating Claudia and Pyotor."

I barely processed the bounty part because I was too appalled by the first bit. "The remaining council is meeting together now? All of them? Tell me they're not meeting at the official court location on Mount Lycabettus?"

Her gaze widened with understanding. "Yes, they are—"

"Fucking hell!" I shouted, leaping off her wrists. "Ian!"

He was there before my voice died away, his grim expression revealing that he'd overheard everything.

"They're serving themselves up for slaughter," he said.

"Unless we stop it," I replied, yanking on the car.

Ian's hand landed on it, stopping me from freeing Xun Guan. "First, swear by your blood that you will not try to kill or arrest Veritas," he said to Xuan Guan.

"Ian!" I shoved at his arm. It didn't move. "We don't have time for this. The council could *die*."

"Then she'd best get to swearing that, shouldn't she?" he replied, not looking away from Xun Guan.

Her mouth curled in contempt. "How dare you demand my word of honor when you have no honor yourself?"

"Very little," he agreed with a wolfish smile. "But you're awash in it. So give your word, or I'll bounce up and down on this car until I grind your bones to dust while the council probably gets murdered."

If I could teleport, I'd have left them both behind for their stubbornness. Still, only Ian could get us to the top of Athens's famed Mount Lycabettus in seconds, and even at that speed, we might be too late.

There was only one way to hasten this standoff.

"He'll do it," I said to Xun Guan. "He didn't like the council before they branded me a fugitive. Now that they have? He couldn't care less if they died."

Ian's grin said, *all true.*

"So swear it, Xun Guan," I went on. "Saving them is more important than arresting me, and now that you know I didn't murder Claudia or Pyotor, you're not going to hurt me anyway."

I also wouldn't hurt her, now that I wasn't defending myself against her impressive attempts to kill me. Ian might want to grind her bones into dust for that, but I wouldn't let him. Not that I'd tell her that. After believing I'd murdered two of them, the council *really* wouldn't be inclined to listen to me, so we needed Xun Guan. But if she couldn't bring herself to make such a simple promise, I'd leave her behind.

Xun Guan's gaze promised vengeance as she stared at Ian. I'd be tempted to make her swear the same concerning him, if she were his match. But she wasn't, and we were out of time.

Ian must have agreed. "Now or never," he said, giving the car a warning jostle.

"On my blood, I do swear to your conditions," she said, then ripped her lower lip with a fang and spat the blood at Ian.

He only grinned as he yanked the car off her with one hard tug.

"Now, hold on to Veritas since neither of us wants your hands on me. We've got a slaughter to stop."

Chapter 27

When the blinding whirls ceased, we were at the top of Mount Lycabettus, on the gravel path above part of the amphitheater. The cable cars, church, restaurant, and other attractions across the way were closed, emptied, and with their lights off, leaving only the theater illuminated on the famed peak. Normally, that was a subtle statement to all Greece's vampires that the council was now in session. This is where the council had met for centuries, even before there were electric lights to turn on or an amphitheater for them to meet in.

That was the point. Everyone knew that Mount Lycabettus was the official court for the council, and no demon, ghoul, or vampire had ever dared to attack here. But this was no normal conflict. We were fighting against gods, and they didn't care about honoring the old rules. Right now, the theater lighting up the famed mountain's peak might as well have been a neon sign flashing "Attack here!" to Phancs.

Xun Guan took a step toward the amphitheater, and promptly fell on the weathered stone. Either her legs hadn't finished healing during the brief moments it took Ian to transport us here, or she was unsteady after her first time teleporting.

I knelt at once, too, but I wasn't checking on her. I was keeping low as I sent my senses out to discern who else might be on this peak with us. So far, I felt nothing but vampires. Over a dozen were inside the open-air amphitheater, and at least that many were also around its perimeter. To my relief, I didn't hear any sounds of violence. Only talking from inside the amphitheater, too low for me to make out individual words.

Ian knelt next to me. "Nothing but vampires so far," he whispered. "A few spotted our movements and are closing in."

"We should teleport inside," I whispered back.

"No," Xun Guan hissed in an equally low voice. "They'll think you came to murder them. Let me handle this."

"Halt!" a familiar voice ordered moments later.

"Hands behind your backs," Xun Guan ordered, now so low I could barely hear her.

I did, glad to see that Ian followed suit. Then, Xun Guan rose from her crouch and strode toward the guard.

"Stand aside, Vachir," she said to the tall, bearded Law Guardian, whose new look reminded me of Leonidas from the movie *300*. "I have captured the murderess and her miserable jackal of a husband.

Now, I am bringing them before the council to face their judgment."

Ian's mouth quirked; the closest he'd come to expressing his admiration for how she'd found a way to insult him and waltz us in before the council all at the same time.

Vachir's swarthy complexion darkened further when he looked at Ian and me. "Where are the prisoners' bindings?"

"You think I would trust regular metal on these two?" Xun Guan scoffed. "Magic binds them."

"Announce them," he ordered to Priscilla, another Law Guardian I'd long been friendly with.

The blonde Viking gave me a look that said she'd blood-eagle me herself, if she could. Then, Priscilla went farther down the path around the theater, which was in the shape of an open ladies' fan and was tucked into the side of one of the mount's rugged peaks. Even from our higher vantage point, we couldn't see inside the theater, but it was easy to know when Priscilla told them we were here. Voices erupted in anger, and she returned with satisfaction stamped on her ivory features.

"Bring them in, Xun Guan."

Vachir spat at my feet as I walked past him. "Traitor."

I didn't take offense. I'd spit at me, too, if I believed what he did.

We circled around until the terrain sloped down to the base level of the theater. Behind us, the city of Athens shone brightly, while in front of us, row after row of seats in the open-air theater surrounded the stage. The rocky section we'd recently stood on rose past them, blocking out the lights from the rest of the surrounding city.

The stadium seats were all empty. The only people seated in the entire theater were in the large, ornate thrones spread out on the circular stage. There were eleven thrones, but two were empty, and the malevolence coming from the remaining council members was palpable as Ian and I came closer.

"On your knees," Xun Guan barked, pushing us down.

"Bit much," Ian muttered as his knees hit the floor.

I didn't care. We were exactly where we needed to be. Phanes would get a hell of a surprise if he attacked the council now. I almost hoped he would. I couldn't wait to give him a taste of what he deserved, if Ian didn't beat me to it.

Until then, we'd reason with the council about the real dangers facing them. If they didn't believe us, we could always do a snatch-and-grab. Ian had the teleporting ability; I had the magic. We'd get them to safety whether they liked it or not—

Ian vanished. Gasps barely had time to sound before he reappeared behind Haldam's throne. Then, Ian stabbed Haldam through the heart and twisted the knife.

Over the instant war cries from the horrified Law Guardians and multiple crashing sounds as thrones hit the floor from fleeing council members, I heard Ian shout, "Freeze this room, Veritas!" before he disappeared again.

I felt almost numb as I released my power, covering the amphitheater and immediate perimeter around it.

Instantly, everything froze as if it had been turned into a living photograph. Council members were suspended in mid-run or mid-flight, depending on their abilities. Silver knives that the Law Guardians had flung were also suspended in the air. One must have reached me because my back now stung. I moved away, turned, and saw Xun Guan holding a silver knife with a bloody tip. From that now-fading sting in my back, she'd been in the process of knifing me through the heart.

I couldn't really blame her. Ian had murdered the council's appointed spokesperson right in front of her, and she'd been the one to bring both of us in here armed and unrestrained. She probably would have turned the knife on herself next.

Ian reappeared, proving that he was still immune to my time-freezing abilities. He paused to give a disgusted look at Xun Guan before he yanked the bloody knife from her hand.

"One simple vow, and she couldn't keep it for five minutes. So much for her fabled honor."

I stared at him. "She thought we tricked and betrayed her so we could murder the rest of the council! After what you just did, why would she think anything else?"

"Can you release the council member's heads while leaving their bodies frozen?" Ian asked, ignoring that. "Or would that take too much power?"

Even for him, this was going too far. "You are *not* going to gloss over murdering a council member, Ian!"

He cast an unconcerned glance at Haldam, whose expression was frozen in a mask of horror as he stared at the silver knife that Ian had twisted in his chest.

"He's fine," he said in dismissive tone.

Eating that cursed fruit must have warped his mind. That was the only explanation. "Dead is the *opposite* of fine."

"No need to shout," he said with infuriating amusement. "Besides, didn't you tell Xun Guan that Haldam would be the first council member you killed if you went on a murder spree?"

Did he think murdering Haldam was . . . was akin to being chivalrous? Dear gods, he *had* lost his mind.

"That didn't mean I wanted you to kill him," I began, only to stop as Ian held up a hand.

"Trust me, luv. I do know what I'm doing. Now, can you release the others' heads alone, or not?"

I already felt like a door being hammered by a battering ram since the power I'd sent out kept crashing back into me before reverberating out to envelop the amphitheater again. Freeing the council members' heads while keeping the rest of their bodies in time-suspended animation? That would hurt so much worse.

Trust me, luv.

"Bring the pain," I muttered, and did what he asked.

Awareness returned to the council members' expressions. Then, fear followed as they realized they were completely immobilized from the neck down. Shock was next when they looked around and saw the rest of the amphitheater in the same freeze-frame state, right down to the dust particles suspended in the air next to them. When their gazes finally settled on me, I schooled my features while I inwardly braced.

It still didn't take away the sting of being looked at as though I were pure evil.

"See what she can do?" Ian's clear voice broke the silence. "Despite all your power, your many protectors, and your bloody inflexible laws, she could slaughter the lot of you if she wanted, and you couldn't even lift a finger to stop her."

"Ian!" This was hardly the way to open things!

"No, they need to know," he continued in a cruelly cheerful tone. "They created laws to oppress people out of fear that one day, they'd be the ones oppressed. You have all the power they feared and more when they outlawed magic and blending the races, yet did you oppress them? No. You served under them for centuries despite being worlds more powerful than all of them. Even when they arrested you, you didn't strike out to defend yourself. No, instead you're still trying to save them even while they're meeting to put a bounty on your head."

"Haldam's death and our current immobility hardly seems proof that she is here to save us," Hekima said, with an emphatic glance down at her time-frozen body.

She'd long been the council member I was friendliest with, but Hekima's hard stare my way reminded me that she was also a formidable opponent. As a vampire, she was the council's first female judge. As a human, she'd been Japan's first empress regnant back when she went by a different name.

"I'm sure Ian is building to a point," I said, while thinking, *Please, let him be building to a point instead of this being a sign that the cursed fruit that is slowly killing his body has overtaken his mind.*

"I am. Release Haldam's entire body, Veritas."

I hesitated for a moment, and then again chose to trust that he did have a logical reason for all of this. With a painful burst of power, I freed Haldam while keeping everything else frozen in the same previous moment in time.

At once, Haldam's body slumped forward, and he fell off his throne to sprawl onto the floor.

I concealed my shudder as I absorbed the power that slammed back into me from what I'd done. This ability was one of my most dangerous ones, and it was also my most draining. Unfreezing parts of people while keeping the rest of them in suspended animation only made it worse, as did encompassing the entire amphitheater and the immediate space around it. I wouldn't be good for much after this, and I doubted I could hold it for more than another twenty minutes—

Haldam groaned.

My shock almost caused me to drop the entire room from suspended animation. Dead vampires didn't groan. They also didn't sit up, snatch the knife from their chest, and hurl it aside, but that's exactly what Haldam did.

My gasp was echoed by the other council members. Even if Ian hadn't twisted that blade in him—and he *had*, we'd all seen it—no vampire whose heart had been pieced with silver would have had the strength to do that. Haldam should be shriveling into a vampire's state of true death, not looking at the time-suspended room around him with amazement.

"Behold." Ian's voice rang out in the stunned silence. "Your real traitor."

*H*aldam immediately tried to run. Ian teleported over and caught him before he made it one step.

"Not so fast, mate. You're my Exhibit A."

Haldam struggled with a surprising display of strength. I refroze him without even pausing to think about it. His latest lunge at Ian ended with him flat on his face.

Ian swung around to face me. "Really?" he said with exasperated amusement.

"I know, you could've handled it," I replied, sheepish. "What can I say? It just slipped out."

He rolled his eyes and then grabbed Haldam by his long, white beard. He dragged him by that beard over to the center of the stage. Once there, he began to strip him.

"What are you doing now?" Hekima asked.

I was wondering the same thing.

"We're at court," Ian replied, yanking Haldam's shirt off to reveal his parchment-pale skin. "Courts require proof, so I'm getting it for you. Bet it's in his trousers. Few would want to venture near his hairy old arse."

With that, Ian ripped Haldam's trousers up the back, revealing that Haldam's ass was, indeed, hairy. That wasn't what made me stare. It was the small, tight cluster of smoke-colored swirls under his left buttock.

"Haldam has Dagon's brand," I breathed out.

It seemed like forever ago that Ian had gotten a spell to detect anyone with traces of Dagon's power in them. Ian had thought he'd felt the spell activate before, when the council arrested me weeks—no, months—ago, in this timeline. But Ian hadn't been sure, because he'd barely been conscious after breaking us out of Dagon's trap.

When we arrived here, that spell must have activated again, giving Ian his proof. Haldam coming back after being stabbed through the heart was proof for the rest of us.

"Demon brand," Ian said, holding Haldam up and walking him around so that the council members in various frozen states of flight could all see him. "Haldam sold his soul to a demon for supernatural perks, all the while voting to kill any vampire who practiced magic, and while casting the deciding vote to kill a child merely for being a combination of races. Isn't it always the most bigoted sods that are also the most hypocritical?"

"Can this be true?" Sanjay, one of the newer council members, whispered.

Ian flipped Haldam right side up and shoved his chest in front of Sanjay. "Stab him in the heart with silver yourself, if you don't believe me. He'll come back from it every time, because there's only one way to kill someone who is demon-branded."

"Demon bone through both eyes," Hekima said in a flat tone. "Give me some of his blood to taste, young man."

Haldam's blood would certainly offer more proof. As soon as Dagon branded him, Haldam would have become infused with part of Dagon's power, and demon blood was a narcotic to vampires. Even now, after Dagon's brand was gone, Ian's blood was still mildly intoxicating because it contained traces of the power that Ian had absorbed from Dagon.

Ian dropped Haldam to fetch the bloody knife he'd stabbed him with. Then, Ian held it next to Hekima's mouth.

"Bottoms up," he said lightly.

Hekima licked it, grimacing as soon as her tongue touched the blade. It would have burned since the knife wasn't made from the lower-content silver that Ian used in his personal piercings. No, this was high-grade, vampire-killing silver, and if Hekima had doubted that before, she wouldn't now.

"His blood is indeed tainted," she said, spitting it out.

"Altered," I corrected her. "No one's blood is 'tainted' from merely being a combination of more than one species."

The faintest smile creased the deep lines in her face. Hekima hadn't been young when she was changed over, but she refused modern options to lessen her wrinkles, and she also didn't dye her black hair to conceal the liberal amounts of white. She'd once told me both were reminders that life had battled against her at times, and that she had battled back.

"Altered, then," she finally replied.

I inclined my head in appreciation of her amendment. Then, I looked at the rest of the council.

"As my husband has gone to extreme lengths to illustrate, I mean you no harm. I also didn't kill Claudia and Pyotor. A lesser deity named Phanes did. He's a powerful illusion master, and unfortunately, he has even more powerful friends."

With that, I gritted my teeth, and unfroze all the Law Guardians from the neck up. It would've been easier to release my power over the amphitheater entirely, but then Ian and I would have over a dozen highly skilled guards trying to kill us before we could explain that we weren't the bad guys here. This way was better, even if it did feel like lying down on the freeway to let rush hour traffic run over me.

Once everyone was able to listen, I brought them up to speed on Phanes, Morana, and Ruaumoko. Some of them already knew the lore about the three, which saved me a lot of questions. Others, however, were more scornful.

From Phoenix, our youngest council member: "This goddess Morana can cool the entire planet? That would fix our global warming problem," he added with a derisive grunt.

"Oh, it will," Ian said in a silky tone. "It'll fix all the problems created by humans, because few of them will be left once Morana reaches full strength. Ice killed nearly all life on earth before. Fancy giving that another go? Morana likely does."

"If these gods are as powerful as you say, what chance do we have against them?" Sanjay asked, to murmurs of agreement.

Ian swept his hand toward me. "Look at what one vampire from a mixed bloodline can do. She's the only one brave enough to reveal herself to you, but decriminalize mixed bloodlines and magic, then sit back and watch even gods fall before you."

"We will not change thousands of years of peace-sustaining laws for one unproven threat!" Lucius snapped.

No shock that Lucius would be the council's biggest objector. He'd been Haldam's closest friend for centuries, and the "birds of a feather" saying was true for a reason.

"Then our continued infighting and criminalization of those we needlessly fear will propel our enemies to victory," I said curtly. "Add the additional power struggles that are inevitable now that two council seats have opened up for the first time in centuries, and Morana, Ruaumoko, and Phanes can sit back and watch us destroy ourselves for them."

"Not to mention your only other hope of victory is allying with the ghouls," Ian said in a mild tone.

Lucius's head jerked as if he'd been slapped. "An alliance with filthy flesh eaters? Never!"

"You'd rather risk the safety of the entire world than abandon your precious, prejudiced laws? Of course you would," I answered my own question. "You've been comfortable letting others do the fighting and dying for you since your days as a rich, pampered aristocrat back in Julius Caesar's Rome!"

Lucius's cheeks puffed out in outrage. "How dare—"

The ground fell out from beneath me. Everyone else stayed suspended in their time-frozen state, but I dropped several meters before landing on the remains of the circular stage, which was now splitting like a smashed plate. Metal screeched as the scaffolding supporting the stands crumbled, sending the stands tumbling down around me.

I started to release my time-freezing hold on the amphitheater so that everyone could flee, then immediately snapped it back when scalding ash and gases rushed up to burn me and a deadly reddish-orange glow destroyed the floor.

Ian grabbed me and flew me above the amphitheater. Only then did I realize what had happened. Mount Lycabettus had somehow been instantly transformed into an erupting volcano.

That shouldn't be possible, *especially* since Mount Lycabettus wasn't a former volcano! Still, I knew a magmatic eruption when I saw one, even if I'd never before had a terrifying bird's-eye view of it.

Ruaumoko.

He was here, not Phanes, and he'd decided to take out the council by blowing up the whole damn mountain!

$\mathcal{I}$ sent everything I had into extending more of my time-bubble over the mountain. Only suspending everything in a single, frozen moment would hold back the fiery eruption. Vampires could survive a lot, but being blown to bits and immersed in red-hot lava would *definitely* kill us.

Agony bashed me from the extended effort, until I felt like I'd explode along with the mountain. I tried to hide that from Ian as I gasped out, "Save the council. Can't . . . hold this long."

Ian cursed in three different languages, but set me down at the base of Mount Lycabettus, away from the immediate eruption danger. Then, he teleported away.

The ground shook. People started pouring out of their houses shouting, "Earthquake!" I looked around in despair. All the lights that had made up the gorgeous skyline when viewed from Mount Lycabettus now seemed like potential headstones. This was one of the most populous areas in Athens.

Even if the residents somehow escaped the exploding rock and deadly lava flow from the eruption, the wide-spreading gasses and ash would still kill thousands.

I stretched my power to the limit. I had to stop this long enough for the people to evacuate to safety.

Ian reappeared with Hekima and Sanjay. He dropped them near me and disappeared again. Hekima came closer, freed from immobilization now that she was outside of my time-bubble.

"Veritas," she said in concern. "You're badly burned."

I didn't spare the concentration to reply. I would heal, if we survived this.

"Are you not speaking because you're somehow trying to stop this?" she asked in a sharper tone.

My head jerked in a nod.

"Sanjay," Hekima said in that same sharp tone. "We must clear the surrounding buildings of as many people as possible."

Ian reappeared again, almost throwing Lucius and Fion, another council member, down. Lucius grabbed on to Ian's leg before he could teleport away.

"I demand to know what's happening!"

Ian gave Lucius a savage look. "One of those 'unproven threats' you were dismissing just detonated a volcano under your arse."

Lucius's eyes bulged. "Impossible!"

"Not for a god of earthquakes and volcanoes. Now, release me, or I'll throw you into the volcano's flaming center like I'm sacrificing a bloomin' virgin!"

Lucius let Ian go as if he were suddenly scalding him. Ian disappeared, and Hekima took Lucius and Fion by the arm.

"Come, help us get the people to safety."

They left, Lucius still arguing that this couldn't be happening. Sweat burst out of my skin as more agony rolled over me. I tasted it on my lip and felt it beneath the remains of my burned clothes as it drenched my body. I hadn't broken out into a sweat since I was human. I hadn't known I still could. My time-freezing power had reached its limit; it wasn't enough. The volcano Ruaumoko had instantly transformed the mountain into was too big and volatile for me to hold back much longer.

Ian appeared with two more council members, dropping them and vanishing almost instantly. The council members peppered me with questions that I ignored, using all my concentration to hold back the deadly eruption as long as I could.

Hekima called out, directing them to come down to her. They left, and moments later, Ian dropped off two more council members, and then in mere moments, reappeared with Haldam and Xun Guan. Haldam's eyes were still smoking from the demon bone sticking out of them. Ian must have decided to finish him once and for all.

He'd saved the council, but there were over a dozen Law Guardians up there. Ian could probably save them before I lost control, and Hekima and the other council members might be able to get a few hundred people to safety, but that still left tens of thousands in the eruption zone. I couldn't keep the mountain from detonating long enough for the majority of the people to evacuate. I could already feel my control slipping, but . . . this didn't have to all be on me, I realized.

As Ian had repeatedly reminded me, I wasn't alone anymore.

I summoned up the additional energy to whisper. "Ian."

He knelt by me at once, shoving Xun Guan away.

"Mencheres and Vlad." I could barely get their names out from how tightly I'd clenched my jaw against the pain. "Vlad can . . . extinguish lava, while . . . Mencheres holds . . . mountain together."

"You're barking mad," he snapped. "Even if they both *could*, I'm not leaving you alone long enough to fetch them. Ruaumoko is clearly here, and Phanes and Morana could be, too."

"Have to," I gritted out. "All those innocent . . . people."

Xun Guan pushed herself to her feet. Then, she faced Ian.

"Go. I will protect her."

Ian looked at her as if she'd suggested he lop off his own head. "Think I trust you? You tried to stab her heart out half an hour ago. If I didn't think she'd hold it against me, I would've left you right in that blast zone, and good riddance!"

Ian was shouting, and still, it was getting harder to hear him. I was folding myself into the power to maintain it, which meant everything else was fading away.

"I love her, too," I heard Xun Guan snarl. "And I was *not* trying to kill her. I was incapacitating her to protect the rest of the council, but I swear on my life that she will survive this, even if I have to fly her away and leave everyone else."

"Swear on more than your life." Even though I could barely hear Ian's words anymore, the death that stalked his tone was clear. "Swear it also on everything you hold precious because I *will* destroy all of it if she dies."

"If she dies, everything I hold precious is already gone," I thought I heard Xun Guan say, but I couldn't be sure.

Hands gripped my shoulders, and then a mouth pressed against my ear.

"Listen to me, Veritas." Ian's voice, raised and insistent. "Someone threatens you, you rip open the netherworld and hurl them into it. Don't bother about more veils cracking. We can fix whatever you break later, but you survive now, understand?"

After that, something soft brushed my cheek that might have been his lips, but I couldn't be sure. My vision had narrowed to pinpricks, and the white-hot pain made me feel like I was being blasted by those superheated gases again.

Hurry, Ian. Hurry!

I repeated that as shudders wracked me. More sweat ran down me, making my clothes feel sodden.

The ground shook harder, faster, until its insistent vibrations felt like a heartbeat pounding in my chest. Pain took turns turning my blood to ice one moment and fire the next, making me almost insensible. Even my brain ached as if trying to split through my skull.

I couldn't stand this. I had to drop the time-bubble. I had to. It was too much, too much, too much . . .

Cool fingers dug into my temples and face, finding pressure points and massaging them. Hadn't Ian left yet? What was he waiting for? Didn't he know I was at the end of my strength?

Above the roar in my ears that could have been the mountain breaking apart or my skull shattering from power overload, I caught snatches of words, and realized they came from Xun Guan.

". . . can do this, my beloved. Nothing has ever defeated you. Nothing ever will. Hold on a few moments longer, just a few . . ."

A few moments longer. I ground my jaw tighter, ignoring the continuous taste of blood. Yes, I could do this for a few more moments. The council members might be able to save another dozen more lives in that amount of time . . .

"What fresh hell is this, Ian?" an annoyed voice said with a noticeable Romanian accent.

If pain wasn't ripping me apart, I would've smiled. Vlad Dracul, better known by his hated moniker, Dracula, had just arrived.

"See that mountain?" I heard Ian reply. "A mad god turned it into an erupting volcano. Unless you want to see thousands of people burn, use your fire-controlling abilities on a real challenge instead of just incinerating anyone who annoys you."

"If I did that, you'd be ashes," Vlad muttered, but then I felt a blast of power that knocked me back against Xun Guan. Before I could recover, I felt a second blast. My hold over the time bubble splintered. The ground heaved like it was vomiting.

"Keep the mountain together, Mencheres!" Ian roared. "She's losing her grip on it!"

Not losing, I thought as agony smashed me apart. *Lost.*

$\mathcal{I}$ opened my eyes. Ian's face was the first thing I saw. At some point, he'd knelt and gathered me into his arms.

At once, I looked beyond him. Mount Lycabettus still rose over Athens like a huge stone sentry. Relief almost made me pass out again. No poisonous gases, no deadly pyroclastic flows, no building-smashing tephra, and no molten lava. Just the familiar landmark that had towered above Athens since before the wheel was invented. The only sign that anything ominous had happened were a few new boulders around the base of the mountain and the small, fading plume of ash rising above Lycabettus's peak.

"They did it," I whispered with overwhelming gratitude.

Ian's light snort tickled my cheek. "Only after you did."

Then Ian leaned back, and Vlad Dracul came into view.

Vlad's espresso-colored hair reached the shoulders of his storm-cloud-gray suit, where a charcoal scarf hung with casual elegance around his neck. His jaw was shadowed with one of those growths that was more stubble than beard, and the dark contrast against his pale, creamy skin made his cheekbones look even more chiseled. Vlad could be mistaken for any other handsome man in his mid-thirties, if you ignored how his hands were alight with blue-white flames that somehow didn't burn his jacket. Vlad's control over fire was all-encompassing, down to it never even scorching a hair on his head.

"Veritas." A faint, sardonic smile curled Vlad's mouth, and his eyes darkened from glowing emerald back to their normal coppery color. "My compliments on an unusual morning. I've never been tasked with extinguishing an erupting volcano before."

I smiled, though even that simple gesture felt exhausting. "Next time, I'll have Ian kidnap you for a nice brunch instead."

"Xun Guan is gathering the council. Once they reach us, we should leave," Mencheres said, moving into my line of view next. His long black hair blew around his shoulders as if from a strong breeze, when in reality, it was from the crackling energy Mencheres still emanated. Vlad's pyrokinesis might have extinguished the volcano, but Mencheres's telekinesis had kept the mountain from blowing apart from all that building pressure.

"Yes, so does anyone have a flask?" Ian asked.

Vlad gave him censuring a look. "Why would we have portable containers of liquor on us at *six* in the morning?"

I let out a tired laugh. "Ian isn't trying to get drunk. He must want to summon Ashael to help teleport the council."

Vlad stiffened. "Ashael the demon?"

"Ashael my friend," I corrected him.

I didn't trust Vlad enough to tell him about our shared lineage. Ashael was still passing as a full demon among his kind, and demons were even less accepting of mixed races than vampires and ghouls. Still, exhausted or no, I wasn't going to let the disgust in Vlad's tone go unchallenged.

"Eh, someone in one of these houses must have a bottle," Ian said, then disappeared.

Vlad turned to Mencheres. "You have no objection to him summoning a *demon* here?"

Mencheres opened his mouth to reply. Ian returned before he could get a word out, holding a half-full bottle of ouzo.

"Don't," Vlad said in a warning tone.

"Sure," Ian said sarcastically, and then took a drink. "Ashael, we need you!" he said right after he swallowed.

Ashael seemed to leap from the shadows, wearing only silk pajama bottoms in, of all colors, baby pink.

"Thought I could sleep now that it was almost dawn," Ashael muttered, and then stopped short when he saw me. "Veritas," he said in a conversational tone. "Why are you half barbecued and covered in blood?"

"She was sweating it while time-freezing a volcano that Ruaumoko detonated beneath us," Ian replied.

That had been blood? I glanced down. My burns had healed, but yes, my remaining clothing was charred, and I also looked like I'd rolled around on a slaughterhouse floor.

"Someone tell Mr. Sparky Hands to put his flames out," Ashael added without even glancing behind him at Vlad.

I looked. Yes, Vlad's hands were alight again.

"Do you mind?" I asked in the testiest tone I could manage.

"I do," Vlad replied coolly. "The last time I saw Ashael, he was trying to convince me to sell my soul to him in exchange for removing a deadly spell on my wife."

My eyes widened, but all Ashael did was laugh.

"I was so close, too!" he said, finally turning to face Vlad. "I would've been the toast of my species if I'd negotiated *that* deal. Ah, well. Maybe next time."

Vlad's expression darkened, and the temperature suddenly spiked around us.

"Vlad," Mencheres said in a stern tone. "Do *not* attack him. Ashael is a new ally of mine."

"A demon?" Vlad let out a harsh laugh. "You're joking."

"I'm not," Mencheres said, his hand on my shoulder silently adding, *Let me handle this*.

If I weren't having trouble sitting up, I would've argued. Since I was beyond exhausted, I gave Mencheres a "go for it" wave. Mencheres was Vlad's honorary sire, so if anyone could control the world's most bad-tempered vampire, it was him.

Besides, all my abilities except my soul-ripping one felt depleted, and I wasn't about to do that, no matter how Vlad's rudeness annoyed me.

"You would not disrespect me by attacking an ally of mine without provocation, would you?" Mencheres asked Vlad.

"No," Vlad said after a seething silence. Then, he flashed a cold smile at Ashael. "You'll never get another chance at my soul. My wife discovered what she needed to know after your foolish attempt to drive up the price on your information."

Ashael laughed again. "That's what you believe I did? Aren't you supposed to be brilliant as well as deadly?"

"No insults, Ashael," I said as Vlad's hands blazed again.

Ashael rolled his eyes. "Fine, but I liked his wife, so it was no accident that I directed Leila to the one person who had the information she needed."

"Change the subject," Ian said, spotting Xun Guan leading Hekima and the rest of the council up the hill to us. "Ashael, I need your help getting the council to safety . . ."

Ian stopped talking and slowly turned. I followed his gaze, but I didn't see more council members. I didn't see anyone after them except humans milling around outside the entrances of their houses, still wary about entering because they thought the previous shaking had been an earthquake that might not be over . . .

My arm suddenly stung as if I'd been bitten. I looked down, expecting to see a snake slithering away. No, nothing moved on the ground near me, so what was it . . . ?

My tattoo rose from my skin, unwinding itself into a three-dimensional set of wrist cuffs attached to a long, steel-colored chain. Mencheres stepped back with a hiss.

"What is that?"

A big damn *Heads-up!* from my father, that's what. I'd wondered how I would get the cuffs out of the arm tattoo to use them. I should have known the Warden had a solution. He'd also made it a perimeter warning system for Ruaumoko or Morana, judging from the cuffs' sudden appearance.

I followed Ian's gaze again. He hadn't looked away to see what was happening to me, and he'd been the only one not to.

There. Not on the ground, but on the roof of one of the taller buildings tightly clustered around this section. A dark-haired man of average height, medium build, and indistinguishable features. I wouldn't have even noticed him except for his eyes. They were lit with a vivid orange glow.

That alone would've told me who this was. Vampire eyes glowed green, demon eyes glowed red, my father's eyes glowed silver, as did mine and Ashael's on occasion . . . but I'd never seen orange before.

"Ruaumoko," I whispered.

"Ashael, get the council out of here now," Ian said in a low, urgent tone. "With them gone, he won't try to blow up another mountain. Mencheres?"

"My powers don't work on him. I've tried," the former pharaoh said, sounding slightly baffled.

Mencheres's powers might not be effective on Ruaumoko, but my handcuffs were supernaturally made for him. I staggered to my feet. Ian's hand landed on my arm without him once looking away from the ancient god.

"No. You're too knackered to fight him right now."

"Doesn't matter," I gritted out, trying to knock Ian's hand away and failing. "This could be our best chance—"

Ian's grip tightened, and the city spun away before I finished the sentence.

When it stopped, Ian and I were back in Spade and Denise's house. In their parlor, to be exact. One of Spade's servants nearly tripped in shock at our sudden appearance, but Ian just dropped me onto the nearest couch and said, "Tell Charles that Veritas is here."

"Wait," I said, trying to grab Ian.

He twisted away and vanished.

$\mathcal{D}$ammit, Ian!" I shouted at the space where he'd been.

Spade came into the room, wearing a long dark blue robe. "Veritas," he said with a touch of wariness. "Before we get to why you're here, tell me something that proves this is you."

"I'm going to kill Ian for dumping me here when I'm the only one who can stop the deranged escaped god!" I snapped.

Spade relaxed. "Good enough. Only the real Veritas would be that brassed off at Ian."

"Oh my God, Veritas. Look at you!"

Denise ran into the room next, concern pinching her lovely features. She was still in a nightgown, reminding me that England was two hours earlier than Athens.

I tried to wave Denise away. It didn't work, and I was too weak to do more. She covered me with an embroidered silk blanket even though the blood and char on me would ruin it, and fussed at Spade to get me something to eat.

"I'm not hungry," I said.

Spade ordered that some blood be brought despite my protests, and also some hot damp towels.

I was going to get sponge-bathed, too? That was it. I really *was* going to kill Ian for this.

"We heard voices," Cat said, coming down the staircase with Bones behind her. They both looked like they'd been in bed, too.

"Where's Ian?" Bones asked, thankfully not commenting on my appearance.

"Soon to be murdered," I muttered, and then added, "By me, metaphorically," when Cat's expression grew alarmed.

"What happened?" Denise asked.

I was spared from answering when Silver flew into the room. He flew around me in his usual excited way, and then practically dove into the crook of my arm to snuggle.

Denise gave Silver an adoring smile. "He is the sweetest thing! I'd fight you for him when it comes time for Silver to leave, but Spade didn't love him sleeping in bed with us last night, so I guess I have to let him go."

Spade's expression confirmed this statement.

I scratched Silver as I told them what happened. It took the last of my energy, but they deserved an update after having me literally dumped onto their couch. Besides, Denise had cuddled Silver in bed the way he liked when I couldn't, so I'd burn down an enemy's house for her after that.

That's why I let Denise wipe away the dried blood on my face and hands with the hot towels Spade's servant brought. I also sipped from the wrist of one of their human blood donors because I didn't want Denise to worry that I'd be tempted to eat her again. When I was finished, I was so tired, I felt like passing out was a real possibility.

Maybe I wouldn't kill Ian. He might have been right that now wasn't the best time for me to fight Ruaumoko.

"We've struck out over here, too," Cat said, sounding frustrated. "Marie still won't agree to a meeting. My texts to her are also being ignored. But I did have some luck with the ghosts. My friend Fabian is talking to all his specter friends, and I have a medium on the way to pump out the bat signal even more."

"Bat signal?" I asked, confused.

"Comic-book reference," Bones said.

"Of course," I murmured. "Sorry, I'm very tired. If I subconsciously revert back to my original language of Sumerian, just ignore me."

"You're welcome to rest. We have several guest rooms available," Spade said.

"Thank you, but I can't sleep until I know Ian's safe."

No one argued. From their expressions, they all understood.

"Denise, may I use your mobile phone?" I wasn't good for much right now, but I could make a call.

She gave it to me. I closed my eyes, needing to concentrate to remember the number to Marie's private line. Gods, even my brain was fried from burning myself out on the time-freezing spell. Finally, I remembered it and dialed.

"Who is calling me?" asked a smooth, feminine voice in lieu of a hello.

The sweet notes of her Southern accent made the question sound less threatening than it was. Few people had Marie's personal line, so she probably wasn't used to getting calls from unfamiliar numbers. I couldn't imagine what she did to cold-call telemarketers. They must have their own unmarked graves.

"Marie, it's Veritas, Law Guardian for the council," I said, ignoring how Cat shot to her feet. "I have an urgent matter to discuss, so I need an audience."

"Don't you mean former Law Guardian and current council assassin?" Marie's tone was still sweet, but so was hard candy, and that could also break your teeth.

My eyes briefly closed. Of course Marie knew. She had the best spies in the world because they weren't of this world.

"Your ghosts are incorrect," I said. "I didn't murder anyone on the council. I was framed."

"Interesting, but not my problem," Marie said. "And I'm not receiving audiences, as I'm sure Cat must have told you."

Were her spies here *now*? I glanced around. No ghosts that I could see, but that was what made ghosts the best spies. They were masters at hiding. Then again, Claudia and Pyotor had been murdered days ago. Maric could have heard about that despite the council keeping it quiet. Perhaps she thought Cat had called on my behalf before? If so, I needed to fix that assumption.

"I'm not calling about myself. There are dangerous gods on the loose," I said before she hung up.

Silence for a moment. Then, "What kind of gods?"

I almost sighed in relief. She'd hear me out, and once she did, she'd agree to see me because this was too important.

"Ancient, elemental ones. Ruaumoko controls volcanoes and earthquakes, and Morana's power is ice and—"

"Bless your heart," Marie interrupted with a laugh. "I already know that *those* gods are here."

The line went dead. I stared at the phone for a second, trying to absorb the implications of what just happened.

"What did Marie say when you told her about the gods?" Cat asked in an urgent tone.

I looked at her, still feeling dazed. "The Southern equivalent of 'I know, and go fuck yourself.'"

Cat paled until her complexion resembled curdled cream. "Shit. You think she might be planning to align with them?"

That's exactly what I thought. If I was right, we'd be fighting against gods *and* ghouls, which meant we'd be doomed.

*I*an didn't return for over an hour. If I'd had the strength, I would have been pacing from anxiety by then. As it was, I had the energy only to drum my fingers against the couch.

A burst of smoke-scented air preceded Ian's sudden appearance. He still wore the same clothes, but the bloodstains looked dry, so they were probably from my blood, earlier. Volcanic ash streaked his russet hair with gray, but he was unharmed, and I was so relieved by that, I could have cried . . . right up until his gaze found me, and he made an exasperated sound.

"You're still awake? Thought you'd be resting by now."

Really? "And *I* thought you'd be back sooner," I snapped.

He laughed. "From you, poppet, that is beyond ironic."

Okay. I deserved that.

He came over and pulled me into his arms. I had never been so glad to be there, and also had never felt so limp. He may as well have held one of the wet towels Denise had cleaned me with.

"Ruaumoko got away," he said to the room at large. "Mencheres couldn't hold him, Vlad couldn't torch him, and Ashael and I were busy ferrying the council and Law Guardians away. They're all safe, but that's what took so long. Ashael's still finishing up, since we're keeping them all in separate places. The fewer who know where the others are, the better."

I agreed, but I didn't reply, despite having important news myself. It felt so good to be in his arms. I wanted to savor it for a few moments longer.

Spade cocked his head. "I hear a car. Expecting anyone?"

Cat pulled back the drape and glanced out the window.

"Good, it's Tyler. My medium friend," she clarified for me. "Oh, wait, he's got another guy with him I don't recognize."

"Sun's not up yet," Spade said, rising. "No one invite them in. We need to be sure this isn't a trick."

Cat nodded, and then went to the front door and opened it.

"Hey! We're in here, guys," she called out, and left the door open behind her.

Not an invitation, but a greeting that left them no reason to stay outside waiting for one. Clever.

"We're coming," a masculine voice sang out with an American accent.

Moments later, two men came into view. One was tall, with black curls cropped so short, they barely hugged his head. His stylish shirt had golden designs at the cuffs and collar, complementing the amber undertones in his dark brown skin. The other man was shorter and bald, with umber-brown skin and a reserved air that matched his conservative blue suit. But his charcoal-colored eyes were warm, even if his smile looked a little forced when he saw all of us in the parlor.

"The party can now begin!" the taller man said.

Bones eyed the shorter, handsome man. "Who's this, Tyler?"

The tall man grinned. "My husband, Harrison. Told you I had a surprise. I'm hitched! He's a doctor, too. Mom was so proud."

I didn't trust the sound of their beating hearts or their breathing. Those could be faked. I used the last of my strength to feel for any blood or water inside them—something Phanes lacked—and my senses roared back in the affirmative.

"Neither is Phanes in disguise," I said. "Both these men have juices running all through them."

"You said vampires were different," Harrison whispered to Tyler. "You didn't mention that they'd know how . . . *juicy* I am."

"Don't worry, sugar, I won't let you die twice," Tyler replied, winking at him.

"Twice?" Cat cocked her head.

"We have the best meet-cute story," Tyler said, beaming. "Harrison didn't know he was allergic to bees. Imagine being his age and not knowing that? Anyway, he got stung while jogging in a park, went into shock, and crossed the veil for a few minutes. I was doing a séance nearby and boom! In pops this hottie."

"No!" Cat said appreciatively.

"Yes." Tyler grinned. "Since Harrison's a doctor, he guessed what had happened, and told me to send paramedics with an EpiPen. I wasn't sure if he was pranking me, but I did it, then ran to the park to see for myself. I beat the paramedics there, gave him mouth-to-mouth until they arrived, and . . ."—another grin that Harrison returned—"we haven't stopped kissing since."

"Congratulations," Bones said, shaking Tyler and Harrison's hands.

Cat chose a hug for each, and then Spade and Denise came over and shook their hands. Ian, did, too, saying, "Good on you, mate. I'm a married man myself now."

"No!" Tyler said in shock. "Where is she?"

Ian swept a hand in my direction. "Right there."

"Hello," I said, managing a wave. If I tried to get up, I'd fall on my face, and that wouldn't be the best first impression.

"Oh, honey," Tyler said with sympathy. "You're a beauty, but you also look like hell ate you up and spat you out." Then, he rounded on Ian. "For shame! You can't take better care of your wife than this?"

"You could raise the dead before convincing her to let someone take care of her," Ian said, with a knowing look at me.

Harrison cleared his throat and stepped forward. "Ma'am, if you're in need of medical attention . . ."

I stifled a laugh. "That's very kind, but I died over four thousand years ago, so I'm beyond any help you could give me."

"What you need is rest," Ian said, coming over and scooping me up. "Charles?"

"If you're actually letting her sleep, second floor, third room on your right," Spade replied. "If you're feeling amorous, back into the groom's quarters with you, where you've already done enough damage that more won't be noticed."

Ian began climbing the stairs. He was almost at the second floor when Harrison shouted, "Jesus!" with clear alarm.

Ian turned. Ashael was now in the main hall, shadows and the scent of volcanic ash still clinging to him.

"No," Ashael said with a dark chuckle. "Though many people have indeed screamed, 'God, yes!' while in my arms."

Tyler turned to Bones. "Is younger, hotter Idris with you?"

"He's with us," I said, squirming in Ian's arms. "Bring me down. I'll fill both of you in about Marie before I pass out."

Ian shook his head but went back down the stairs.

Ashael's grin slipped, and he gave me a concerned glance. "Veritas, you still haven't slept or bathed?"

"You, too?" I said. "Believe me, I'd love nothing more than to fall asleep in a hot bubble bath, but new shit storms keep interrupting that. Marie is just the latest."

"I told you I could set up an audience," Ashael began.

"She's refusing all audiences, and she already knows that Morana and Ruaumoko are here," I said.

Ian's brows rose. "She told you this?"

"Right before hanging up on me," I confirmed.

Ian's sigh ended in a hiss. "Bugger me bent and broken."

Cat gave him a sympathetic look. "We'll all be buggered bent and broken if Marie allies the ghouls with those gods."

Ashael pulled out his mobile and walked out of view.

"Marie, *ma belle*," I heard him say moments later. "*Comment allez-vous?*"

Ian teleported us next to him before I could blink. Ashael held up his free hand in the universal "not now" gesture.

"I apologize for the interruption, Marie," Ashael said, still speaking French. "But I must see you as soon as possible." A pause. "That is unfortunate, for my business is urgent."

Another pause. I could hear Marie's voice, but I couldn't make out what she was saying. Either my exhaustion was stymieing me, or Ashael had the volume turned way down on his mobile.

"I understand," Ashael finally said, regret in his tone. "Alas, you leave me no choice except to call in my marker . . ."

I sucked in a breath. His marker? Had Marie made a *demon deal* with Ashael?

"Tomorrow night?" Ashael's tone was bright again. "Of course that will be sufficient. Our usual place? Perfect. I'll see you then, *ma belle*."

He hung up. Cat appeared in my peripheral vision, her mouth ajar from the same disbelief I felt.

"How did you do that? Marie hung up on Veritas and me when we tried to get a meeting with her!"

Ashael gave her an arch look. "Told you to let me handle this. When a job requires a demon, accept no substitutes."

"I'll put that right on a tee shirt, but it still doesn't answer my question," Cat said, her tone turning hard.

"Ashael," I said in a quieter tone. "What sort of debt does Marie owe you?"

"Not that kind." His wave dismissed a demon deal as a possibility. "But if you think I wouldn't have made it my business to know a beautiful, powerful woman whose meteoric rise up the undead ranks made her queen of the entire ghoul nation in a mere two hundred years, you underestimate my intelligence."

"Ah," Ian said simply. Then, "Know her well, do you?"

Ashael caught the inference and grinned. "Not as well as I'd prefer, but well nonetheless." Then, he patted my shoulder. "May as well rest now. We don't see Marie until tomorrow night, so there's nothing you need to do until then."

"We?" I said in surprise while Ian tensed.

Another grin, this one shameless. "Didn't I mention that part? The debt Marie owes me includes my bringing a plus-one, and you, my sister, are it."

The French Quarter in New Orleans was one of the few spots in America that felt like preindustrial Europe to me. Maybe it was because the Quarter had kept the narrow streets that had originally been designed for horse and carriage instead of cars. Or how gas lanterns still flickered in golden-orange rebellion against the harsher brightness of electric lighting. Or how the eighteenth- and nineteenth-century architecture lining much of the famed streets prioritized beauty and whimsy over the modern tendency to stuff as many people as possible inside a building.

It could also be the ghosts. Aside from former battlefields, America tended not to have an abundance of ghosts concentrated in the same spot. New Orleans, however, was filled with them, from residual ghosts that were mere snapshots of energy repeating the same moment to sentient ghosts like the newly deceased guy who kept chasing our car because he thought it was the Uber he'd ordered.

I didn't have the heart to tell him that he was dead. He'd figure it out soon enough. Hopefully, he would move on to the next phase of his journey once he did. Sentient ghosts usually remained on this side of the veil for only a short amount of time before they crossed over, though some lingered for decades, and every so often, some never crossed over.

New Orleans had one of the highest concentrations of sentient ghosts I'd ever seen. They came from all around America and even the world, drawn by the otherworldly power of the city's most famous resident, Marie Laveau.

"How long have you known Marie?" Ian asked Ashael.

Ian had come even though he wasn't able to attend our "audience" since Ashael had only a plus-one invitation, not a plus-two. However, having Ian on the outside came with its own advantages. Marie guaranteed safe passage to and from any meeting with her, but in case this was the one instance where she revoked that, Ian was our backup. Marie didn't know Ian could teleport, so he could warn Ashael and me of danger faster than she could sic one of her infamous Remnants on him.

"Since she was human," Ashael replied, his mouth curling at my surprised expression. "Yes, I knew Marie was special even then. She channeled ancient mambo magic like no mortal had done in centuries. When someone pulls that hard on the veil, our bloodline allows me to feel it. You would have felt it, too, if you hadn't been suppressing that part of yourself."

Interesting. "You don't think Marie could be another one of our father's secret offspring, do you?"

"Blazes, no," Ashael said with a chuckle. "I've seen the source of her magic. It might be netherworld adjacent, but it's definitely not netherworld descendant."

"If not a demon deal, what did you do for her that she owed you this 'marker'?" Ian asked in a casual tone.

I'd wondered the same. When I saw the look Ashael leveled at Ian via the rearview mirror, I knew we weren't getting an answer.

"That's between me and Marie," Ashael said with finality.

I was surprised when Ashael drove out of the French Quarter and toward the Garden District. Ian must have been, too, because his brow arched as if to say, *know what he's up to?*

I shook my head. Marie's formal audiences were in St. Louis Cemetery Number One, in the underground sanctuary beneath her crypt, and we were going in the opposite direction of that.

"Sightseeing, are we?" Ian asked in a casual tone.

Ashael grunted. "No, but I'd kill for a beignet and a café au lait right now. Pity that Café Du Monde is closed."

At this hour, it certainly was. Midnight was the time Marie set for our meeting, proving she still had a sense of the dramatic.

After several minutes, Ashael pulled onto Prytania Street. We passed row after row of beautiful houses before he pulled over and parked in front of an ornate, wrought-iron fence that bordered the grounds of a stunning pale pink mansion.

"Here we are," Ashael said.

Ian and I exchanged a look. I spoke first. "This isn't Marie's normal meeting place."

"That dank hovel?" Ashael shuddered. "I wouldn't have worn these shoes if splashing through secret cemetery tunnels was on my agenda for tonight."

He had dressed up, wearing a black suit with a snowy white shirt open at the collar. Black diamond cuff links glittered at his wrists, and yes, his shoes were polished to a fine sheen.

Ian and I again wore borrowed clothes from Spade and Denise. Lucky for us, they had plenty to spare, though Denise wasn't a fan of pantsuits the way I was. If she had to conceal multiple weapons the way I usually did, she'd become a fan. Since we were visiting Marie, I wasn't armed. That was against her rules. My only weapons were my abilities. After I slept for fourteen hours straight, it felt like most of them were back to normal.

Thus, my attire was a dark silver Bergdorf Goodman column gown with long sleeves so my supernatural tattoo was covered. It also hung to my ankles, where instead of the heels Denise offered me, I wore a pair of black leather boots. Hey, I thought I would be traveling through crypt tunnels. Open-toed heels might have looked better, but I hadn't wanted to spend an hour scrubbing rat feces from under my toenails.

Ian's suit was deep sapphire. The contrast with his creamy skin, sunset-colored hair, and lighter turquoise eyes nearly grabbed your gaze with all the color. Looking at him, I suddenly wished we'd had more time alone at Spade and Denise's, but between my marathon sleep session and trying to convince the ghosts that Tyler summoned via séance that they should join our side, our plate had been full.

It always seemed to be full, and I was struck with a sudden longing for what most couples had after they were newly married.

"If we make it through this, we should go on a honeymoon."

A smile spread across Ian's face. "Smashing idea. Where do you want to go? Because we *will* make it through this."

The most remote place on earth sounded good, since I didn't want to be near anyone except him. Still, Antarctica was hardly a romantic honeymoon destination.

"I don't know," I finally said. "Is there any place you'd like to go that you've never been to?"

"Yes," he said instantly. "Your home."

"Where I was born?" I let out a short laugh. "That's somewhere in modern-day Iraq, to the best of my knowledge."

"I'm not talking about location." He reached between us, taking my head. "No matter where you were born, how much you've traveled, or how many properties you may own, everyone has a place that's home to them. I took you to mine in Manhasset. I want you to take me to yours, wherever that is."

For a moment, I couldn't speak past the new lump in my throat. Yes, I had a place that was as close to home to me as a building could get, though it had always felt as if something was missing. Now, I knew what that was.

It had been missing Ian.

"Then, when this is over, we'll go to my home," I said in a newly husky voice.

He raised my hand and kissed it, his eyes never leaving mine. "There's nowhere else I'd rather be."

Ashael cleared his throat. "Hate to interrupt, but in two minutes, we'll be late, and Marie does not tolerate lateness."

I didn't need to give her another reason to side with the gods over the vampires. So, with a final look at Ian, I left the car, squared my shoulders, and accepted my brother's arm.

Time to negotiate with the ghoul queen.

We walked right up to the front door without anyone stopping us. Marie didn't appear to have any guards, either of the ghoul persuasion or the ghostly one. Then again, she probably didn't need them. I'd seen Marie's abilities firsthand. They were so formidable that one would be a fool to attack her.

Ashael rapped on the door. A handsome ghoul with a ruddy sepia complexion opened the door. His suit, ascot, and white gloves covered every inch of his skin aside from his face. Not that it needed covering. The word "ghoul" might conjure up images of rot and decay, but ghouls looked as hale and healthy as any human. They also had a pleasant, earthy scent that reminded me of herb gardens.

Bet it had been a vampire that had first started calling them ghouls. That they'd kept the term just showed how little they cared about our attempt to be derogatory.

"Greetings," he said. "I am Jacques." His gaze didn't even slide to me when he added, "I'm afraid that Majestic was only expecting you, so she will need to wait with the car."

"She is my sister," Ashael answered. "Majestic can confirm that any family of mine was long ago included in her marker to me."

"Wait here, sir," Jacques said, and shut the door.

"You didn't mention the family requirement for your plus-one before," I said in a low tone.

Ashael grinned. "Wait until she realizes who you are."

True. Marie, or Majestic, as her people called her, had never seen my real appearance. She wouldn't recognize me as Veritas the Law Guardian now. She'd only see a stranger.

"I hope she loves surprises," I murmured.

The door opened, revealing Jacques again. "Come in," he said. "Majestic is expecting you."

One glance inside was enough to know that the house was well over a century old. The abundance of tall, narrow windows was only common before the invention of air-conditioning, not to mention the steps we'd climbed to reach the front porch. Back before the pump system that kept this city dry, homes had been elevated to avoid being ruined from the area's common floods.

Once inside, eighteenth-century Creole influences were also apparent in the lack of hallways. Jacques opened double doors to lead us through the twin parlors into the living room, where crown molding bordered the high ceiling, a mantled fireplace added a touch of coziness amidst the formality, and one of the walls was entirely made up of windows overlooking a lovely garden.

Jacques nodded at the beige suede couches arranged to face that window. Ashael and I sat. I declined Jacques's offer of refreshment, but Ashael asked for a café au lait and a beignet. Guess he hadn't been kidding about his craving.

Jacques left. Ashael and I sat in silence. Even if this room wasn't being monitored, and it probably was, ghouls had great hearing. After five minutes, Marie entered.

She wore a long, pleated burgundy skirt and a sleeveless, cream-colored silk blouse. The skirt's rich color accentuated the subtle pink glow in her light brown skin, and her thick black hair was swept up on both sides with a ruby-studded comb, showing off her high cheekbones, full mouth, and walnut-colored eyes.

Marie might have been in her mid-forties when she was changed. She might have been a decade younger, too. It was hard to tell. Her skin had the kind of ageless beauty that cosmetic companies promised to their customers, and most failed to deliver.

"*Ma belle*," Ashael said, rising.

I got up, too. Marie accepted a kiss on each cheek from Ashael, but after a brief, appreciative glance at him, her gaze was all for me.

"I don't believe I've had the pleasure, sister of Ashael," she said, extending her hand. "I am Marie Laveau, and you are?"

"Ariel," I said with the briefest smile as I shook her hand. "But you'll know me by my other name, Veritas."

With that, I briefly donned my usual glamour, showing her a glimpse of my slender blonde disguise before dropping it for my real appearance again.

Marie didn't flinch, but for an instant, she was haloed by an innumerable amount of writhing, translucent Remnants.

Remnants were made up of the darkest types of energy, and they consumed pain and vitality with the merciless ferocity of sharks during a feeding frenzy. No one was immune to them, living or undead, and Marie commanded them with absolute authority.

Just as quickly, the Remnants vanished, leaving Marie haloed by nothing more than her elegant furnishings and then Jacques, who'd come back into the room bearing a china coffeepot, cups, and beignets on a silver platter.

"Not now," Marie said curtly.

Jacques turned on his heel and left. Ashael sighed in disappointment.

"You deceived me, Ashael." Marie's tone was smoother than honey, yet each word landed with the slam of an anvil.

Ashael spread out his hands. "Never, *ma belle*—"

Remnants flashed behind her again. "Do not 'ma belle' me!"

I had to stop this before Marie had them attack. Shadows ripped out of me while my gaze flashed from emerald to bright silver.

"I am not what you thought I was, Marie," I said with all the icy calm of my other nature. Then, I lightly tugged on her blood so she'd know the darkness spilling out of me and my glowing silver eyes were no trick of glamour.

Her face, chest, and arms flushed a deep red as her blood rushed to the surface. I released it before any drops broke her skin. I didn't want her to bleed for my proof, and besides, her power over Remnants resided in her blood. I might be able to glimpse the Remnants always hovering near Marie because of my abilities, but they wouldn't become manifest to attack without her drawing her blood and commanding them.

My non-vampire side now revealed, I rescinded my shadows and let my gaze return to normal.

Marie said nothing for a moment. Then, to my surprise, she laughed until she held her sides as if they'd split otherwise.

"All this time, you've been *that*," she said, gesturing at me. "I wish I could have seen the vampire council's faces when they discovered their longest-serving Law Guardian was a walking embodiment of their most-feared crime!"

"They weren't nearly as amused as you are," I confirmed.

"Now I know why they issued that death sentence against you several months ago," she said, regaining control of herself. "My spies couldn't discover why, and normally, people talk no matter how sacred the secret. But you humiliated the council so badly that they didn't even discuss it among themselves. Ah, Veritas, or Ariel, thank you for that. They richly deserved it."

"Not all of them," I said, trying to steer the conversation away from vampire bashing. "Almost half the council wanted to decriminalize mixed-species people. It was Haldam who cast the tie-breaking vote against the tri-bred child not too long ago, and now, Haldam is dead."

Marie's left eyebrow twitched—the only indication that Haldam's death was news to her.

"You already know that Pyotor and Claudia are dead, too," I went on. "As I told you before, I didn't kill them. I was framed by the gods I was trying to warn you about."

Her shrug was careless, but her gaze was hard. "Again, what business is that of mine?"

"They tried to take out the vampire species' rulers. You rule the ghouls, so you could be next," I said bluntly.

A smile ghosted across her lips. "Someone has wanted to kill me since my youth as a human. If I cowered in fear at every new attempt on my life, I would never leave my bed."

This wasn't going in the direction I'd hoped. What might cause Marie to rethink her "not my problem" take on this?

"I told you Haldam cast the deciding vote that kept mixed-species people outlawed. Now, Haldam's seat and two others are vacant. If they're filled with three more moderate-thinking council members, any number of discriminatory laws might be overturned."

"Or they could be filled with three more bigots," Marie said in a sharp tone. "I'm more inclined to bet on that."

"Vampires don't have a monopoly on being prejudiced," I said evenly. "It wasn't long ago that your people were ruled by a rabid bigot who nearly brought ghouls and vampires to all-out war twice over mixed-species people. Then, he was killed and you took the throne. Positive change can happen. You're proof of that."

"Besides, these gods won't stop at taking out the vampire hierarchy," Ashael said in a dark tone.

"Won't they?" Marie had a new gleam in her eye I didn't like. "What makes you think they're enemies of *my* people?"

"They tried to rule the world once before," I pointed out. "Now they're back, and they're already blowing up mountains, cooling the arctic, and cracking open the earth. That's not in celebration of discovering Internet porn, so what do you *think* they intend to do with such incredible powers? Allying with vampires against them might be the only way to stop them."

Marie let out a sharp laugh. "As if I would ever trust *vampires* for my people's liberty."

Nothing I said would change her mind about that, and with good reason. Vampires couldn't stop discriminating against other vampires at the moment.

Until that changed, Marie had every reason to believe we wouldn't treat ghouls equitably because we didn't even treat each other equitably yet.

"As I said, positive change can happen," I settled on. "Besides, you don't have to trust vampires to align with them. 'My enemy's enemy is my friend' is a saying for a reason."

"That's right, *your* enemy." Marie's tone was silky as she glanced at the Rolex on her wrist. "Not mine, and I remind you that I guarantee all my guests safe passage to and from a meeting with me. Anyone who violates that safe passage guarantees themselves an immediate, painful death."

What caused her to make that threat . . . ?

My arm burned the instant before a knock sounded at the door. Jacques streaked over to answer it. In the seconds that took, my fitted sleeve had bulged from a pair of cuffs and chains that hadn't been there moments ago.

I didn't need Jacques to open the door to know the identity of Marie's new guest, nor did I require what he said next.

"The goddess Morana is here to see you, Majestic."

I an teleported in, sword drawn. Magic made the sword's blade gleam with inner lights as he planted himself in front of me. Then, I felt his power build to heights that had Marie casting first an interested and then a wary look at him. Ian must be drawing on the cursed fruit he'd consumed, and doing so might make him unbeatable, but it could also kill him.

"Ian, don't!" I said as Remnants burst from Marie in response. "Morana can't harm me. I'm also Marie's guest, so her 'safe passage or else' rule applies to me, too. Right, Marie?"

The Remnants stopped before attacking Ian as if Marie had suddenly yanked on a hundred invisible leashes. Then, tinkling laughter interrupted whatever Marie had been about to say.

"Is that the death demigod I hear, Marie?" Morana asked. "If so, what a delightful surprise!"

A hooded, cloaked figure opened the doors to the living room, ignoring Jacques's sputtered protests that Majestic hadn't authorized her entrance yet. The Remnants haloing Marie shot toward Morana before Marie's hold stopped them short again. They coiled above Marie, their diaphanous forms a silent, deadly threat.

Morana threw off her cloak when she entered the living room. I blinked, an involuntary reaction to seeing too much beauty, too fast.

Sapphire hair shimmered around Morana's shoulders as if a massive jewel had been divided into thousands of strands. I barely had the time to register Morana's crystalline skin, her red lips, the dazzling pearl-encrusted bodice over a full blue skirt, or her almost eerie loveliness before her wings unfurled.

Jacques gasped.

I bit mine back, but only just. Morana's wings glittered more than the crystal chandelier above her, but that wasn't what was almost mesmerizing. Her wings were made of ice, and though their length and breadth didn't alter, the icy shards contained within them seamlessly formed into different, intricate patterns, like a living, magnified slideshow of snowflakes.

I didn't know how Morana had transformed the body she inhabited to reveal her true, goddess appearance, but she had. Then again, transforming a host body was probably easy compared to her other abilities.

The supernatural cuffs my father had given me now almost burned against my skin. I glanced at the

Remnants above Marie. They swirled and writhed with greater urgency, as if begging to be freed so they could feed from our pain and life force. Only Marie's power held them back, and I could no longer freeze time to stop her from unleashing them. I'd burned myself out on my time-freezing skills when I held back that volcano. I'd be lucky if I regained that ability within the next two weeks.

I would also ensure an enemy for life in Marie, if I survived the Remnants long enough to cuff Morana and send her back to my father. I might be willing to risk that, but the vampire nation couldn't, and Marie would *definitely* take her grudge against me out on them. She already didn't trust vampires. I didn't need to give her another reason to hate them, too. Not when there were two more renegade gods on the loose who would take full advantage of any ghoul animosity toward vampires.

That left doing nothing, which burned me more than the supernatural cuffs that now felt white-hot against my arm.

"Ian," I said in a quiet tone. "Stand down."

Maybe he'd also realized all the reasons why we couldn't attack Morana, because his power whooshed back into him, and he sheathed the sword in one swift, fluid motion. Then, he bowed in a courtly way to Marie.

"Pleasure to see you again, Majestic."

Marie gave him a look that had me poised to rip all her blood out if even one of her Remnants twitched toward Ian.

"You dare say that when the last time we met, you were blackmailing me with pictures you'd just taken of me?"

Ashael's palm slapped against his forehead. "You didn't."

I hadn't known this, either, or I *definitely* would've tried stopping Ian from coming in here. Then again, how could I? I wasn't faster than teleportation even on my best day.

"Did," Ian said, flashing an unrepentant grin at Ashael. "Come, now," he added to Marie. "You admire cunning, and that was cunning. Besides, you agreed with the cause behind the blackmail, or I wouldn't have lived out the day after that."

"You're fortunate that you're correct," Marie said in her frostiest tone. "Now, get out before I decide against forgiving you for trespassing, too."

Ian doffed an imaginary hat. "Ladies," he said before sauntering out instead of teleporting away.

Morana watched him leave, proving that my vampire side was back at the helm because I had the sudden urge to slap the lustful look off her face.

"Do you know I recently discovered chocolate?" she said with a flirty little smile. "As it turns out, I love white, milk, and dark," she added while looking from Ian to Marie to Ashael.

The inference was obvious, and my hackles rose again.

"Modern tip," Ashael said in a genial tone. "Never compare black people to chocolate. That got old decades ago."

"Ah," Morana said, nodding. "Thank you. There's still so much I need to learn."

"Yes, like mass murder being wrong," I almost purred.

Morana only laughed as if I'd told a joke.

"Ashael, did you have business with me beyond sneaking Veritas in under your plus-one marker?" Marie asked him.

My brother's brows lifted in feigned affront. "As if seeing you isn't reason enough . . ."

"I thought not," Marie interrupted, though her tone was less sharp than her normal annoyed one. "Go. It appears that we three women have important issues to discuss."

"Men do tend to muck up the waters," Morana agreed, though her instant grin added, *But not you, I'm sure,* to Ashael.

I ground my teeth. She was flirty, charming, faery-queen gorgeous, and a homicidal maniac. If Hollywood knew about Morana, they'd sign her up for her own reality show on the spot.

Ashael's glance at me was casual, as if he weren't looking for the barely perceptible nod I gave him. Then, he let out a defeated sigh and bowed low in much the same way Ian had.

"With regret, then, I take my leave of you, *ma belle.*"

I waited until Jacques closed the two sets of doors behind my brother before I spoke.

"How did you know that I was the death demigod?" I asked Morana, using the words she'd chosen to describe me.

"Your voice," she replied with another musical laugh. "I was in quite the state when Phanes pulled me and Ruaumoko out of the netherworld, but you screamed at Phanes long enough and loud enough to be very memorable."

Marie's side-eye had me inwardly cringing. My being in the netherworld when they escaped was a detail I *really* wished Marie wouldn't have been informed of.

"Yes, well, Phanes betrayed me and left me for dead when he broke you two out," I said so Marie would know that I hadn't been a willing participant in their escape.

Morana's cerulean gaze grew hard. "Phanes excels at lethal betrayal. You were fortunate to escape from the consequences of that very quickly. I, as you know, was not."

Oh, so there was trouble in god paradise? That was my first piece of good news tonight.

"Where is Phanes, by the way?" I asked in a neutral way.

Her hand flicked as if shooing an imaginary fly. "With Ruaumoko. I told them not to make a spectacle of our return, but did they listen? No. Some things, as they say, never change."

Marie was being unusually quiet. Probably sitting back and doling out rope to see if we hung ourselves with it.

"So, you disagree with the earthquakes in Iceland and New Zealand, and the volcanic eruption in Athens?" I asked.

"Athens, too?" Morana said with a ladylike snort. "Busy bees."

"You didn't know about Athens?" Marie asked, brows raised.

Morana gave her a languid look. "Should I have?"

"Since they tried to murder the entire vampire council there, yes," I said, watching her carefully.

Morana only laughed again. "Ruaumoko must still be angry at vampires for our deaths. Your people helped, too," she said to Marie, as if the ghoul queen might feel left out otherwise. "They trapped us in that gorge, but flesh eaters can't fly, so it was vampires who swept in with the final killing blow."

"And Ruaumoko can't let that go, but you've gotten over it?" I asked with open skepticism.

"Thousands of years to think can reset your priorities." A diffident shrug. "I see now that I was too ambitious before. Ruling the world is . . . unnecessary. Now, I only want my lands. Ruaumoko of course wants his, and Phanes wants that wretched little stretch of the Mediterranean, which he's welcome to." She paused to shudder. "It's so hot there. It's so hot everywhere now. How do you people stand it?"

"You learn to adapt," Marie said. "Tell me, what is your land, Morana? Russia?"

Another shrug. "That, and the rest of the upper half of the continent they now call Eurasia. Ruaumoko is claiming Oceania and the neighboring islands. Once sea levels drop, Zealandia will reemerge, too. We were both shocked to discover how much of our world has been overtaken by the waters. I'll fix that."

Dear gods. She was discussing divvying up a quarter of the world with the casualness of slicing a pie thick or thin. Worse, Marie didn't look appalled. Instead, she looked intrigued.

"You intend to lower sea levels by drastically cooling the earth to rebuild all the melted glaciers and arctic ice, yes?"

"Not immediately," Morana replied, a touch of frustration entering her tone. "My powers have not yet fully returned. It could take me the better part of a year to accomplish this."

I couldn't hold back my horror any longer. "Such cataclysmic climate change would kill millions!"

Morana looked bored. "Mortals' lives are so short that ending them a few decades early hardly matters. Most vampires would survive. So would most flesh eaters. In fact, flesh eaters would flourish, since large parts of the world would be, what is the expression? Ah, yes. Freezers full of meat."

"How dare you?" My voice shook. "Yes, mortals only live for a scant collection of decades. That's why it's abhorrent to cut even one of their years short. Only monsters take all from those who have little. Vampires and flesh eaters might be creatures from their mythology, but we are *not* monsters."

The temperature abruptly dropped until ice crystals formed in the air around us.

"How interesting that you mention monsters."

Morana's voice was almost lilting, but the new iciness in the room told a different story about her mood.

"At first, I was dazzled by the advances mortals had made. From flying machines to transplanting body parts to landing on new planets . . . I thought such wonders meant that mortals had truly changed." Her voice darkened. "Then, I realized only their achievements had advanced. Mortals themselves are the same. The strong still oppress the weak, and those with too much amass even more while taking no pity on those struggling to survive. You speak of monsters?" Now her tone was scathing. "That is more monstrous than the culling I will do in order to finally set things right again."

I gripped the cuffs beneath my sleeve and tried to hold back the river of darkness that almost burst out of me.

"I won't let you. The moment you leave this city, Morana, the 'safe passage' requirement that protects you now will be fulfilled, and I will hunt you down and stop you."

She only smiled, and turned to Marie. "You're already queen of the flesh eaters. Not nearly enough, in my opinion, for a person of your caliber. How would you like to be queen of everyone residing in North and South America, too?"

Ice rippled up my spine, and not from the new, frigid temperatures. From how Marie tilted her head with interest.

"Go on," Marie said.

*M*orana clapped with delight. Meanwhile, I had to fight against the bile rising in my throat.

"I told you, I don't want to rule those continents," Morana said, as if she were being very magnanimous. "I do, however, want someone I can trust to rule them. You would be that ruler, Marie. Think about it."

Ice suddenly formed into a globe that floated between Marie and Morana. More ice formed into familiar-shaped continents and islands, with frost serving as oceans, seas, lakes, and rivers. The globe spun until North and South America faced Marie, with the words "All Yours" forming across it.

"Think about it," Morana repeated in a seductive whisper. "You wouldn't only be queen of the flesh eaters. You would be queen of the entire western hemisphere. Mortals, flesh eaters, vampires . . . all would bow down to you. Enact any laws you desire. Mete out whatever punishment you deem fitting.

All will be yours . . . if you and your people refrain from joining in her foolish, doomed rebellion against me."

"Marie," I began.

Her hand sliced the air. Remnants followed, surrounding me until I could hardly see through their endless loops around me.

Oh, shit. That looked like a "yes."

I started yanking power from the water that thankfully was all around New Orleans. I'd use every ability necessary to stop this, barring only one.

"You would give me this?" I heard Marie ask.

"Gladly," Morana crooned in response.

"But it isn't yours to give."

The Remnants snapped back from me to swirl around Morana, their mouths open in silent, ravenous hunger.

"What?" Morana asked, sounding wary now.

"I said, you can't give me what you don't own," Marie replied in a flinty tone. "Those lands were already stolen once, at irreparable damage to the people they belonged to. I'll have no part in such evil again, nor will I partner with anyone who would. Leave now, Morana. Our meeting is concluded, and your invitation to my city is hereby revoked."

Morana's voice hardened. "If that is your answer, allow me to leave you with a parting gift."

Instantly, I was blind and every nerve ending screamed as ice replaced blood and tissue. I tried to move and couldn't. I couldn't even speak, and my mind felt dangerously sluggish.

She did not *just flash-freeze us!* my other half thought.

She'd been quiet for a while, but now she was back, and her incredulous rage felt like a tiny fire within.

Bitch sure did, I thought hazily. *Gonna stand for that?*

No we are not, she replied, and detonated with power.

Morana didn't know it, but she had made a critical error. Ice was made of water, and water was my—*our*—specialty.

Ice smashed within and without. Agony dropped me to my knees, but I was moving again, and after blinks that felt like someone held a blowtorch to my eyes, I could see again. Piles of ice shards were now at my feet, glittering much like Morana's stunning wings had.

Ian and Ashael appeared before my next blink. Ian's aura was so charged with power that being near him hurt, and Ashael's shadows billowed like dark thunderclouds behind him.

"Are you hurt?" Ian asked, grabbing me.

Yes. All over, and his aura stabbing the air like thousands of tiny knives wasn't helping.

"No." My voice was raspy. Vocal cords must still be in the process of healing. "Morana?"

Ian and Ashael blocked most of my view. Still, the supernatural cuffs sliding back into my skin seemed to indicate that she was now gone.

"Vanished." Ian's tone turned savage. "Don't know where to. Ashael felt the ice blast the instant before it hit, and teleported us away."

"Smart," I murmured.

"Wrong because it left you helpless," Ian countered, with a furious glance at Ashael.

"Clearly not," Ashael responded, with a meaningful glance at the melting ice around me. "Besides, you and I becoming popsicles like those two would not have helped Veritas, either."

Those two? I turned around, and then almost slipped on the wet floor as I staggered toward Marie, who was frozen solid inside a thick pillar of ice.

Ian caught me, holding me against him. "Take a moment first. You'll be stronger for it."

I sagged against him, letting my body catch up to my mind. Being a vampire, it didn't take long. Still, I didn't move away. Even the stabbing force of Ian's aura wasn't enough to make me want to leave him as I focused my power on Marie first, decimating the ice within her and around her.

She came to with a gasp that immediately turned into an impressive curse in Creole. Then, Marie sliced her finger on a hidden razor in her ring. At once, more Remnants tore into the room with the force of a tornado. They skipped over Ian and Ashael to rush through the house, obviously seeking out Morana.

"She iced us and left," I said.

Marie flung her hands out. Even more Remnants appeared before vanishing in a rush through walls and doors.

"They'll search the city in case she didn't get far," Marie said in a crisp voice. "If she's here, they'll find her." Then, she turned to Ian and Ashael. "Which one of you freed us?"

"Neither," Ian said, kissing the top of my head.

Marie gave me a raking look, and then pointed at Jacques. "If you would?"

"Of course," I said, and ripped away the ice that both trapped Jacques on the outside and froze him within.

Her gaze narrowed as she watched. Seeing it, I realized her reason for asking me had been two-fold: to get her butler free and to see my abilities in action. Now she knew that I could decimate a Jacques-sized ice block and unfreeze a person with my mind alone. Maybe I should've waved my arms around and made up a fake magic chant first.

"My queen!" Jacques said, rushing to Marie as soon as his limbs worked again.

She let him kiss her hand, and then said, "Gather my lieutenants and bring them here, Jacques. We are at war."

He left. Marie and I faced each other across her living room. Morana hadn't stopped at turning us into ice sculptures. She'd also iced the entire house and exterior gardens, too.

"Thank you," I said very quietly to Marie.

The look she gave me was harder than the ice that now blanketed every centimeter of her home.

"My decision to war with Morana and her allies has nothing to do with you. If I refuse to trust vampires with my people's liberty, I certainly won't trust an egotistical god who intends to murder millions simply because they're an inconvenience."

Not a friendly alliance, but the ghoul race would now fight against Morana, Phanes, and Ruaumoko. That was fucking *great*.

"To kicking their asses," I said, and held out my hand.

Marie didn't move. "You know how to defeat them. Tell me."

I wasn't about to play coy when she'd just committed her entire species to this fight.

"Netherworld handcuffs," I said, pulling my sleeve higher so Marie could see the supernatural restraints etched into my skin. "The Warden himself gave them to me. I put these on Morana and Ruaumoko, and they get a one-way ticket back to their prisons. As for Phanes . . . we'll figure something out."

She stared at me. "You had these, and didn't use them on her when you could have."

I let out a short laugh. "Regretting that a bit now, but you were emphatic that Morana was under your safe passage rule, so I didn't. I don't want war with your people. I never have."

Marie finally took my hand, her grip strong and sure. "You should have shown me the real Veritas long before this. I don't trust vampires, but I might one day trust you."

"My queen!"

Jacques ran back into the living room, startling all of us.

"What is it?" Marie asked him.

His expression alone said that it was more bad news. I braced, and Ian's arm tightened around me.

"Morana did not attack you and your residence alone. She froze the entire Garden District."

I started to run for the door, but Ian hauled me back.

"Wait."

His voice was so urgent that I stopped. "What?"

"Didn't notice it before because I was too focused on you." Ian lowered his voice as if someone outside this room might be listening. "Now, I'm certain of it. Someone else's scent is here, and it wasn't before when Ashael and I left."

I sniffed, but all I smelled was ice, our scents, and Marie's delicate, floral perfume that was light enough even for a vampire's oversensitive nose.

"Phanes," Ian suddenly spat.

I stiffened. I didn't smell him, but my senses still felt off after being flash frozen, so I didn't trust them over Ian's.

"I still have to help those people," I said.

"I'll go," Ashael replied. "My power over anything liquid-based is greater than yours, and I'm much faster, too."

Both true, except for one large drawback. "You can't get inside homes that you haven't been invited into."

"I back the banks that finance every loan in the district," Marie said in crisp tone. "Therefore, technically, *I* own these houses. Ashael, I hereby invite you inside every home in this district. Go. Save all who can be saved."

He bowed to Marie, gave me a look that said not to worry, and then vanished.

Ian's arms relaxed around me. "Don't fret. If they set a trap for you or Marie in one of those homes, Ashael can teleport out of it. If they're watching, they won't bother with him because they don't yet realize they have a quarrel with him, too. Phanes doesn't know that he's your brother, remember?"

No, he didn't. Ian was right that Ashael probably would pass unnoticed, whereas if Marie or I went and Morana and Phanes were waiting to ambush us, that would put more innocent people in danger. It was already horrible that some had been murdered in their sleep simply for living near Marie's house when Morana dropped her deep freeze bomb. Ghouls and vampires could come back from being flash frozen. Humans couldn't.

From Marie's expression, she was thinking the same thing.

"I'm so sorry," I said softly.

Marie gave a sharp nod.

"They will be avenged to the last drop of their blood. My only cause for thankfulness is that it's the middle of the night, so there are no tourists. Also, it's hurricane season and very hot, as that vile creature noted. Because of that, many of the nearby homes will be empty of mortals, since they prefer the safer, cooler months of fall, winter, and early spring."

A slight comfort, but not enough. Marie wasn't the only one who felt responsible for each death. And Phanes! Oh, how I wished I would have broken free from that ice shell before he and Morana fled. I would have ripped into both of them . . .

Wait. *Phanes had been here.*

I'd been so distraught over more innocent people dying, I hadn't digested the implications of that, but I did now.

"That clever bitch," I growled.

Ian raised a brow. Marie looked around as if to say, *Who?*

"Morana," I said. "She went on and on about how she hadn't forgiven Phanes for betraying her, and how he was with Ruaumoko and not her, but he didn't *accidently* show up because he ran across her while touring the neighborhood!"

"He was waiting for her signal," Marie said, her hard gaze turning knowing. "That's why she froze the entire district. She wanted that signal to be too big to miss because she didn't want us to see him waiting for her."

"Yes, if we survived." Agitation had me pacing. "She didn't know I'd be here, so this setup was for you. Morana probably intended to take you back with them like an ice-covered trophy if you refused to join her. Or kill you while you were immobile. She didn't change the plan when she saw me because she didn't know I could manipulate ice and water. My breaking free probably startled her and Phanes into bolting."

"Ashael and I were only gone seconds," Ian said. "They must have teleported away during that time. I'd have seen them if they flew."

"They sure as hell wouldn't try to get away by running," I muttered, and then stopped in my tracks.

"What?" Ian said.

"Running." Holy shit, that was it! "No one runs away from vampires because that's too slow, even for a god. Back when Morana was talking about her and Ruaumoko's deaths, she said that ghouls had trapped them in a gorge, but Ruaumoko hated vampires the most because they'd *flown in* to strike the killing blow."

Ian began to smile. "Did she, now?"

"What of it?" Marie asked, sounding impatient.

"Means Morana and Ruaumoko can't fly," I summed up.

I should have realized that the moment I saw her. Yes, Morana had wings, but Phanes had flown both of them out of the netherworld when he broke them free. At the time, I'd thought Phanes had done it because their confinement had left them too weak, but how could ghouls have trapped Morana and Ruaumoko in a gorge if one or both of them could fly?

"Must not be able to teleport, either," Ian said, dark expectancy sliding through his tone. "That's how Phanes betrayed them. He left them to die instead of teleporting them away."

"Then took credit for their deaths, probably by slaughtering the people who did kill them," I added.

"That would tie up the necessary loose ends," Marie said in a diamond-hard tone. "It would also explain why I couldn't discover more about their demise despite extensive research."

"When did you do that?" I said, surprised.

She gave me a look. "The moment my spies told me new gods had arrived. By the time Morana contacted me to request this meeting, I knew everything ever written about her, but"—she shrugged—"at best, history only ever whispers at the truth."

That was a fact, as was its frequent twisting based on who was writing it.

"Someone powerful must have suspected that Phanes wasn't the hero he claimed to be, because he was exiled to his realm not long after Morana and Ruaumoko's deaths," Ian said.

Yes, and all that time with only his illusions and the people he teleported into his realm had made Phanes pine for the good old days when he and his warmongering pals had ruled down here. Then, he'd felt me crack the veil, and begun to plan.

"My father must have eventually suspected Phanes, too," I said, looking at Ian. "He said Phanes was supposed to be my shelter, but later, he cloaked me so Phanes couldn't find me."

Not unless I used *that* power, which my vampire sire had forbidden me from doing in terms so strong that they had scarred me emotionally for thousands of years. But maybe Tenoch had had another reason for his appalled reaction to my ripping open the veil when I was young. Had my father warned him that doing so would cause disastrous results?

Was it . . . was it possible that Tenoch's horror hadn't only been caused by seeing what I could do? Could part of it have come from Tenoch trying, as he'd done so many times before, to protect me from people who wanted to use me for my power?

I wished Tenoch was still here so I could ask him. He wasn't, though. He was dead, and far too many others would join him if Morana, Phanes, and Ruaumoko weren't stopped.

"They don't realize that we know their secret," I said. "We can use that against them."

Marie smiled, and though it made her face even lovelier, I had never found her more terrifying.

"Then let us find another gorge to trap them in, and this time, they won't come back from their deaths."

Ashael returned within the hour with the grim news that ninety-six humans had frozen to death, and it was now snowing in all of New Orleans. By then, Jacques had rounded up Marie's lieutenants and brought them to her house, where she directed them to immediately do damage control on the deaths and the supernatural aspect of the new snow. Before they left, she also informed them that ghouls were temporarily allying with vampires against the new gods who'd dared to strike in her city. No one dared to object, at least not to Marie's face.

Marie then dismissed them and turned to me. "I will dispatch all my ghosts to look for Morana. Wherever she is, the others won't be far."

I nodded. "We also have ghosts looking for them, so with luck, they won't be able to hide for long."

A smile hovered over her lips. "No one can hide from the dead for long, which is why you only have twelve hours to bring the vampire council on board with this new alliance."

I acted as if I wasn't startled that she knew I'd come here without the council's approval. "Of course."

Her look became pointed. "They also must make their confirmation of this alliance public and official, as I have."

They still hadn't even rescinded their death sentence on me, but what was another impossible task on my to-do list?

"I understand." I wanted to offer to help with the people who'd lost their lives, but Marie would probably take offense to that. She considered them hers to avenge, so she'd consider them hers to bury and provide for their dependents, too.

No, all I could do was try to ensure that no others lost their lives, which was Impossible Task Number One on my list.

"Ashael, we'll need you to take us to the council," I said.

Ian took my hand and placed his other one on Ashael's shoulder. "Start with Hekima. She's the most intelligent."

Very true. I also placed my free hand on my brother, who inclined his head at Marie.

"Until next time, *ma belle.*"

Whatever she replied was lost as Ashael teleported us away.

THE NEXT THING I saw was row after row of cherry trees. We were on a balcony overlooking a street that was famous enough for me to recognize it even without the tall, white obelisk of the Washington Monument spearing the sky.

"You brought the vampire council's most senior member to the humans' seat of power in America?"

Ashael grinned. "Twisted, right?"

Ian high-fived him. "Love it."

I shook my head. At least this swanky hotel on Pennsylvania Avenue would be one of the last places that Morana, Ruaumoko, or Phanes would look for Hekima.

"You have to knock," Ashael said. "I spelled her hotel room so that only Hekima could open the windows and doors."

Smart. I knocked on the sliding glass doors to the balcony, though Hekima had probably heard us already. After a moment, the drapes were pushed aside to reveal her familiar salt-and-pepper hair. She frowned at us, but she opened the doors.

"Your clothes are wet," she said to me in lieu of a customary greeting.

I glanced down. Yes, they were. I hadn't noticed before now because it hardly mattered, but some of the ice left over from Morana's attack had clung to me and then melted.

"It's nothing," I said.

She walked away, gesturing for us to follow her out of the bedroom. The four-poster bed was still made and Hekima was in elegant leisurewear instead of sleep wear, so we hadn't woken her up. For vampires, three in the morning wasn't that late.

"Your business must be urgent to show up un-announced, but you can discuss it in dry clothing," she said to me, and opened a closet in the hallway. "Since I was dropped here without my belongings and I've been forbidden from leaving, I purchased several items from the hotel's stores. I will of course reimburse you," she added to Ashael. "In the mean-time, Veritas, choose one."

"Don't bother reimbursing me," Ashael said with a grin. "So many politicians have demon deals in this city that our entire race practically has an open tab here."

It would be rude to refuse her gift, so I thanked Hekima, selected something that I thought would fit since I was taller and curvier than she, and changed in the bathroom.

When I came out, Ian and Ashael were helping themselves to bourbon from the tall, well-stocked bar in the living room, and Hekima was sitting on one of several couches. Ashael had certainly set her up well. The bedroom had been sumptuous, the bathroom had been wall-to-wall marble, and beyond this spacious, luxurious living room was a full-size formal dining room.

Maybe he hadn't been joking about demons hav-ing an "open tab" in this city.

"Thank you," I said, accepting the bourbon Ian handed me. After one taste, I set the glass down and gave Ashael a censuring look. "You spiked it with drops of your blood?"

His brow arched. "If you couldn't use a real drink after what happened tonight, you'll definitely need it for what has to happen over the next twelve hours."

Hekima's gaze narrowed. "What has to happen?"

I picked my glass back up. Ashael was right; I'd need a real drink for this.

"Nothing much," Ian said in a genial tone while I swallowed. "The council need only not bollocks up the new alliance that Veritas has arranged with Marie."

If I were human, I would have choked on my swallow. He did *not* just say that to Hekima!

"What Ian means—" I gasped out through an esophagus still full of liquor.

"Is that, for the first time in thousands of years, vampires have a wartime alliance with ghouls," Ian continued. "One we'll need, because Morana is offering the western hemisphere to whoever helps her defeat vampires, and there are many powerful creatures that will join her to collect that prize."

"Is this true?" Hekima demanded of me.

I finally got the last of the liquid down to speak in full sentences. "Yes. Morana froze the entire Garden District in two seconds, killing dozens of humans, just to show Marie that she didn't like being refused. She's also claiming half of Eurasia, giving Phanes the Mediterranean, and Ruaumoko's taking Australia, New Zealand, and whatever the hell Zealandia is."

Hekima's dark eyes widened. "Gods or no, three people cannot dream of conquering so much!"

"It's easy when you don't care how many people you kill." Ian's casual tone didn't match his gaze as he set his glass down. "Let's forget about Morana for a moment, which, with her ego, would incense her, but that's off topic. All Ruaumoko needs to do is set off one, maybe two super volcanoes, and then we'd have a worldwide nuclear winter that would kill most plant, animal, and human life. Now, vampires and ghouls could survive the poisoned air, water, and extreme cold, but how long do you reckon it would be before we tore each other apart over the few humans left to feed from, hmm? Years? Or only months?"

Hekima's features hardened. Ashael, however, whistled.

"That'd make worldwide conquering easy, all right. Demons haven't wanted to eradicate humans, because they're too much fun to trick, but Morana and Ruaumoko have no such reservations."

I was going to be sick. I'd been focused on Morana chilling the world to where millions would die, but yes, Ruaumoko could bring about total annihilation. He'd transformed a mere mountain into an erupting volcano in only one night. Setting off a couple sleeping super volcanoes would be child's play for him.

"The council *has* to agree to this alliance," I said. "Vampires can go back to bigotry as usual later. Survival comes first. Otherwise, none of us will be left to document how, like so many other cultures, we were defeated because we couldn't stop fighting with rivals long enough to assemble against the greater threat poised to destroy us."

Hekima held out her hand. I was confused until she nodded at my half-empty glass. I slid it across the table to her, and she drained it in one swallow.

"Smooth," she said in a choked voice when she was finished.

Ashael hid a smile as he pricked his finger and splashed a few more drops of his blood into a fresh glass. Then, he filled it with bourbon and set it in front of Hekima.

She sipped instead of draining it this time, but she was still drinking what amounted to an entire bottle of vodka for a human. I didn't know if that was a good sign or a bad one.

"Even with the ghouls as allies, how can we hope to defeat them, if they are so powerful?" she asked once she'd finished half of that glass, too.

"A mixed-species vampire has a weapon that will drag Morana and Ruaumoko back into the netherworld," Ian said. "She just needs to get close enough to them to deploy it. So, while you're convincing the council to ally with ghouls, you'll need to overturn the law making people like her illegal, too."

"That's not necessary," I began.

"Oh, but it is," Ian said at once. "Yes, you'll risk your life to take them down anyway, but that is exactly the point. You'll risk it all while asking nothing from the same group that will let you save their lives and then cheerfully murder you for the imagined crime of your existence afterward."

Hekima sighed. "I would overturn that law in an instant. You know that, Veritas. But if I tried, I would be outvoted, again."

"You don't have to be." Ashael's rich baritone voice became even smoother. "You're now the most senior-ranking council member, so if you invoke article seven, you can appoint the next two council members yourself, without the customary vote."

Hekima gasped. "How do you know about article seven?"

I'd never heard of it, either, and I'd been the longest-serving Law Guardian in council history.

Ashael gave Hekima a tolerant smile. "Demons have sparred with vampires since the days of Cain. Think Haldam was the first council member that was a demon mole? I probably know more about the secret articles of your laws than you do."

"Then you know it has never been invoked before," Hekima said in a stiff tone.

"Yes, but it was created for circumstances such as these," Ashael countered. "There is a direct threat to the vampire species, and council seats have been unexpectedly vacated, preventing the passage of emergency laws needed to save your species. Simple, legal, and irrefutable. Come now, Hekima." His voice deepened further. "You've thought of this already. I'm only saying it out loud."

Hekima said nothing for a long moment. Then, she picked up her glass, drained it, and said, "Someone get the ghoul queen on video call for me."

Ashael dialed Marie, and handed his mobile to Hekima.

"What?" Marie said when she answered, sounding both busy and annoyed. Then, surprise flickered over her features when she saw Hekima staring back at her instead of Ashael.

"Greetings," Marie said in a new, formal tone.

"Greetings," Hekima replied with the same formality, which was impressive considering that she must have quite the buzz now from Ashael's blood. "I am calling to verify the offer of alliance with your people that Veritas presented to me."

"I verify the offer, which is valid for the next eleven hours, and if accepted, stands until the resolution of the war against the three renegade gods," Marie said.

Hekima gave a short nod. "Thank you for your verification, and for the clarified details of the terms. The vampire council will render our decision to you by dawn."

Marie inclined her head. "Until then."

"Until then," Hekima echoed.

When they hung up, Hekima handed the mobile back to Ashael. "You're keeping us in separate locations and you confiscated our mobiles so they couldn't be tracked, but I know you have people watching us. Contact them, and use their mobiles to get the remaining council on video conference."

"We'll need a laptop," Ashael said. "I can't get all nine members on simultaneous video conference on a mobile."

Ian flashed a smile at me. "Off to steal a laptop, then."

He left, and I gave the bourbon-and-demon-blood mixture a longing look. However, I didn't pick up the glass. If this went well, I'd need every last bit of my wits for the upcoming battle. If it didn't . . . well, all the spiked beverages in the world wouldn't make a difference.

*H*ekima now wore a multicolor brocade jacket shot through with silver thread, with a peacock-blue silk blouse and black pants. Her hair was in a sophisticated knot, and her makeup was subtle and artful. No one looking at her would guess that fifteen minutes ago, she'd been doing shots of demon-spiked liquor.

Squares containing video feeds from the eight other council members plus five Law Guardians including Xun Guan filled the screen of the laptop that Ian had swiped from a hotel guest. Hekima didn't waste time on pleasantries. She detailed Morana's attack on Maric, Morana's plans to split up the globe, Marie's offer of alliance, and what Ruaumoko could do if he grew impatient. Hekima closed by saying she was invoking article seven of the vampire charter, and then let the objecting council members scream for the next fifty minutes.

"I haven't heard any objections based on law," Hekima said, interrupting Lucius's current tirade.

"Without that, article seven is in force, and I appoint Xun Guan and Priscilla to the council as its newest members."

Both women looked shocked. Lucius's eyes bulged, and if he scrubbed his hands through his blond locks any harder, he'd rip out his own hair from his rage.

"I refuse to accept this!"

"You would be a child?" Hekima's tone turned scathing. "Very well, I will speak to you as a child. What did the one dinosaur say to the other dinosaur about the new, bright light in the sky? Nothing, because then the asteroid hit and vaporized them both! Likewise, our destruction *is* coming unless we act now to prevent it."

Sanjay finally spoke. "I accept Hekima invoking article seven, and welcome Xun Guan and Priscilla as council members."

Five more council members voiced their acceptance. Only Lucius, Phoenix, and Rolfe refused.

"You go too far selecting vampires whose opinions align with yours," Lucius hissed.

"Do I?" Hekima said in dangerous tone. "Article seven gives me the power to appoint any vampire I wish. Both Priscilla and Xun Guan have impeccable service records, so if you waste more time that endangers our people, I will appoint *this* vampire"—her head jerked at Ian, and my mouth fell open—"instead even though I shudder to imagine him as a council member."

"I withdraw my objection," Phoenix said at once.

"As do I," Rolfe chimed in.

Ian swiveled the laptop so that Lucius could see him. "Do it," he urged. "Object. I'll wreck your whole bloody life."

"I withdraw my objection," Lucius said in one of the most sullen tones I'd ever heard.

"Wise," Hekima said, and then swore in Priscilla and Xun Guan. Both women looked stunned as they repeated the oath that made them the vampire council's newest members.

"I now call for an immediate vote on allying with the ghoul nation for the duration of this war against the gods," Hekima said as soon as she was finished. "All in favor, say aye. All in dissent, say nay."

Nine "ayes" and two "nays" followed. No surprise, Lucius and Phoenix were the nays.

"I also call for a vote rescinding the illegality of magic," Hekima said, surprising me. "Magic saved us from the volcano, and magic protects us now. We will need more to ensure our victory against our adversaries, yet we can hardly expect it while simultaneously condemning the vampires who use it."

"Once more, you go too far," Lucius growled.

"No, this law did," Hekima countered. "Continuing to make something illegal simply because it makes vampires like you uncomfortable is nonsense. All in favor, vote aye! All in dissent, vote nay."

I clenched my fists as the replies came in, thinking of all the vampires I'd helped into hiding because of this law. Far too many more hadn't lived long enough to hide. They'd been killed or had taken their own lives out of despair. *Please*, I thought. *Please, let this injustice end!*

Ian took one of my closed hands, squeezing it. When the voting was finished, I almost burst into tears.

Seven ayes, four nays. Magic was now legal for vampires.

"I now call for a final vote to rescind the illegality of mixed-species persons," Helena said.

"I will not stand for this!" Lucius shouted.

"Then leave, and forfeit your chance to vote," Hekima replied in her stoniest voice. "Any others are welcome to forfeit as well. The motion will pass or fail based on those who stay, as per article seven of the emergency powers because a mixed-species person holds the only weapon effective against Ruaumoko and Morana."

"Lies," Lucius said in a hiss.

I rolled up the sleeve of my top and showed the council members the cuffs embedded in my skin as if they were thick tattoos.

"When I am near Morana or Ruaumoko, these manifest into restraints that I will use to send them straight to the netherworld." Then, my voice roughened from thousands of years of unnecessary self-loathing: "But that isn't why you should decriminalize mixed-species people. Do it because this law never should have been written in the first place since we are worth more than the worst prejudices of people who hated us enough to make our very existence illegal."

With that, I walked out of the hotel room. I had endured many things, but I couldn't endure hearing how many council members would vote for the continuation of violent hate under the guise of maintaining the "purity" of our species.

I'd made it all the way to the first floor of the hotel when I heard Ian's voice.

"Veritas!"

He was in front of me in the next moment. I only had an instant to see his face before he crushed me in his arms, but that single glimpse told me everything.

I didn't hug him back. I didn't even move because I felt too numb, but it was a beautiful, shocked kind of numb. It felt so long since I'd been surprised by joy.

"They didn't," I choked out.

Ian pulled away enough for me to see his blinding smile.

"Six ayes, five nays, with the nays still screaming when I left, but sod 'em. You're no longer illegal, little Guardian. You and all other mixed-species people are finally free."

We ended up staying at the same hotel for the next few days. Right now, there wasn't much that we could do beyond waiting. Marie's ghosts as well as the ghosts we'd enlisted were scouring the globe for Ruaumoko, Morana, and Phanes; we were watching the news for any new "natural" disasters that might indicate their presence; and everyone had warned their people and their allies to keep an eye out for the three gods.

Normally, I'd be frustrated by the waiting. Now, I considered it the calm before the storm. Ashael fetched Silver and brought him back to the lovely new suite he put on his tab for us, calling it a belated wedding present. It certainly felt like one to have Ian and my beloved pet under the same roof with nothing to do except enjoy being together.

No, more than a present. It felt like being part of a family, and I hadn't had that for nearly seven hundred years since Tenoch died.

I knew it couldn't last, but I didn't realize how much I wanted it to, even just a little longer, until I saw Cat's name flash up on Ian's new mobile.

For an incredibly selfish moment, I considered not answering it. Ian was in the shower, so he didn't hear or see Cat's call. I could squeeze out a few more hours with him, if I just turned his phone off until later tonight . . .

I answered on the fourth ring. "Yes?"

"The ghosts came through," were Cat's first words. My stomach turned to lead. "The gods are in the Tov province of Mongolia, hiding out in the Togchin temple ruins."

"That's good news," I forced myself to say, then meant it as I added, "No super volcanoes are located nearby, and if memory serves, that area has a very low population density."

Cat grunted. "Low as fuck as far as people go. I looked it up. There's a restoration group for the former monastery and a small hostel near the ruins. That's it for miles. We never would have found them, except that area had lots of slaughters in its history, so it's got ghosts. Thankfully, one of them talked."

I closed my eyes, steeling myself. "We need to hit them there as quickly as possible."

The selfish part of me still wanted to stall, but I couldn't bear to see more innocent people killed.

"Agreed, but your brother and Ian can only transport two people at a time, and we'll need to attack in much larger numbers to take them down," Cat replied.

I heard the bathroom door creak, but I didn't turn around. "We know a guy who can transport over a hundred people at a time."

"Really?" Cat sounded skeptical.

"I've seen it myself. Ashael went to seek him out two days ago, but there's no guarantee that he'll help. He, uh, kind of blames Ian and me for his secret island hideaway getting wiped out."

Another grunt. "You both do tend to leave a trail of destruction behind you."

She wasn't wrong, and if we were lucky enough to survive this, I didn't think that would change.

"Hey," Cat said, sounding more tentative now. "I want you to know that I'm glad you and Ian found each other. I think you both deserve to be happy. So know that when you don't see me in this final battle, it's not because I don't care."

"You're not coming?"

She sighed. "I want to, but Bones and I talked, and Katie can't lose both her parents if things go south. She's already spent most of her life trapped and experimented on like a lab rat. I didn't even know she existed until she was seven. Now, she's just starting to act like a little girl instead of a trained killing machine, and I can't . . ." Her voice broke.

"I understand," I said at once. "It's also very logical. Bones's telekinesis is much more advanced than yours, and this will be a fight of powers, not brawling abilities."

She let out a sound that was half sniff, half laugh. "I'm glad you see it as logical. I see it as ripping myself apart and hoping the pieces will be rejoined because if I lose Bones, I lose the best half of myself."

I finally turned around. Ian's hair was still wet, making it look darker and longer. Water ran down his creamy skin in rivulets, highlighting the muscles, ridges, and hollows of his body. If not for the dark crimson scars that streaked his back and zigzagged over to his taut stomach, he'd look like a flawless statue come to life, and all that was nothing compared to what was in his eyes.

He was my real home. He was also my deepest love, my wildest passion, my truest friend . . . he was everything I'd never dared to dream for, yet now had.

And now, I could lose him. Again.

"I know how you feel, Cat," I said in a voice that cracked at the edges. Then, as I had many times before, I forced the crushing weight of my emotions back. In a steadier tone, I said, "We'll contact Ashael and call you back."

I hung up. "They found them."

"I heard," Ian replied.

We stared at each other. From the other room, I heard Silver whine as he sensed the new tension in the air. It gave me an excuse to take a moment to collect myself, so I left the bedroom and went into the living area to pet Silver. If I touched Ian instead, I might grab on to him and refuse to let go.

He followed me. When would I learn that he wouldn't stay behind when he knew I needed him?

His arms came around me, and his chest was a hard, welcome wall behind me.

"We've got this, luv."

His voice rolled over me in its own caress. For a moment, I closed my eyes, willing myself to believe him.

"I know," I said while thinking, *Actually, we probably don't, but we still have to try. Too many lives are at stake.*

"This is different from the other times. We're no longer taking on enemies by ourselves," he replied, guessing at my doubts. "I kept insisting that my friends stay out of our battles, but I was wrong. Just as you and I are stronger together, so the pair of us will be stronger with allies at our sides. This time, I'm confident that all truly will be well."

I gave up trying to pretend that I wasn't wracked with nerves. He knew me too well to fall for it, anyway.

"The last time I was confident that all would be well, you ended up dead. So, no offense, but I'll stick with being paranoid and anxiety ridden. I've had much better luck with those two."

Breath from his laughter tickled the back of my neck. "Whatever you prefer, then."

I leaned back against him, allowing myself to sink into this moment. It wouldn't last, but for now, all *was* well. I shouldn't waste a second of it.

"This is how we first met, remember?" he murmured, his hands starting to roam. I only wore one of the hotel's robes, and it fell open beneath his touch. "Only then, it was a life-and-death battle between vampires and ghouls."

I did remember, although it was getting harder to think with him seeking out my most sensitive spots.

"You looked bored before the fight," he went on, voice deepening, "and I thought, 'Ah, another useless politician.'"

"Understandable presumption," I said, arching to give him better access. If I was risking losing him forever, I at least deserved a quickie before summoning Ashael.

"Then, on the battlefield," Ian said, his strokes becoming more possessive, "you tore through a group of ghouls until all I saw was flying body parts. At that moment, I had my first premonition about you, and it seared through me as if I'd been branded from above: she is mine."

"Yours," I agreed, turning around to kiss him.

Three hard knocks on the balcony glass doors shattered the moment. Ashael stood outside, wearing two thick, hooded coats that covered all his skin except for his face, which now had a very baleful expression.

"I didn't spend the last thirty-six hours straight convincing Yonah to help us only to stand out here and burn while waiting for the two of you to finish copulating."

"Come in," I said, reluctantly stepping away from Ian.

Ashael teleported into the bathroom while I closed the drapes. With a sigh of disappointment, Ian put on his trousers.

"Yonah agreed to help?" I asked Ashael.

He peeked out, saw that the sun was now blocked from streaming in, and threw off his cloaks, revealing a designer jacket, a sleek bronze shirt, and black denim trousers.

"Yes, mostly. He'll drop off the reinforcements, but he won't stay to fight, and convincing him to reveal himself to so many strangers after he's been in hiding for thousands of years was the opposite of easy."

"Well done," Ian said. "Hope that Yonah has nothing important planned right now, because we attack within the hour."

Both Ashael's brows rose. "You found them?"

"Yes."

Ice rolled over my nerves. This was it, so I had to be ready.

"Get Yonah," I said to my brother in a steady voice. "I'll call Marie so she knows to have her people ready. Ian will call Bones and the others, and then Yonah can mass transport us."

Ashael grasped my shoulders. "Yonah can take Marie and the others. I'll take you and Ian. Where are we going?"

"Drop us about a kilometer outside the Togchin temple ruins in Mongolia." The site of a former, awful massacre. With luck, history wouldn't repeat itself.

Ashael nodded. "I know the place. Make your calls. I'll return with Yonah."

With that, he threw his cloaks back on and vanished.

I stared at Ian. "Promise me you won't use the power from the cursed fruit tonight. Promise me."

His mouth curved in the barest of smiles. "I can't make that promise, and you know it."

Dammit! I did know that, but I'd had to try.

"Then don't. You dare. Fucking die," I said, biting off each word.

Now, his smile widened. "Have no intention of it, but I *will* murder Phanes. That, I can promise you."

"He's unkillable," I began, only to have another set of sharp knocks come from the balcony again.

I glanced out, saw the hooded figures of Ashael and a bald man with a prominent Roman nose. Ashael had been fast, and we hadn't even begun making calls yet.

"Come in!" I said, bracing myself again.

Time for talking with Ian about personal concerns was over. Now, it was time to gather everyone and fight for all our lives.

$\mathcal{T}$he Bogd Khan Mountain cradled the Togchin temple ruins as if still attempting to shelter them from the outside world. This mountain had long been considered sacred, leading to its protected status banning hunting, mining, and other industries. Forests of larch trees dressed the high peaks in green and gold while the tall grasses were brown from the chilly temperatures. Winter had come early to this part of Mongolia.

It would be winter everywhere if we failed, and it wouldn't leave for hundreds or even thousands of years. That's why we couldn't fail.

The Togchin ruins were about a kilometer above the tree patch that Ashael had teleported us behind. Between us and them were the remains of the Manjusri Monastery, a former Buddhist complex consisting of nearly two dozen temples plus housing for hundreds of monks. Now, the original structures were reduced to intermittent stacks of blocks and the occasional weathered Buddha statue, barely hinting at the place's previous size and glory.

Time and cruel people had that in common. Both could ravage without mercy, leaving nothing but ruins in their wake.

"Ready?" Ashael asked, so low that I could barely hear him even though he was standing right next to me.

I nodded. My cuffs hadn't activated yet, but the skin on my arm now felt . . . itchy. I'd take that as a sign that Morana and Ruaumoko were still in one of the ruins above us.

"Remember, I'll focus on Phanes," Ian said, equally low.

I gave a sharper nod. It was agony not to watch Ian's back while he went up against such a formidable foe, but only I had the cuffs that could send Morana and Ruaumoko back to the netherworld. Plus, more practically, only Ian could match Phanes's teleporting skills, and we had to keep Phanes from teleporting Morana and Ruaumoko out of here at all costs.

Ashael had another job. One that was equally important.

It would have saved us so much trouble if we could've cast a spell over this area to prevent anyone from teleporting out of it. However, those spells took time we didn't have, and this place was so wide open, we'd be spotted before we set even half of the ten necessary anchoring gems.

No, we had to do this the hard way.

Ian tensed right before I felt prickles against my skin, like I was being hit with an invisible, sand-filled wind. I recognized the type of power at once, even if its source was unfamiliar to me. There was another vampire on this mountain, and he wasn't with us. Yonah hadn't arrived with our backup yet.

Before I could react, another wave of power rolled over me, even stronger, and it left a sour taste in my mouth. Not just another vampire. A vampire who practiced dark magic.

Looked like we were doing this the *really* hard way.

"Where's the bloody ghost?"

Ian's growl barely disturbed the air since there was at least one creature nearby with hearing as great as ours. If we hadn't tamped down our auras to barely detectable levels, we would have announced our presence to this unknown vampire via our power level, too. The good news was, this vampire must not know we were here, to flaunt their aura that way.

"He'll be here," Ashael whispered.

Separating them before Phanes teleported Morana and Ruaumoko away required a surprise precision strike. That required knowing exactly where to strike, and for that, we needed intel. The same ghost who'd notified Cat's specter friend, Fabian, about the trio of gods being here was also supposed to tell us which ruin they were hiding in. We were in our predetermined meeting spot, in the clump of trees just south of the newly rebuilt museum. Where was he?

A few minutes later, Ashael frowned. "Perhaps he

meant that other patch of trees," he murmured, and teleported over.

Power immediately snapped around me before pulling tight like a snare net. I tried to run and couldn't. Flying didn't work, either. It only tightened the net. At once, I knew what had happened. We hadn't had time to rig a magic trap over this place, but someone else had, and we'd just activated it.

Ian grabbed me, and then rage flashed over his features.

"I can't teleport both of us out."

I cursed as I looked around. I could feel the net, but I couldn't see it. Why? My other half should be able to see the magic in it, and my father had made sure I was immune to illusion.

"Ashael?" Ian called out softly.

No answer. I craned my neck as far as the trap would allow, but I didn't see him.

"Maybe he made it out," I whispered.

"Perhaps."

Ian wasn't looking at me now. His attention was fixed on the steeper terrain above us. Power began building in him, so intense that the air crackled and my skin ached.

"Don't," I said, realizing what he was doing. "We don't need that, and if the others feel it, it could ruin our chance. Let them get close." I tapped my arm for emphasis. "Real close."

He ground out a curse, but that deadly spike of power diminished until he felt like a normal, albeit very pissed off, Master vampire.

My sigh of relief was interrupted by infuriating laughter that still managed to sound as bright as the tinkling of bells.

"Welcome! I hope you enjoyed the surprise. You didn't think killing me would be that easy, did you, little demigod?"

I turned toward the sound.

Morana hadn't been there moments ago, but now she was standing near the lowest of the ruined temples, her sapphire hair a vivid splash of color against the faded beige blocks. She wore a pearl-encrusted corset over a black velvet dress that was more suited for a formal ball than hiding in this desolate patch of mountainside, but far be it for her to wear sand-colored camo gear to blend in with the landscape like Ian and I had.

"Only one person gets to call me 'little' anything," I replied, raising my voice so she'd have no trouble hearing me. "And that isn't you, you blueberry-headed bitch."

She laughed again, and Phanes appeared next to her. His large wings seemed to attract the moonlight, making them look ethereal as those pale silver beams shone through his golden feathers. He wasn't wearing a shirt—again—and only had swaths of purple silk crisscrossed in an X pattern over his bare upper body while black trousers and boots covered his lower half.

"This looks familiar," Phanes drawled. "When I last saw the two of you, you were also trapped and about to die."

"How did that work out?" Ian asked in a contemptuous tone. "Think this will fare any better for you?"

Phanes smiled. "Let's find out."

"Bring them in!" Morana sang out.

The magical net I still couldn't see tightened until Ian and I were mashed together. Then, we were hauled up toward Morana and Phanes, each bone-jarring bump no accident. If someone had the power to rig this kind of trap, they had the power to glide us over the steep, rocky terrain instead of having the magic drag us like a proverbial sack of potatoes over every rut, boulder, and crumpled ruin along the way.

When we were finally in front of Morana and Phanes, my clothes were bloodstained and torn in places, and my lip bled from how hard my teeth had repeatedly clanged together. If we'd missed bumping over a single stony obstacle on the way up the kilometer-long trek, I'd be amazed.

A third figure joined Morana and Phanes. My gaze skipped over them to study him. Even though I'd only glimpsed him once before from far away, I knew this had to be Ruaumoko.

No surprise: the god had also transformed his host's body to reveal his true form, which was eye-catchingly handsome, with a wide, full mouth, high cheekbones, rich brown skin, and teak-colored eyes, now that they weren't lit up with that unique orange glow. His full facial tattoos were inked in patterns reminiscent of the Maori culture, where his legend was still celebrated. Half of Ruaumoko's black hair was up in a bun while the rest trailed down past well-muscled shoulders. Unlike Morana and Phanes, whose loud-colored clothing jumped out from the landscape to announce their presence, Ruaumoko dressed with a warrior's mindset of blending into the terrain, wearing tan trousers and a pale yellow shirt that matched well with the dried grass and weathered stones from the ruins.

As if I needed more confirmation that he was the smartest one among them, Ruaumoko also never looked away from me and Ian, even though Morana and Phanes kept exchanging self-congratulatory glances.

If I get the chance, he dies first, I thought.

"Impressive trap," Ian said. "Who do I compliment for it?"

"That would be Genghis," Morana said, waving forward a thickly built vampire with light brown skin and purple streaks in his short black hair. "He flocked to my side when he heard what we were offering."

"Our side," Ruaumoko said pointedly.

"Yes, of course," Morana replied in a soothing way.

Ian's gaze raked over the vampire, who grinned at us the way hungry fishermen grinned at a large catch.

"Genghis? I think not," Ian said, dismissing him.

I had no trouble seeing the magic that sparked around his hands as he glowered at Ian. "It isn't wise to anger the Great Khan."

"You're a poser, not the Great Khan," I said bluntly.

Morana cocked her head. "No? He said he was."

"I am," Genghis insisted.

I snorted. "You're absolutely not. I met the real Great Khan once. If he were still alive, he'd slaughter you for the comparison. *He* founded the largest contiguous empire in history, and you're slumming for scraps from these three."

Genghis smiled. "I will have far more than scraps soon. I set the traps that caught you, earning me my promised reward."

"Your magic was unusual," I allowed. I still couldn't see the net around me, but I could feel it, and if I tried, I could squeeze a hand through it in places.

"It wasn't his magic," Morana said, her voice turning to a purr. "It was mine. He just fashioned it into the trap we used."

That's why I couldn't see it! My father gave me the ability to see through Phanes's illusions, which let me see normal magic, too, but Morana was, to put it mildly, not from around here, so her magic was far from normal.

"Trapping us isn't the same as keeping us," Ian said in a light tone. "Even in this net, two against four are odds I'll take all day."

Morana smiled. "Not two against four. We aren't alone."

Ruaumoko held out his hand. The ground shuddered and parted, revealing a network of hidden tunnels filled with scores of vampires and at least as many ghouls.

My teeth ground from how hard I clenched my jaw. Genghis might be a fake Khan, but he wasn't as stupid as we'd thought. He'd only let us feel his aura so we'd underestimate their numbers, when there were many vampires here and that same number in ghouls.

Wait until I saw the ghost who'd told us that the gods were here! He'd left out a *lot* of important information.

"Mind if I crash the party?" a familiar deep voice said.

I tried to turn around, but only ended up seeing a very close view of Ian's shoulder.

"Kill the demon!" Phanes hissed.

Genghis lunged forward, and Ashael appeared in my view.

"Oh, you don't want to kill me," Ashael said, with a wag of his dark brows at Morana, Phanes, and Ruaumoko. "After all, I'm the person who activated the trap that caught them."

*T*he stunned silence was broken by Ian's snarl.

"You scurvy son of a bitch! That's why you went to that other patch of trees. You knew where the magic trip line was!"

"Guilty," Ashael said, with an apologetic look my way. "I really am fond of you, but the chance to rule the entire western hemisphere was too good to give up. You understand?"

I let all the hatred I was capable of fill my voice. "I understand that I should never, ever have trusted a demon."

"I know!" Now Ashael laughed. "And now *you* know how demons trick people into selling their souls even though everyone knows that doesn't work out for the seller. We tell you what you want to hear, all while pretending that we're making exceptions to the rules for you because you're so special to us." Another laugh. "Works every time, be it human, ghouls, vampires . . . or other."

Morana came closer, an interested expression on her face.

"Don't." Ruaumoko's voice was hard. "We don't know him, and he just demonstrated what happens to anyone who trusts him."

Once again proving you're the smartest, I thought.

"You don't need to trust me," Ashael replied with a grin. "I already proved my worth by delivering your enemies to you, and by giving the other demon the wrong location to show up at with their reinforcements, so now they're all alone."

"I will rip off your limbs and use your own bones to stab your eyes out," I said, darkness pouring out of me.

Ashael jumped out of its path. "Don't let that touch you, either," he said to Morana and Ruaumoko. "Getting any of that on you is like a bad acid trip combined with a paralyzing agent."

"He's right," Phanes said, looking at Ashael with surprise.

Everyone now gave the roiling darkness a wide berth. I tried to stretch it further and couldn't. Dammit.

Ashael winked at Phanes. "I'm always right, and if your friends don't renege on my reward, I'll even throw in how Ian beat your pet Minotaur. Spoiler alert: he used secret magic."

"I knew it!" Phanes said, pounding his fists on his thighs. "How did he do it? How did Ian trick me?"

"Shut it, demon," Ian said in a deadly growl.

"Annoying, isn't he?" Ashael said, flicking his fingers in Ian's direction. Then, he danced them along the edges of Phanes's wings until the other deity gave him an aggravated look. "But, annoying or not, Ian carries incredible magic within him," Asahel went on. "You must not be able to see it, or you'd know that. Probably because that magic predated even you. Pity you don't see it, because if you knew how powerful it was—"

"Ashael, don't!" I said, straining against the net.

"—you'd want to use that delicious ability of yours to rip spells out of people to take it for yourself," Ashael went on, ignoring me as he walked past Phanes.

Phanes stared after Ashael with the intensity of a denied child watching the neighborhood ice-cream truck pull away before he could get his favorite treat.

"What kind of magic?"

"What kind, indeed," Ashael said in his most caressing tone. "You already know it can turn a mere vampire into a Minotaur-defeating badass, so imagine what it could do for you?"

"Give him the prize, Morana," Phanes said hoarsely.

"That reward is mine," Genghis hissed. "I set the traps."

"Traps that would still be empty without me," Ashael replied. "Which is worth more to you, my gorgeous trio of gods? Empty traps, or full ones?"

Genghis barreled toward Ashael. "I won't let you—"

Ashael's hand flashed out. Genghis fell backward, the hilt of a silver knife buried in his chest. Ashael gave a cool glance at the scores of vampires and ghouls in the tunnels beyond him.

"Who wants to die next? Or, who wants to be smart, and I'll appoint you overseer of areas I don't particularly like?"

"Overseer sounds good," a redheaded, ivory-skinned vampire with an Irish accent said.

More murmurs of assent, until the tunnels began filling with the sounds of vampires and ghouls backing Ashael.

I struggled against the net. It held with impressive strength. Morana watched, a smile playing about her lips.

"I offered you peace under my rule. You chose war. Now look at you. With all your power, you're helpless. You can't rip another hole in the netherworld to throw me back down; that will only crack the veil wide in hundreds of places and let more of my allies free, my *little*, deluded demigod."

Phanes met my widened gaze with a nasty smile. "Yes, I told her about the cracks. I couldn't only see into the netherworld. With enough power, I could speak into it, too. I told Morana and Ruaumoko that I'd be coming for them ever since your power put the first crack in the veil. Now, you die."

"Yes," Morana purred. "I won't even bother doing it myself. You don't deserve the honor of me killing you. Instead, I'll let one of my vampire or ghoul followers send you back to that miserable piss river you call a father."

The ground suddenly trembled. Morana glanced at Ruaumoko as if to ask, *Did you do that?*

He shook his head, his dark eyes narrowing as he looked past us down the mountain toward the Manjusri Monastery remains.

Morana followed his gaze. "What?" she breathed out.

Ashael vanished and reappeared next to Ruaumoko, grabbing him before they both vanished. I yanked out the cuffs that had been burning beneath my sleeve this whole time. Ashael reappeared in front of me. He shoved Ruaumoko against me, and I slapped the cuffs on his wrist through one of the net's holes.

Ruaumoko's scream was echoed by Morana's roar of rage as fire swept over Ruaumoko's body, until his skin glowed as orange as his gaze. That fire turned into liquid that disappeared into the earth like water sucked down into an endless hole.

Ian teleported out of the net, confirming my suspicions that he'd always been able to leave. Before, he'd only said that he couldn't teleport *both* of us out. He reappeared by Morana and grabbed her. I ripped out the next pair of cuffs, stretching for her . . . only to have Phanes appear between us before Ian could shove Morana within my reach.

I felt another, stronger vibration as hundreds of sets of feet took another step forward.

"Guess what, Morana?" I said while still stretching for her through the net. "We *didn't* come alone."

*B*itter experience had taught that even the best-laid plans could get ruined by a clever trap. That's why Option B was Ashael's fake betrayal, if we failed to take Morana and Ruaumoko by surprise. I thought that Ian and I did well with our acting, but Ashael had been a bit over the top. Still, he'd succeeded in getting Morana, Phanes, and Ruaumoko to trust in his greed . . . and, more important, to trust in their superiority over the situation to let Ashael maneuver Phanes away from them.

Turns out that Phanes wasn't the only one with a massive ego that could be used against him.

But Phanes was using all his strength as well as the great expanse of his wings to keep Morana out of my reach. Only Ian's grip on his hands kept Phanes from teleporting Morana out of there, too.

Ashael tried to grab Morana and instantly froze into a tall, wide block of ice. Another freeze blast caught me in it, instantly blinding and immobilizing me. I used my power to force the ice away, regaining my vision to see that Morana's latest blast had been so intense, it had frozen both Ian and Phanes into solid blocks of ice next to Ashael.

"Whoever kills her wins the western hemisphere!" Morana shouted as she ran away.

The vampires and ghouls began pouring out of the tunnels, and I couldn't run because I was still stuck in this damned net.

I used my power to unfreeze Ian, and Ashael blasted out of his ice prison himself. Morana had been so panicked that she'd left Phanes frozen on the ground behind her. I soon lost sight of her as my attackers swarmed me, and I cursed freely as they stabbed me with silver knives through the net.

"Get her, I'll be fine!" I shouted as Ashael and Ian began hacking at the vampires and ghouls attacking me.

The sky suddenly filled with so many Remnants that they blocked out the stars. More filled the perimeter, until our entire area was domed under the writhing, deadly mass. All the while, the ground kept trembling as Marie's army ran toward us.

Morana might be running, but with Phanes still frozen on the ground, Remnants blanketing the perimeter, and Marie's ghoul army marching up the mountain, she was trapped.

She must have known it, because she threw another freeze bomb at us. Several moments of blinding pain later, I unfroze myself and Ian as fast as I could, hearing Ashael shout, "Don't worry, I'll get her," before his voice was suddenly cut off.

My blindness cleared and I screamed. A jagged bone knife now jutted from Ashael's eye, which blackened and smoked. The ghoul next to him yanked it out, drawing his weapon back for that second, final stab—

Ian teleported over and yanked the ghoul's arm away with such force, his limb tore off. His head followed suit with a brutal fly-and-twist maneuver that would have impressed me, if I wasn't so horrified by seeing Ashael slump to the ground.

Only one thing could kill demons: stabbing through their eyes with bone from another demon. With one eye remaining, Ashael would survive, but he couldn't teleport anymore. He'd barely be able to move. Every part of me screamed with vengeance.

How dare they harm our brother!

I ripped the blood out of the vampires and ghouls, which is what I should've done as soon as they'd swarmed, had I not been distracted by Morana's freeze bombs. Ian slipped in the new pools of it before teleporting over to grab Asahel. They both disappeared, only to reappear inside my net.

Before I could gasp out that I was being crushed by their combined weight, Ian was gone, and Ashael was curled next to me.

"You guard his remaining eye, and you guard her heart," Ian said. "I'm getting Morana and ending this."

"You can't touch her, she'll freeze you solid!" I snapped. "She's going subzero on everyone. Look!"

I gestured down the mountain. Marie's army was now being swept aside by huge sheets of ice that rushed down the mountain like an endless, glittering avalanche. Bones and Mencheres were farther up the mountain, standing side by side, the ice forking around them as their power swelled. Moments later, the ice broke around Marie's army, too, as the vampires' combined telekinesis shredded it into something that resembled snow.

Then Remnants began falling from the sky. I was shocked until one glance at Marie explained why. She'd been hit by a freeze bomb, and the Remnants were controlled by Marie's will and her blood. Right now, both were frozen solid.

"If you touch Morana, she'll freeze you so hard that you'll shatter," I said to Ian as I blasted Marie free. "I'm the only one that can survive her, so find a way to get me free."

Ian cursed, but began to teleport among the vampires and ghouls, alternatively ripping through their hearts with silver or tearing off their heads. With all their blood on the ground turning into crimson ice from the freezing temperatures, they were no match for Ian. Soon, they were all dead.

Morana must have realized that, because ice began shooting at us like it was coming from a warship firing on all guns. I screamed as countless shards ripped into me, making me deranged with pain.

What are you waiting for? my other half snapped. *Fight ice* with *ice!*

I pushed past the pain enough to form a barricade around my net that was so thick, Morana's ice bullets didn't get through. After a few moments, I healed enough to see and hear again . . . and let out a scream when I realized that Ian was on the outside of the barricade. Not protected within it.

Liquid darkness shot out of me with the same velocity as the ice bullets that kept chipping deeper dents into my barricade. That darkness flowed past the hole I'd made at the bottom of my barricade without even thinking about it. From there, the darkness spread out in search of Ian.

I didn't need to see him to know when it found him. As soon as it did, I could *feel* Ian, and I grabbed at him with hands made of liquid midnight instead of flesh.

I pulled Ian into the barricade, closing it around him and building up the ice thicker against the endless barrage of bullets. Next to me, Ashael groaned, and tried to flip over.

"Is he . . . ?"

"He'll be fine," I said, watching as countless holes over Ian's body began to close and the smashed pieces of his skull knit itself together. He'd been hit so fast that he hadn't had time to use his cursed fruit power, and for that, I was glad.

Then, I was blind, deaf, and immobilized again as another freeze bomb hit me. I broke out of it, but it took longer this time. All the freezing, unfreezing, and healing was taking its toll, especially on my wits, and all the while, the temperature kept dropping.

Morana wouldn't need individual freeze bombs soon. This whole place would be a massive, frozen prison.

"We need heat to counter this," I said to Ian as soon as I unfroze him and Ashael, since Ashael's injury left him too weak to do it himself. "You have to teleport away and get some."

Ice shards fell off Ian's brows from how sharply he drew them together. "Leave you? Are you mad?"

"Not yet," I said, and made a doorway in the ice dome around us before remembering that Ian could teleport away. Gods, my brain must be getting freezer burn, like a poorly packaged piece of meat!

"Behind you," I shouted when I saw a glint of silver as someone rushed through the door I'd made.

Ian spun around, and I slapped out a wave of the inky darkness still pooling beneath me. The advancing vampire screamed when it touched him and fell to the ground, clawing at his body as if his own skin were attacking him.

Ian picked up one of the discarded silver knives and ripped through the vampire's heart with it. Then, he teleported back to my side, but his movements were a little slower than normal. I wasn't the only one suffering side effects from being repeatedly flash-frozen, and the temperature just kept getting colder.

I grabbed Ian through the net. "Leave me and *go get heat*," I repeated. "Only massive amounts of heat can counter this, so don't take no for an answer from him."

His eyes widened in understanding. Then, he shoved a silver knife in my hand, gave me a hard kiss, and disappeared.

The sudden quiet was unnerving. I couldn't see what was going on outside without lowering my ice barricade, and from the repeated chipping sounds, Morana was still spraying down ice bullets.

I'd have to lower it, though. It was too quiet outside. That meant Marie, Bones, Mencheres, and Marie's army was probably frozen. I was the only one who could unfreeze them, so I had to drop the barrier and—

Pain ripped through me, followed by instant blindness and immobility. Sonofabitch! Another freeze bomb.

I burst the ice within me and around me. As usual, it felt like being stabbed by a thousand burning knives at once. When I was free, I broke the ice away from Ashael, too. Then, I gripped my brother's hand.

"This is going to hurt, but I have to do it. Brace."

With that, I tore down the barricade, keeping only a half dome above us to, hopefully, protect our heads. Ice bullets immediately tore into me, their velocity flinging me against the sides of my net trap. Wonderful relief followed when Ashael wrapped his arms around me, covering half my body with his. He was taking my fire, so I had to make this count.

I forced my head to turn so I could see down the mountain. Once I did, I was appalled. *Everything* was covered by ice. I couldn't even see the tallest points of the ruins anymore. For several kilometers in every direction, there was only smooth, white, deadly sheets of ice.

Morana wasn't just raining down ice bullets and freeze bombs. She was forming a fucking glacier right on top of us!

I sent my power out to break apart the ice. Between the sounds of it shattering and the ringing from the endless rounds bouncing off the ice roof above me, let alone the ice bullets that hit me, I couldn't hear anything else. Dizziness filled me, competing with ripping pain as more and more bullets hit me despite Ashael's selfless efforts to shield me.

I couldn't see Morana, but she must have been able to see me, and she was unleashing arctic hell.

Another blinding flash of pain later, everything went black.

*W*ake up. Wake up!

I will, I thought groggily to my other half. *In a moment.*

We don't have a moment, was her pitiless reply. *Can't you feel her coming toward us? She's almost here, so wake up!*

I tried, but while I could hear my other half, I couldn't access our power to do what she said. I could feel it, and yet somehow, the power seemed to be far away.

I tried again, harder. Now, it felt almost within my grasp . . .

I exploded. At least, that's how it felt. I didn't actually blow up, because a few blinks later, I could see again. I was facedown in the net, Ashael's body draped over mine, and . . . what was all this water? And how was I free from Morana's latest freeze bomb? I hadn't done that. Had I?

"Veritas!"

I turned toward Ian's voice, catching a glimpse of him next to a dark-haired man. For a second, I couldn't make out who that was because of the thick clouds of steam pouring out around him. With a start, I realized that steam was billowing around me and Ashael, too, and shockingly, the puddles of water beneath our net were warm where before, there had been solid ice.

Ian teleported over and pulled me into his arms through the holes in the net. "Brought you your heat," he murmured.

Now I knew what had happened. Vlad Tepesh, who'd once signed his name Dracula, meaning son of the dragon, had turned the ice into steam so fast that it had exploded away from me.

"Yes, and the next time your husband fetches me, it had better be to bring me to my promised brunch," Vlad growled.

"It's a date," I said with a weary laugh.

Vlad raised his hands. Blue flames licked them as he stared at the tons of ice that had buried the entire mountainside.

Ice bullets rained down anew upon us. I tried to marshal my powers to throw up another shield, but then the ice bullets turned to warm rain. Moments later, they vanished entirely as Vlad spread out a canopy of blazing fire above us and around us.

The blast of warmth felt so good that I had the insane urge to get close enough to burn myself. I didn't, not the least of which because I still couldn't get out of the damned net. Instead, I kissed Ian through the net until I felt a different, even more wonderful form of heat. All the while, sounds of ice shattering merged with the shrill whistles of steam under compression as Vlad tore into the glacier with fire and heat.

I finally broke our kiss, murmuring, "Think I'm well enough to help now."

"Oh, let him keep showing off," Ian said, with a low laugh. "It's what he lives for."

"I can hear you," Vlad said in a grating voice. "And while it might be true, it's still rude to say it."

I pushed Ian back, my eyes widening when I saw through the door-shaped hole Vlad had made in his fire wall to the mountain beyond. What had been kilometers of glacial ice was now rivers of water raging down the slope, carrying along pieces of ruins, trees, and people in its path.

Then the wall of fire parted in a new place and Mencheres strode through, looking as pissed as I'd ever seen him.

"Thank you for coming," he said to Vlad. "My powers didn't work on the ice goddess, and the polar vortex she dropped on us was . . . debilitating."

Vlad grinned. "I saw. Froze you into your own tomb, did she?" Then, his smile was wiped away. "No need to thank me, Mencheres. Ian told me you needed me. That's all I had to hear."

Mencheres touched his forehead to Vlad's for a silent moment. Then, he stepped back.

"My powers might not work on Morana, but they can still move things around her, and this landscape is full of trees."

I gripped the invisible chords of my net. "If you can get her to me, Mencheres, I can stop her forever."

Ian stood up, flashing a cruelly expectant smile at his sire. "Club Morana with a whole bloody forest, if need be."

"I'll cover you," Vlad said to Mencheres, opening another fire door for him.

Mencheres nodded at Vlad and left through it. Moments later, I heard the sound of multiple trees snapping.

"She'll use more freeze bombs," I warned Vlad.

He flashed a charming smile my way. "We'll see how many of those she can muster while I'm fire-bombing the ass off of her."

Another set of explosions punctuated his threat. I thought I heard a scream, but I wasn't sure. Between Vlad's bombs and Mencheres knocking down trees, it was too loud to tell.

Next to me, Ashael finally stirred. "What did I miss?" he asked in a drowsy tone.

My throat briefly closed from the gratitude that swelled in me. "You missed our friends helping us when we needed it."

Why had I fought so hard against relying on others for help? Everyone needed help sometimes, no matter how old, strong, or powerful they were. If only it hadn't taken me thousands of years to learn that.

"Ah, look, there's Bones using his telekinetic powers to go ghoul fishing," Vlad remarked in a conversational tone. "He just pulled Marie and two of her people from the river."

"I should help," I said, giving Ian a light push back. "I'm feeling better, and water is easier for me to control than—"

Power blasted out, so explosive that Ashael and I were hurled backward toward Vlad's flaming barricade. The fire wall vanished only an instant before we hit it, and we rolled to a stop against a crumpled block that used to be part of a far larger set of temple ruins. At once, we were pelted with ice bullets that stopped when another fire canopy was flung over us.

"What?" I gasped out.

Frenzied movement right outside the original fire barricade caught my eye. Then, I gasped again.

Phanes and Ian were locked in battle, blipping in and out of my vision as Phanes tried to teleport away, and Ian kept forcing him back. Oh. My. Gods. Phanes must have defrosted when Vlad heated up this area, and I hadn't even noticed!

"Hit Morana with everything you've got," I shouted to Vlad. "If she blasts Ian with another freeze bomb now, Phanes could get away and take Morana with him!"

Another blast hit me like a full-body punch. At first, I thought it came from Vlad, because, from the deluge of explosions outside, he was taking my advice seriously. Then, my heart seized up when I realized the source of the incredible bursts.

They were coming from Ian. He was using the cursed fruit power to fight Phanes, at levels that I'd never felt before.

"Ian, don't!" I screamed.

He either didn't hear me, or he didn't care. His power grew, until even the flames making up Vlad's barricade seemed to shrink back in fear from it. Then, Phanes and Ian fell out of the sky, hitting the ground hard enough to make it shake.

Phanes roared in rage as they rolled over the terrain, pummeling each other, making sounds more akin to rocks smashing together than fists meeting flesh.

"Fool!" Phanes shouted. "You cannot best an immortal!"

"Can't I?" I didn't even recognize Ian's tone for its new savageness. "Let's find out."

Another blast of power rocked us back. I grabbed the nets, trying to right them so I could see what was happening. Even when we stopped rolling, it was hard to make out because Ian moved so fast. I caught a glimpse of a brutal, twisting shape, and then Phanes screamed, a high-pitched, agonized sound.

Ian jumped back from him, and my jaw dropped. Ian was now holding up one of Phanes's large, golden, severed wings.

He threw it aside as if it were garbage. Phanes spun and fell as he tried to retrieve it. Ian was on him in a flash, ripping off Phanes's remaining wing while more power boiled out of him. Even after he threw that aside, he didn't stop tearing into Phanes, who was now nearly limp on the ground beneath him.

"He has to stop," Ashael breathed out. "He's using too much power. It will kill him."

It absolutely would. I could see it in the new scars that ripped over Ian's body like the ground opening up from a violent earthquake. His body was dying even as the power swelled to such astonishing levels that it stripped the bark off the nearby trees.

"Ian, stop, please!" I screamed.

He didn't turn his head. Maybe he didn't even hear me. From the look on his face, I doubted he could hear anything at all. He seemed utterly lost to the power as he tore at Phanes, trying to rip him limb from limb.

"If you want to live, take the source of his power from him!" Ashael shouted to Phanes, and stretched out his hand.

A red glow appeared below Ian's ribs, no bigger than a peach pit. Phanes's gaze fastened on it as if it were a diamond.

"There it is. Take it! He's becoming too powerful, and he'll kill us all!" Ashael continued in a hoarse shout.

Hope crashed through me. Ian was too lost to the power to stop, but Phanes could tear off any spell from someone. He'd proved that the first time he met Ian, and the cursed fruit was, in essence, no more than a very powerful spell.

"Don't, Ashael!" I yelled, while hoping that Phanes would do exactly what Ashael said. "If

Phanes rips that power out and keeps it, he'll use it to heal his wings!"

That galvanized Phanes into flipping over and grabbing at the red glow beneath Ian's sternum. All the while, firebombs continued to go off, and trees crashed to the ground as Vlad and Mencheres aimed their combined, fearsome abilities at Morana, keeping her from ending this battle with another freeze bomb.

Ian grabbed Phanes, power spilling out of him so fiercely, Phanes's skin began hyper-extending away from his frame. I sucked in a horrified breath. Ian was going to kill him, and killing an immortal would make his power go supernova, taking both of them out at the same time.

"Ian!"

All my hope, fear, and love came out as a scream that made his head tick ever so slightly in my direction.

"Ian, please, if you love me, *don't do it*!"

He paused. Very slowly, his head turned toward me.

Phanes plunged his whole fist into Ian just below his sternum and then ripped it out.

The shockwave knocked all of us backward. When my net stopped tumbling, I frantically pushed past Ashael's body to look where I'd last seen Ian.

He was still there, though now he was on his back instead of standing. Phanes was on his knees, smacking himself in the stomach with his fists while that red light waned and dimmed beneath his clenched fingers.

"It's not working, it's not working, it's not working!" Phanes cried out in frustration.

Ashael let out a tired laugh. "Of course it's not, fool. You can't reabsorb that power back into yourself. You should have known that, but you believed me because demons are the world's best liars, and I told you what you wanted to hear, same as I've told every human, vampire, ghoul, or *other*."

Phanes staggered toward us. "I'll kill you. I'll—"

"You'll do nothing."

I leapt into a standing position at Ian's voice. The tight net knocked me right back down into Ashael, but I didn't care. Ian was alive, gloriously alive, and rolling over to grab Phanes by the ankle so that the former deity tripped.

"You'll do nothing because nothing is all you're capable of now," Ian went on. "That power showed me how to neuter your abilities. Your wings were the source of all your greatness, and now, you've been snipped."

"What? No!" Phanes said, swinging at Ian.

He caught the punch one-handed. Phanes's eyes widened, and then he screamed as Ian bent his wrist back until it snapped.

"Can't stop me, can you, even though I currently am as weak as a new vampire," Ian said in a tired but conversational tone. "You can't teleport anymore, either. Or do illusions, or fly, or heal instantly, or live an immortal life span, or—"

"That isn't possible!" Phanes shouted, sounding as if he might burst into tears.

Ian let him go and laughed.

"It's more than possible; it's done. I'm not even going to kill you. Living a regular life span while as weak as a human will punish you far worse than a quick death at my hands."

"Cruel," Vlad said with an approving smile at Ian.

A tremendous crash jerked all our attentions to the left, where an enormous, floating pile of burned, snapped trees knocked down the remaining line of larches. Remnants also swarmed it, diving through the pile in a continuous, deadly flow to a chorus of fainter and fainter screams.

Now, Vlad's smile aimed my way as that huge pile floated closer to me.

"Special delivery from me, Mencheres, and Marie."

The cuffs in my skin unwound. They pulsed with power as I grabbed them and stretched my hands through the net, waiting.

Morana spilled out of the pile and landed on my net. She was soaking wet and also burned in places, reminding me that effigies of her were still drowned in parts of Russia to this day to herald the coming warmth of spring. Perhaps water and heat was the secret to undoing Morana's power, just as ripping Phanes's wings off had been the secret to undoing his.

I didn't pause to ask. I didn't even wait for her to open her eyes, breaking my previous claim that I'd never kill an enemy in their sleep. Unconscious or no, and weakened or no, Morana was too dangerous for me to hesitate for a second.

I slapped the cuffs around her wrists and held on to make sure that she didn't freeze blast them off.

The cuffs glowed a bright, vivid orange that seemed to leak onto her skin before it raced over her entire body. Her eyes opened then, and she screamed as that glow turned into liquid flame that drained her straight down into the hole I hadn't made because I hadn't used any of my netherworld-splitting powers.

None of the veils would crack today. They wouldn't crack because of me ever again. Some powers weren't worth their cost.

When that hole vanished, Ashael and I abruptly fell to either side. It took me a second to realize why, and then I smiled as I stood up to my full height.

Morana had bragged that the magic used to make these nets had come from her power. Now that she was dead, that power had died with her, freeing me.

I was free in so many ways now. For the first time in my life, my very existence was no longer illegal. Neither was the magic I practiced. What would my life be like, now that I didn't have to hide my real self? I couldn't wait to find out.

I ran over to Ian, who caught me and then laughed as my momentum knocked us both backward.

"Well, hallo, my strong blonde sweeting," he murmured as his arms curled around me. "Going to grab my cock and say 'surprise' like you did when you found me at that bordello?"

"Sure," I said, and did. "Surprise."

A grin slid across his lips. "Careful, little Guardian. You know I don't care if there's an audience."

"Right now, neither do I," I whispered, and kissed him.

"Get a room," I heard Ashael say, but he sounded like he was laughing.

"Good idea," I said, drawing away to stare at Ian. "How are you feeling? Good enough to teleport, do you think?"

"Why?" he asked, with a stifled laugh. "Somewhere else you need to be? Another apocalypse to stop, perhaps?"

"No," I said, holding his stare. "Just a promise to you for me to fulfill."

"Ah."

Ian smiled and then gave a brief wave at Bones, Marie, and the couple dozen of her very soaked troops who'd finally made it back to our spot on the mountain.

"Sorry, can't stay to have a chin wag about all this. We have somewhere very important to be."

Bones let out an amazed snort. "Really? Where is that?"

"Home," I said, and whispered the location in Ian's ear.

I felt his grin against my cheek. Then, I felt the chaotic drop of teleportation as everything else slid away.

I smiled because I didn't need to wait for us to arrive at the location I'd given him. Even in the midst of the whirling chaos, as long as I was in Ian's arms, I was already home.

Author's Note

As you've read by now, there's a certain plot point contained herein that is similar to what happened after Justice Ginsburg's death in late September 2020. I want to assure my readers that any similarities to those events are coincidence and not by design. I finished writing *Wicked All Night* in June 2020, the manuscript was copyedited in July 2020, and in production by mid-September, all before Justice Ginsburg's passing. However, it wasn't released until late February 2021, so I'm adding this note to avoid any misconceptions that the scene/plot points in question were influenced by Justice Ginsburg's demise. As a feminist, I hold the utmost respect for Ruth Bader Ginsburg, and I would never have exploited her legacy that way.